The Amours of Philario and Olinda

Anonymous

The Forced Virgin

Anonymous

Narzanes

Anonymous

The Unparallel'd Impostor

Anonymous

with a new introduction
for the Garland Edition by
Malcolm J. Bosse

Garland Publishing, Inc., New York & London

1973

The new introduction for the

Garland *Foundations of the Novel* Edition

is Copyright © 1973, by

Garland Publishing, Inc., New York & London

All Rights Reserved

Library of Congress Cataloging in Publication Data
Main entry under title:

The Amours of Philario and Olinda.

    (Foundations of the novel)
    Reprint of 4 works, the 1st originally printed in 1730 for F. Cogan, London; the 2d originally printed in 1730 for W. Trott, London; the 3d originally printed in 1731 for and sold by T. Payne, London; and the 4th originally printed in 1731, London.
    1. English fiction—18th century. I. The forced virgin. 1973. II. Narzanes. 1973. III. Moore, James. The unparallel'd imposter. 1973. IV. Series.
PZ1.A54 1973 [PR1297] 823'.02 73-170577
ISBN 0-8240-0566-X

Printed in the United States of America

Introduction

Ranging from the idealized romance to the realistic criminal biography, these four works exemplify the brief novel of the first half of the eighteenth century. In the preface to The Amours of Philario and Olinda *the author acknowledges that he is specifically writing for a female audience who "will meet with nothing which even the chastest Vestal might not read without a Blush" (p. 4), and, indeed, his narrative contains a host of elements associated with sentimental fiction: complicated romantic entanglements, young noblemen quick to anger, young ladies slow to reveal feeling, a setting devoid of realistic detail, long soliloquies, physical illnesses caused by emotional frustration, wounds sustained on the field of honor, sudden departures and unexpected returns, misunderstandings and reconciliations, and finally marriage celebrations. Events in this story devoted to the rituals of courtship are patently contrived. For example, Olinda learns of Philario's passion simply by overhearing him declare it out loud while strolling alone in a grotto. Frequent soliloquies notwithstanding, the narrative proceeds at an admirably steady pace, and although passion has temporarily made enemies of close friends and cruel women of sweet girls, the romance ends appropriately with a triple wedding. It is a workmanlike example of the kind of sentimental fiction which appealed to female readers of*

INTRODUCTION

the period before Richardson came on the scene and added psychological realism to pathos and sentiment.

It is interesting to speculate whether Richardson read The Forced Virgin, *the tale of a persecuted maiden. The dedication states that the story's purpose is to illustrate the terrible force of sexual love and the inevitable consequences of a fall from virtue: "Love, when opposed in its directive Way, swells like a rapid Torrent over all little Bounds, and Deluge-like sweeps wide wide Destruction round." Lomina is abducted and raped by a suitor, Lysanor, whom she then stabs to death in a wildly melodramatic scene: "The Blood sallied apace from the Crimson Wound, and the heavy Wings of Death sealed down his lustful Eye-lids" (p. 16). Then the suitor whom she loved also rapes her, first administering a potion in the manner of Lovelace. She blames her resultant pregnancy on the murdered Lysanor, and in despair she kills her own child, only to discover that her true love might well have been the father. A romantic tragedy, written in a flagrantly rhetorical style, this novella presages* Clarissa *in a grim appraisal of unleashed erotic impulses and a harsh judgment of women who lose their virtue no matter how hard they strive to keep it.*

For brevity, the dedication to Narzanes *is rare in the eighteenth century: "To all Sincere Lovers of their Country, the following Sheets are, with the utmost Deference, inscrib'd by the Editor." Although the author uses a story-telling device made popular by satirists of the age — the discovery of a manuscript — his*

INTRODUCTION

narrative is more of a polemic than a satire; his thesis is that great statesmen who have served their kings faithfully become the political targets of envious opponents. Not only is the story a tract, it is also a curious blend of sentimental romance and scandal chronicle in which the story of Narzanes' love affair leads into a roman à clef *treatment of English politics during the 1720s. The plot turns on the contrast between sober Narzanes and licentious Euryphax; the political struggle that develops is a direct result of their earlier love for the same woman. Although the romantic element tends to cancel the effect of the political issues and although the disregard of concrete detail obscures the identity of actual personages,* Narzanes *draws some parallels to the early ministry of Robert Walpole, when his anti-war policy drew fire from political opponents such as Stanhope, Sunderland, and Aislabie, and from the exiled Bolingbroke. The author describes the kind of public resentment and antagonistic press which plagued the Treasurer during those critical years. In this glowing defense of the man whom Fielding would ridicule in* Jonathan Wild, *Walpole is portrayed as serenely aloof to attack; he "would not even suffer any one to write in his Defense, or make the least Reply to the numberless scandalous Libels which were daily publish'd, from dark Corners, against him" (p. 71). Narzanes' economic policy may be an allusion to Walpole's handling of the South Sea Bubble crisis in August 1720, which vindicated his domestic statecraft and caused the downfall of his political rivals.*

INTRODUCTION

The Unparallel'd Impostor, *signed by James Moore and called in the preface "incontestable Matters of Fact, supported by authentick and legal Vouchers," is a realistic narrative obsessively involved with the crime of forgery and specifically with one of its practitioners, Japhet Crook. Moore pleads for severe punishment of extortion, perjury, and forgery which, because they constitute crimes against property, are "Crimes of a deeper Dye, than even Murder it self" (p. 2). Little time is wasted upon drawing Crook's character, although his occupations are listed and a point is made of his Quaker education. An account, principally through letters, is given of Crook's activities as Sir Peter Stranger, a cunning felon who preys upon widows. A plethora of wills and legal terms absorb the major part of the story, and the narrative ends abruptly, promising in an advertisement, however, that a further collection of Crook's barely literate letters will be published. The brevity of this account, the claim to authenticity, the attention to the special mechanisms of a crime, the fabrication of detail and the pretentious moralizing identify* The Unparallel'd Impostor *as a rogue biography, although its author's obvious personal concern with Japhet Crook gives it the added dimension of being a social document as well.*

Malcolm J. Bosse

The Amours of
Philario and Olinda

Anonymous

Bibliographical note:

This facsimile has been made from a copy in the British Museum (12614.d.11)

THE
AMOURS
OF
Philario and *Olinda*

OR THE

INTRIGUES
OF
WINDSOR.

A

Genuine HISTORY.

Turpe est difficiles habere nugas,
Et stultus labor est ineptiarum.

LONDON:

Printed for F. Cogan, at the *Middle-Temple Gate*, in *Fleetstreet* M.DCC.XXX.

TO THE

RIGHT HONOURABLE the

Lady *Diana Spencer*, &c.

MADAM,

HE following Performance, which here presents it self to your Ladyship's Hands, comes recommended by nothing but its Circumstances, which are those of an Infant Production; and altho' I have not the Honour to be known to your Ladyship, yet the Assurance I have of your Candour and Facility, encourages me to hope, that this Piece may meet with a favourable Reception. There is not in Nature a more attractive Quality, than Clemency and Humanity; but when these meet in an elevated, extensive Genius, the Subject of them not only claims, but even commands our Esteem and Veneration.

It might be expected by some, that I should here launch out into the Praises of your Ladyship's Wit, and other Perfections; but as this would look too much like Flattery,

THE PREFACE TO THE READER.

*AM very senfible, that the Difficulties, which attend a Perfon entering upon the barren Province of Poetry, are much greater than moft are apt to imagine; for befides the almoft innumerable Productions of this Sort, the capricious Tafte of the prefent Age is fo hard to pleafe, that Encouragement, the fole Spirit and Life of all Endeavours, is almoft impoffible to be attained. This together with the many Defects I am confcious of in the following Sheets, might well have difcouraged me from printing them; but confiding in the known Candour of my Female*

A 2 *Readers*

PREFACE.

Readers, for whom they are principally designed, I have ventured to publish them, hoping that their good Nature will excuse the Errors of this Performance.

I am persuaded, Ladies, if you will do me the Honour to peruse this Essay, you will meet with nothing which even the chastest Vestal might not read without a Blush; and those of my own Sex, who will give themselves the Trouble to examine it, may possibly find something not unworthy their Notice. Upon the whole, it being the first Fault I have committed in this Kind, I hope if it does not meet with Approbation, it will at least find an easy Pardon.

THE

THE AMOURS OF PHILARIO and OLINDA.

✿✿✿✿✿✿✿✿✿✿✿✿✿✿✿✿✿✿✿✿✿✿✿✿✿✿✿

PART I.

N the Reign of King *WILLIAM* the Third, there lived at Court a Gentleman called LYSANDER, who by his Bravery under his then Majesty while Prince of *Orange*, in *Flanders*, had juſtly merited the Favour and Eſteem of his Sovereign; but ſoon after the Death of that great Monarch, he retired from Buſineſs to his Countrey Seat near *Launceſton* in *Cornwal*; where he enjoyed all the Pleaſure, a Life free from Hurry

Hurry and Cares can afford. But his chief Happiness consisted in a Son called PHILARIO, a most accomplished young Gentleman, inferior to none in Valour and Courtesy. Even in his younger Years he gave evident Signs of an extraordinary Wit and Gallantry, which was very much improved by a liberal Education. For although he was Master of a very affluent Fortune, yet this did not in the least deter him from the laudable Pursuit of Knowledge; which he prosecuted with so much Application, that in a few Years he became a great Proficient in all kinds of polite Literature, and was caress'd by Gentlemen of the greatest Wit and Learning in *England*. It was in this Time that he contracted a very strict Friendship with a young Gentleman named *Horatio*, with whom he passed the softer Hours of Life in the most agreeable Manner.

Being arrived almost at Man's Estate, he began to fix his Thoughts on travelling; and accordingly with *Horatio* he left *England*, and made the Tour of *France*, *Italy*, *Germany*, *Spain* and *Holland*; which they compleated in about five Years, and return'd home very much improv'd both in the Knowledge of Men and Customs.

Not long after their Arrival at *London*, they came intimately acquainted with two Gentlemen, whom we shall style *Neander* and *Mirabell*, both Persons of illustrious Families, and Men of Wit and Learning. But *Neander* was still happier in his Consort, the Pride and Ornament of her Sex, whose fair Perfections we will hide under the Name of *Aurelia*. She was often visited by a young Lady called *Belinda*, of so celebrated Beauty, join'd with the most strict Virtue, that there were not a few who sighed for her Love; and

and among the reſt were *Mirabell*, *Aurelia*'s Brother, and one *Elutherius*, who gave Place to none in Honour and Courage.

Theſe two Gentlemen had been very intimate Friends, and accompanied each other through the greateſt Part of *Europe*; but ſince their Return, falling both paſſionately in Love with *Belinda*, that ſacred Knot, which had ſo long laſted inviolate, was ſoon diſſolv'd. *Belinda* had at firſt entertained a favourable Eſteem of *Mirabell*, which in Time improved, and grew up into Love; tho' ſhe had given him no Marks to diſcern which Way her Affections leaned; as well the more throughly to prove his Fidelity, as to prevent the unhappy Conſequences that might iſſue upon ſuch a Declaration. However this often cauſed great Differences between them, which might have ended in very melancholy Effects, had not the Kindneſs of their Friends interpoſed. For *Mirabell* thinking that *Belinda* expreſs'd greater Reſpect for *Elutherius*, than himſelf, and he imagining the ſame of *Mirabell*, hence a continual Jealouſy between them aroſe, which could never be pacified, unleſs one would reſign up his Pretences to the other, which neither of them ever would do.

This Amour had been carried on ſome conſiderable Time without any, or at beſt very ſmall apparent Advantage gained on either Side: For *Belinda* was as prudent as fair, and without diſcovering in the leaſt her own Inclinations, entertained both their Addreſſes with equal Complaiſance; determining to reward *Mirabell*'s Services in a proper Time, according to their Deſert. For tho' Women for the moſt Part, like Fortune, blindly diſpenſe their Favour without any Regard to Worth and Merit, yet the

wiſe

wife Carriage of *Belinda* seemed to atone for the almost epidemical Fault of the whole Sex, and rendered her not less admired for her Conduct, than the Charms of her Person.

The agreeable Conversation of such Persons could not but be very delightful to PHILARIO; whose sprightly and facetious Temper render'd his Company very entertaining to all, but especially the Ladies; who in *England* for Wit and Beauty bear away the Prize from all the Ladies in the World.

The Season of the Year inviting them into the Countrey, they left *London* and retired to *Neander*'s Seat at *Windsor*; where being one Day at Dinner, PHILARIO started the Proposal of a hunting Match; which being immediately fell in with by all the Company, *Neander* sent Orders to his Servants to have all Things in Readiness, and invited several Gentlemen and Ladies to take Part of the Sport. Accordingly in the Morning they all met at the Time and Place appointed, where PHILARIO was no sooner come, but he was struck with the highest Admiration at the Sight of the most beautiful Lady his Eyes ever beheld. The Sun in all his Progress round the Universe never saw a Creature so exquisitely fair. To describe her would be as impossible as to equal her. What irresistible Charms, what Sweetness appeared in her Looks! Her riding Habit, which was extreamly rich, gave an additional Grace to her incomparable Shape and Air: Her Head was adorned with a Plume of white Feathers, while her flowing Tresses that hung carelesly over her Shoulders, wanton'd in the Wind. She was mounted upon a fiery milk white Steed, who proudly champt the foaming Bit, and paw'd the Ground with Fury and Disdain, eager and hasty

for

for the Courſe; whom notwithſtanding the managʼd with the utmoſt Dexterity.

PHILARIO for ſome Time ſtood motionleſs and ſpeechleſs, like one in a Trance, and found the Infection like Lightning ſeize upon his Heart, which took away his Power both of acting and ſpeaking; but when his Spirits began to return from that Lethargy they had been in, he could hardly avoid diſcovering the Commotion of his Mind by the Diſorder of his Words. However reaſſuming as much as poſſible his wonted Air and Looks, he joined the reſt of the Company, who did not in the leaſt diſcover his Confuſion; and ſo after uſual Ceremonies and Complements, they rid forward to their intended Diverſion. All the way they went PHILARIO endeavoured to entertain OLINDA, for that was the Ladyʼs Name, who ſeemed no Way diſpleaſed either with his Perſon or Diſcourſe; but on the contrary returnʼd his Gallantries with equal Wit and Complaiſance. But by that Time they were arrived at the Place where they intended to begin their Game, a black Cloud ariſing ſpread it ſelf over the whole Heavens, and it began to rain ſo violently, that they were all obliged to ride away as faſt as they could to ſome Shelter, which by good Fortune they happened to meet with at a little Diſtance, where they entered without any Ceremony. The Storm continued above an Hour; when a great Wind ariſing, which began to diſſipate the Clouds, by Degrees it ſenſibly decreasʼd, till it was quite fair, and the Sky reaſſumed its wonted Azure. Then ſatisfying the People of the Houſe handſomely for their Trouble, which with a ſeeming Reluctancy at firſt they refusʼd, but were ſoon perſwaded to accept, they rode home as hungry and tired, as if they had

C   hunted

hunted all Day. *Neander* invited the Company to spend the rest of the Day with them, which was infinitely pleasing to PHILARIO, because he had then an Opportunity of the Conversation of his dear OLINDA; and after Dinner he and *Horatio* entertain'd them with a Relation of their Travels; a particular Account of which I omit here to mention, because it would extend this Essay to too great a Length. At Supper notwithstanding all PHILARIO's Endeavours to be merry and facetious, yet a certain Gloominess sat on his Countenance, and he seemed rather a Spectator of what passed in the Company, than an Actor in it. This was taken Notice of with Surprize by several then present, but especially by *Horatio*, who presently concluded that something more than common disturb'd him, otherwise the Gaiety of his Temper would not suffer him to be dull at such a Time. But the Ladies seeing him wrapt up in such profound Contemplation, began to rally him on the Subject, and particularly OLINDA, who taking it for granted that he was in Love, very pleasantly said to him: " I " cannot but esteem that Lady very happy, Sir, " whose Perfections engage so great a Share of " your Thoughts; but withal very covetous, in " that she will not allow you to throw away one " upon any less deserving Object.

This smart Repartee, attended with so much Grace in the Speaker, effectually rais'd PHILARIO out of that deep Consideration, he seem'd before lost in; who immediately reply'd: " How can " she, fair OLINDA, but possess my most in- " tense Thoughts, when I have not only her " charming Idea imprinted in my Mind, but " even that dear Object her self before my Eyes."
Upon this a universal Smile ensued, and OLINDA
glanced

glanced her Eyes upon PHILARIO with a rosy Blush, that added new Lustre to her incomparable Beauty, and fresh Fuel to the Flame struggling in his Breast.

Neander and *Mirabell* were very desirous he would oblige them with the Lady's Name, who was the Object of his best Wishes; but he reply'd that he hoped a more propitious Minute would occur in which he might whisper his soft Complaints in her Ear, and therefore desired to be excused. But it beginning to grow late, the Company prepared to go home: PHILARIO and *Mirabell* waited on OLINDA and *Belinda*, who he then understood were Cousins, and liv'd both together at OLINDA's Father's.

Upon their Return, PHILARIO went directly to Bed, not to Sleep but to indulge his Thoughts. All Night his Mind was agitated with a thousand different Imaginations; sometimes he ran over her charming Perfections; her Air, her Shape, her graceful Speech, sharp Wit and fine Address; sometimes his Fancy represented her as then in his Arms, and he was in Raptures even at the Idea: at other Times his prophetick Fears represented the Uncertainty of obtaining his Wishes; then a Croud of melancholy Thoughts invade his Breast; he is tortured with the dreadful Apprehensions of her Disdain, and the mournful Consequences of Rage and Despair. Next he revolves in his Mind the most proper Methods of communicating his Passion to her: sometimes he proposes to write to her; at other Times fearing the ill Success of Letters, resolves to speak to her in Person. Thus he spent the whole Night, without being able to determine on any Method concerning the Affair. As soon as it was Daylight, he rose and went to *Horatio*'s Chamber,

(12)

telling him he had a Matter of Importance to communicate to him, and defired him to rife; which he immediately did, and they both went out into the Garden together, where PHILARIO unfolded the whole Matter to him, and afked his Advice. *Horatio* told him it was what he imagined, when he fat fo filent and penfive, while all the reft of the Company were ingaged in the moft agreeable Difcourfe. His Opinion was, that PHILARIO fhould endeavour to fmother his Paffion till he became more intimately acquainted with OLINDA, and that then he might convey his Thoughts to her in whatever Manner he thought proper. This Advice PHILARIO refolved to follow, and therefore, tho' he had frequent Opportunities of feeing and fpeaking to OLINDA, yet he kept his Defires concealed; however they daily increafed, and every new Occafion that prefented her to him, made her ftill more lovely than before: fo that it was plainly perceived by the Alteration of his Countenance, that fomething diſordered him. *Neander* fancied the Air of *Windſor* did not agree with him, and therefore refolved to carry him to the *Bath*; and altho' he ftrenuoufly oppofed this Propofal, becaufe it would deprive him of the Sight of OLINDA, (a Happinefs he prized above the World) yet all he could fay was of no Weight with *Neander*; and his Perfwafions being feconded by *Aurelia*, he was at laft forced to comply. The Day before their Departure PHILARIO paid a Vifit to OLINDA, and invited her to go along with them, but for fome Reafons, which fhe did not mention, fhe was forced to deny him; otherwife, fhe faid, fhe fhould gladly have born them Company. At parting PHILARIO was fcarce able to contain himfelf, and took Leave of her in fo paffionate a

Manner,

Manner, that he was afterwards afraid that he had discover'd his Thoughts; but she imputed it to the Gallantry of his Temper which was easily perceived by all that knew him. However his fine Wit and Address had made so deep an Impression upon Olinda's Mind, that she began to look upon him, as he really was, a Person not unworthy her Esteem.

In his Absence she found an uncommon Uneasiness upon her Spirits, which she her self was unable to assign any Reason for; and others who observed it, imputed it to some Indisposition of Body; but *Florella* her Maid, who was better skill'd in the Mysteries of Love, imagining it proceeded, as it really did, from some quite different Cause, soon found it to be the Effects of that Passion, tho' as yet she could not discover fully the Object. She had for some Time in vain endeavoured to wrest the Secret from her; not that Olinda doubted in the least her Fidelity, but she would fain perswade even her self, if possible, that it sprung from another Cause, than in fact it did. *Florella's* Intimacy with her Mistress gave her the Liberty of speaking her Thoughts very freely, and by what she had observed in Olinda's Carriage, she had no small Reason to believe Philario was the happy Man that was so high in her Favour. Determin'd to be satisfied in this Doubt, as they were one Day walking by the Side of a pleasant Canal in the Garden, she artfully fell into Discourse of Philario; taking Occasion to recommend his Person, his Wit, and Address; narrowly all the while observing each Motion of Olinda's Countenance, if she could from thence discover what she so earnestly sought. She perceived her attend with a great deal of Pleasure to every Thing urged in his Praise,

every

every now and then fmiling, and then again blufhing at the Mention of his Name, which ftill heighten'd her Sufpicion. But refolv'd to be certain, fhe made Trial of another Experiment, which fully confirm'd her.

Having one Day feen PHILARIO taking the Air with a young Lady call'd *Hyppolita*, "I am apt "to imagine, fays fhe, that PHILARIO has a De- "fign of marrying the Lady *Hyppolita*, for I "have often feen him entertaining her with a "great deal of Gallantry; befides it is rumoured "in the Town that he loves her." Upon mentioning thefe Words, fhe obferv'd a ftrange Diforder in OLINDA's Countenance; but taking no Notice of that, fhe purfued her Difcourfe: "I "cannot, continued fhe, but think his Choice "very good, for, except your felf, I fcarce know "any that excells her." OLINDA could no longer contain her felf, but in a great Paffion commanded *Florilla* to leave that Difcourfe on Pain of her Difpleafure. "Heavens, Madam, reply'd "*Florilla*, what have I faid that fhould create "you this Diforder! I hope you have no Inte- "reft in PHILARIO, which fhould make you Dif- "like his Choice." —— OLINDA here ftopping her fhort, reply'd: "And name that Word once "more and I banifh you my Service for ever. "I fay it cannot be, it is impoffible he fhould "love *Hyppolita!*" "Ah, Madam, reply'd "*Florilla*, my Sufpicions were but too true! I "always imagined you lov'd PHILARIO, and "therefore feign'd this Story for a fuller Confir- "firmation of my Thoughts." "How, fays "OLINDA! have you then impos'd a Falfhood "upon me!" "Here, on my Knees, reply'd "*Florilla*, I entreat you to pardon the innocent "Deceit: 'twas my Concern for your Repofe
"that

"that put me upon this Artifice to difcover the
"the Object of your Wifhes: Your Looks, your
"Speech, nay even your very Silence declar'd
"you lov'd, and fancy could not frame a nobler
"Subject of your Affections, than the gallant, ge-
"nerous PHILARIO." OLINDA, while the Tears
ftood in her Eyes, anfwered, "Forgive my
"Warmth, I well know thy Fidelity and Love.
"Thou haft indeed divined aright, and PHI-
"LARIO is the Perfon who poffeffes my Heart.
"But alafs, I am doom'd to be unhappy; for
"Modefty forbids that I fhould reveal my Paf-
"fion, and he perhaps may love elfewhere, and
"then I am loft for ever." "Let not this Fear,
"reply'd *Florella*, difturb you; but when you
"next fee him, attack him with the Force of all
"your Charms; his Heart will never ftand the
"Affault of fo much Beauty, but fall a Captive
"to your lovely Eyes." "I wifh it may, reply'd
"OLINDA, for mine is loft already." They walked a confiderable Time, difcourfing in this Manner, till a Servant came and told them *Belinda*
was return'd home, who had been out a vifiting,
upon which they both went in.

PHILARIO in the mean Time ignorant of his
Happinefs, tho' incircled with all imaginable Pleafure and Felicity, found no Delight in any of thefe
Injoyments, becaufe unpoffeft of the fole Object
of all his Wifhes. To him all thofe Things which
others count the Joys of Life, nay which he himfelf once took Delight in, were grown infipid.
Even Mufick, which, as *Congreve* finely fays,

———— *Has Charms to footh a Savage Breaft*,

afforded him no Pleafure, but rather increafs'd
his Melancholy. His Mind which was ever taken
up with fair OLINDA's Idea, could make no room

(16)

to entertain another Thought; and he who was once the Joy of Society and Life of Conversation, whose very Presence inspired with Wit and Gaiety, was now become enamoured with Solitude and Retirement. This strange Alteration was highly surprizing to *Neander* and all his other Acquaintance, except *Horatio*, who alone knew better the Cause. *Neander* had often press'd him to relate the Reason of his Melancholy, offering to serve him with his Life and Fortune. PHILARIO thanked him for his generous Friendship, but said it was a Trouble which only one Person could remove, to whom, and to none other he would reveal it. But soon after their Return from the *Bath*, chance brought it to OLINDA and *Belinda*'s Knowledge; for as they with *Florella* were taking the Air pretty early one Morning in a pleasant Grotto a little way out of Town, they heard at some Distance a Voice like one in Distress, and drawing nearer to listen, to their great Surprize they found it was PHILARIO, who imagining himself beyond the Hearing of any but Heaven, utter'd these Words:

"O PHILARIO, where is all thy boasted Reso-
"lution now? Love has at length convinced
"me of its Power, and by one Glance from her
"charming Eyes has made a Captive of me. O
"too lovely OLINDA, little dost thou know the
"thrilling Pangs thy divine Perfections constant-
"ly create me! By Day these solitary Groves are
"silent Witnesses of my Complaints; and Night,
"that brings Repose and Rest to all Things else,
"brings me fresh Cause of Pain! But why should
"I despair? for sure that Angel form can ne'er
"be void of Pity, and Pity still foreruns ap-
"proaching Love!" Here PHILARIO broke off his amorous Soliloquy, and the Ladies immediately

diately withdrew for Fear of being seen, not a little pleased with the Discovery they had made. But an unfortunate Accident happening juft upon it in *Belinda*'s Affairs, she was prevented from partaking in the Pleasure of that Morning's Success: for the same Day *Mirabell* and *Elutherius* happened both to meet at her Lodgings, and after the most passionate Expressions of Love and Adoration, they earnestly press'd her to declare who was the happy Man that possess'd her Heart. She told them that she equally respected them both as Gentlemen, and Men of Honour, but Time would show, who best deserved her Love. Upon this *Mirabell*, with Eyes full of amorous Passion, eagerly kiss'd her Hand; which Violence she accepted with so much Grace, and seemed so well pleased with, that *Elutherius* immediately judging himself the slighted Person, quitted the Room, without so much as taking Leave of *Belinda*. And now Rage, Jealousy, and all the savage Passions of the Soul began to boil within his Breast, and, like so many Fiends, spurr'd him on to his almost fatal Ruin. He now meditated nothing but Revenge upon his too happy Rival, who had robb'd him, as he imagin'd, of the beauteous *Belinda*. As soon as PHILARIO came in, *Mirabell* related to him the Adventure; who was of Opinion that this would cause a Quarrel between them, and told *Mirabell* that he might expect to hear from *Elutherius* either that Night or in the Morning; which if he did, he desired that he might have the Honour of serving him with his Sword, if a Second was required. *Mirabell* caused a Man to stand at the Door all the Evening, to bring whoever should ask for him directly to him without farther Examination; but no Body coming that Night, *Mirabell* was of Opinion,

D *Eluthe-*

Elutherius would not send any, because had he designed it, he would have done it, while he was in such a Transport of Passion. However pretty early in the Morning PHILARIO heard some Body knock at the Gate, who was presently let in, and conducted to *Mirabell*'s Chamber. PHILARIO immediately concluded it was a Messenger from *Elutherius*, as it really was; for the Gentleman, whose Name was *Cleanthus*, after bidding *Mirabell* good Morrow, presented him a Letter, which he opened, and found the following Challenge.

SIR,

The sacred Presence of Belinda *hindered me from telling you my Mind yesterday, but this Gentleman will conduct you to the Place, where I expect you with my Sword to decide by a last Combat the Quarrel, that has for some Time been between us. The Friendship we once so strictly did, and, I hoped, should have inviolably maintained, causes me not without some Reluctancy to ingage in this Duel, which in all Probability will be fatal to one of us; but since it is as impossible for Love to admit of a Rival, as for the Firmament to contain two Suns, and no less a Prize, than the charming* Belinda, *is to be play'd for, this must atone for it. I desire you to choose a Friend, who with mine may be Witness of our Actions; and so recommending my self to Heaven, I wait your Appearance without the least Rancour or Malice on my Part, which I am persuaded, through the many Instances I have had of your Honour and Generosity, you will intirely lay aside on yours.*

ELUTHERIUS.

Mirabell strait rose, and sent his Man to call PHILARIO, who by this Time was almost drest; so they presently mounted, and went out with *Cleanthus*,

Cleanthus, who led them to a Meadow about a Mile diftant from the Town, where *Elutherius* waited. As foon as they came up to him they all difmounted and ftripp'd into their Shirts, and *Cleanthus* and PHILARIO taking Leave of their Friends, removed about fifty Yards off. *Cleanthus* gave PHILARIO his Hand as an Evidence, that it was only to ferve his Friend, and not out of any private Malice that he was at that Time his Enemy; which Civility PHILARIO return'd with the like Courtefy: but this was a Time for Action, not for Words. They then drew, and after feveral Paffes, which they both put by, *Cleanthus*'s Sword glanc'd on the Top of PHILARIO's Shoulder, and in Return he wounded him in the right Thigh. *Cleanthus* immediately fell, and in the Fall dropp'd his Sword, which PHILARIO delivered to him again, faying: " Live, brave " *Cleanthus*, fince it is rather Fortune, than my " Valour, that has given me this Victory;" and fo without ftaying for an Anfwer, he ran towards *Mirabell* and *Elutherius*, who that Moment fell down fpeechlefs with a Wound he received in the Neck, after that *Mirabell* himfelf had been wounded in his right Arm. Imagining him mortally wounded, he took him by the Hand faying, Dear *Elutherius* forgive me; but he was unable to make any Reply, and only opened his Eyes and clofed them again immediately. *Mirabell* feeing PHILARIO come alone, began to be touch'd with a fenfible Sorrow, thinking that he had killed *Cleanthus*, but was prefently undeceived; for *Cleanthus* by the Help of his Sword had made a Shift to rife; but when he heard his Friend was, as they all fuppos'd, killed, his Grief was inexpreffible: but this was no Time for fruitlefs Complaints: wherefore calling *Elutherius*'s two

D 2   Servants.

Servants, who waited at a Diftance in the Field, they took him up in their Arms, and carried him to a Surgeon, who examining the Wound, told them he hoped it was not mortal, tho' exceeding dangerous. He was directly put into Bed, and his Wound drefs'd, and in about two Hours his Speech began to return to him a little, tho' very faint, thro' the great Lofs of Blood he had fuftained.

Mean while *Neander* being informed that PHILARIO and *Mirabell* were gone out with *Cleanthus*, whom he knew to be a particular Friend of *Elutherius*, began to fufpect they were gone to fight; and therefore went immediately to *Belinda*'s to enquire, if fhe knew any Thing of a new Difference between them; who relating *Elutherius*'s abrupt Departure the Day before, together with the Occafion of it, *Neander* was confirmed in his Sufpicions; and therefore taking Horfe immediately with *Horatio* and feveral Servants, they rode all about to find the Place, where they were engaged. *Belinda* likewife knowing that fhe was the unhappy Occafion of their Quarrel, and fearful of any Difafter that might happen to either of them, inform'd feveral Gentlemen of the Duel; fo that the whole Town was in a little Time up on Horfeback to hinder them from fighting. But none knowing the Place of Affignation, they were a long Time before they found it, and when they did, the Combatants were all gone. The great Effufion of Blood they faw in the Place, made them believe that fome of them were killed; but they were obliged to return with no more Certainty than they came. *Neander* and *Horatio* pofted back again with all Expedition, hoping they might fee or hear of them by that Time in Town; but tho' Inquiry was made in all Parts, yet

yet no News could be learn'd, for they were all that Time with *Elutherius*, from whom they never ftirred till he came to himfelf; when the Surgeon giving them fome Hope of his Life, PHILARIO and *Mirabell* left him and *Cleanthus*, who was not able to walk, and return'd to Town. PHILARIO went directly to carry the Account to *Elutherius*'s Friends, who were as much overjoy'd when they heard of his Life and Hope of Recovery, as they were at firft grieved at the News of his Danger. *Mirabell* made to *Neander*'s, who had been all that Day in the greateft Concern for their Safety; but feeing him come alone, they were all ready to fwoon, concluding PHILARIO was kill'd. But upon his relating the Succefs of the Combat, all their former Sorrow was difperfed, and a univerfal Joy diffus'd it felf thro' the whole Company. *Mirabell* had fcarce Time to conclude before PHILARIO enter'd the Room, whom *Horatio* and *Neander* embraced with a Tendernefs which fufficiently fpoke their Affection. The Satisfaction that appeared in the Minds of all prefent was not a little heightened in *Mirabell* and PHILARIO by the Company of OLINDA and *Belinda*; who, tho' they blamed their Fighting, yet difcover'd no fmall Pleafure in their happy Return, thanking Heaven they were all come off with Life. But to avoid Reflection, *Belinda* foon withdrew, whom *Neander* waited on to her Lodgings; for fhe would not fuffer *Mirabell*, tho' he earneftly entreated it; alledging that the World might take Occafion to cenfure her Conduct, if immediately after the Duel, fhe fhould permit him that Freedom, as tho' fhe had countenanced their Quarrel: befides the ill Confequence it might be of to *Elutherius*, if it fhould, as it certainly would, come to his Ears, who then lay in fo dangerous a Condition.

The

The Wound in PHILARIO's Shoulder, tho' it pained him pretty much, being juſt upon the Bone, was notwithſtanding no Hindrance to his Mirth in that fair Company; and the Happineſs he then thought himſelf in the Poſſeſſion of, did much more than balance all his former Uneaſineſs. And indeed the Pleaſure OLINDA expreſs'd in his ſafe Return that Day, would have given a much leſs diſcerning Perſon, than PHILARIO, very good Reaſon to believe he was no way diſagreeable to her. The Diſcourſe being chiefly upon the Diſpute which had happen'd between *Mirabell* and *Elutherius* about the fair *Belinda*, the Company were all very deſirous of hearing the whole Relation of that Amour from *Mirabell*; and tho' he at firſt ſhow'd ſome Reluctancy, yet being preſs'd by the Ladies, he was obliged to comply, and therefore began in this Manner.

" My Acquaintance with *Elutherius* is of as early
" Date as our Childhood; it can ſcarce be called
" Acquaintance, ſo ſoon was it ripened into Friend-
" ſhip. His Age and Temper agreeing ſo exactly
" with 'mine, ſeem'd as tho' Nature had deſigned
" us for the neareſt Alliance. As ſoon as we were
" capable of acting with any Deſign, this Inſtinct
" began clearly to diſcover it ſelf to the entire Sa-
" tisfaction of both Families. We entered upon
" our Studies together, and continued till the
" Age of twenty; in all which Time we met with
" no one Accident to hinder our growing Affe-
" ction, which was then arrived pretty near Per-
" fection. We then began our Travels, viſiting
" the Courts of *France*, *Italy*, *Germany* and *Holland*,
" in each of which we ſtay'd ſome Time for the
" Improvement of our Behaviour and Under-
" ſtanding. In ſhort, we compleated our Travels
" in about five Years, and return'd home much

" to

" to our own, and our Friend's Satisfaction. But
" now the laſt Scene of our Friendſhip was begin-
" ning to open; for not long after our Arrival,
" my Siſter *Aurelia* was viſited by the charming
" *Belinda* whoſe lovely Eyes ſoon kindled a Flame
" in my Breaſt, to which, till then, it was abſo-
" lutely a Stranger. It is impoſſible to expreſs how
" great was the Raviſhment and Wonder I was
" loſt in, the firſt Moment I beheld the beauteous
" Maid! And as Love is eagle-eyed, ſo my Paſ-
" ſion was quickly perceived by *Elutherius*, who
" was no leſs enamour'd than my ſelf. However
" diſſembling his Suſpicion, he ſeemed ſurprized
" at the ſudden Change wrought in me, and of-
" ten endeavoured to wreſt the Secret from me,
" which as yet I kept concealed within my own
" Boſom. But of ſo ſtrange a Nature is Love,
" that maugre all Endeavours, it will ſoon diſ-
" cover it ſelf; and you may as eaſily think to
" hide the Light of the Sun from the Univerſe,
" as this Paſſion from obſerving Eyes. *Eluthe-*
" *rius* preſs'd me to declare the Object of my
" Wiſhes, whom he already knew but too well;
" and I not being able to deny ſo reaſonable a Re-
" queſt to my moſt intimate Friend, at once open-
" ed all my Heart to him. But you may eaſily
" imagine the Surprize I was ſtruck with, when
" at the Mention of her Name I obſerv'd his Eyes
" ſparkle like Fire, and his Countenance alter-
" nately change, ſometimes red as Scarlet, and
" then preſently pale as Death. I perceived my
" Error when too late, in making my Rival the
" Confident of my Love. However pretending
" Ignorance, I imputed his Diſorder, which was
" too manifeſt to be hid, to ſome Indiſpoſition;
" and therefore adviſed him to repoſe himſelf a
" little, which might perhaps remove it. Upon
                                            " this

"this I left him to follow my Directions, and re-
"tired into my Closet to consider what Method to
"take in this unfortunate Accident; and after all
"I resolved to continue my Courtship to *Belinda*,
"without taking any Notice to *Elutherius*. Ac-
"cordingly the next Day I waited on *Belinda*,
"and press'd my Passion, which I had some small
"Time before disclosed to her. Her Answer
"was, that since my Designs appeared to be ho-
"nourable, she would admit my Addresses; but
"Time alone could give Proof of my Fidelity,
"which I might expect should not go unreward-
"ed. I reply'd in an Extasy of Joy, that it
"should be the continual Endeavour of my Life
"to merit her Favour and Esteem.

"Soon after I took my Leave, transported
"with the Success I apprehended my Passion had
"gained; but was not got far, before I met *Elu-*
"*therius* coming, as I imagined, on the same Er-
"rand; whom I saluted with my wonted Free-
"dom, as tho' entirely ignorant of his Design.
"But he with an Air much different from what
"was usual, reply'd: I perceive, Sir, you have
"been paying a Visit to Madam *Belinda*, and by
"the Gaiety of your Countenance I read your Suc-
"cess. You are a happy Man, *Mirabell*, to be able
"with so much Ease to win a Lady's Heart, which
"so many with the utmost Labour have attempt-
"ed in vain. I smiling answered, that if I had
"made Choice of one of those favourable Mi-
"nutes, in which Beauty proves propitious to the
"Lover, the Honour of that Conquest was due
"rather to Fortune than my Merit. I intreated
"his Company along with me, but he pretending
"to have Business of Consequence elsewhere, I
"left him to put what Constructions he pleased
"on my Behaviour. At my Return Home, I
"found

(25)

"found him in the Company of *Cleanthus*, who
"had been an intimate Acquaintance of his be-
"fore his going to Travel, and now upon this
"Occafion renew'd.

"All the Evening, tho' *Elutherius* ftrained
"Mirth, even to an uncommon Pitch, yet could
"he not clear his Brow of thofe Clouds that fat
"thereon, and Spite of all his Endeavours dif-
"covered his Uneafinefs. On the contrary, tho'
"the Succefs I had that Day met with, might
"have been fufficient to banifh even the Remem-
"brance of any anxious Cares, yet I could not
"without the moft fenfible Grief think of the
"Lofs of fo dear a Friend, which I plainly fore-
"faw would be the Confequence of this Affair.
"*Cleanthus* being gone home, I retir'd into my
"Chamber, and going to take a Book off the
"Table, I had before been reading in, I found by
"it a Letter, which I opened and found as follows.

S I R,

*I have till now, been always inclined to believe,
that the facred Name of Friendfhip was exempted
from thofe Injuries of Time and Fortune, to which all
other Things are liable ; but I now begin to fear that
even that is fubject to the common Fate of Nature,
which according to a receiv'd Maxim, has its Rife,
Perfection, and Decay. I have indeed frequently entertained my deluded Fancy with the pleafing Profpect
of a long, uninterrupted Amity, and with how much
Pleafure you, whofe Breaft felt the fame more than
fraternal Ardour, are beft judge: and it cannot therefore be fufficiently lamented, that any Occafion has
happened to difturb at leaft, if not deftroy that delightful Harmony, which I hoped would have ever
been kept up between us. But alas, how foon can
Heaven difappoint the Expectations of wretched Mor-*
E. *tals!*

tals! how soon is this agreeable Scene closed! Scarce does our Friendſhip begin to live, but like a beauteous Flower cropt in the tender Bloſſom by ſome untimely Hand, its meets its Fate. Thus are all our growing Hopes of future Bliſs deſtroy'd, and while our Minds have been entertaining themſelves with the Appearance of Happineſs, lo on a ſudden the Viſion diſappears, and in the Room of a ſubſtantial Good, we have been hugging a vain Illuſion!

You will not, I ſuppoſe, be much ſurpriſed at this ſeeming myſtic way of Writing, ſince you cannot but be appriꝛed of my Paſſion for Belinda, *the Cauſe of our preſent Diſſention. That all ſhould admire* Belinda, *is not ſurpriſing; but for me to meet a Rival, where I thought to find a Friend, in whoſe faithful Ear I might have repoſed the Secret of my Love, is diſtracting: nor could any Thing, except the Loſs of* Belinda *her ſelf, create me ſo ſenſible a Sorrow, as the Loſs of your Friendſhip.*

But I too long detain you from enjoying the Pleaſure of your Succeſs to Day with your Miſtreſs, and therefore have done; only conjuring you to preſerve the Name of Friend ſtill inviolate, and aſſure your ſelf, that I will not act in this Affair unbecoming that ſacred Character.

ELUTHERIUS.

" The generous Sentiments with which this
" Letter abounded, did not a little affect me;
" and I ſpent the whole Night in conſidering of
" the way to preſerve (if poſſible) my Friend, as
" well as obtain my Love; but was as much at a
" Loſs, as when I began. For being of all Mankind
" the moſt intimately acquainted with *Elutherius*'s
" Temper, and knowing him to be a Gentleman
" of the higheſt Courage and Reſolution, I con-
" cluded that I ſhould meet with no ſmall Impe-
" dimen.

"diment in the Progress of my Amour; nor was
"I much out in my Conjecture. The next Day
"he visited *Belinda*, who, as I was since inform'd,
"return'd his Addresses an Answer, tho' not al-
"together to his Satisfaction, yet such an one as
"did not discourage him from pursuing his De-
"sign.

"We had frequent Interviews to have compo-
"sed, if possible, this Difference between us,
"which both of us were grieved for, yet neither
"of us could repent of. But alas, Love is a
"Monarch will admit of no Competitor, and the
"Dispute was heighten'd by endeavouring to
"compose it; so that our Dissension every Day
"increas'd, till at length the highest Degree of
"Affection and Friendship was converted into ut-
"ter Estrangedness: from whence I cannot but
"conclude, that Things when once arriv'd at
"Perfection, never continue long in that Posture,
"but return naturally to their original State of In-
"difference. In the mean Time we continued
"our Courtship to *Belinda*, who receiv'd both
"our Addresses with equal Complaisance and Re-
"spect, but refused to name the happy Object of
"her Wishes; wisely considering that the Con-
"sequence of such a Declaration must be fatal to
"one of us. But still this was not sufficient to
"keep us from Jealousy, for each imagined the
"other prefer'd; and hence arose continual Dif-
"putes, which had several Times before this
"ended in a Duel, had not the Kindness of our
"Friends interposed. In this Posture stood our
"Affairs, till yesterday accidentally meeting at
"*Belinda*'s Lodgings, for a very slight Reason
"*Elutherius* left the Room in the greatest Rage,
"meditating the Design he this Morning put in
"Execution; the Consequence of which you all
"know."

Here

(28)

Here *Mirabell* ended, omitting several Particulars in the Narration, unwilling to detain the Company too long; who were all very well pleased with the Relation, tho' they could not help lamenting the Dissension of two such intimate Friends. Afterwards *Aurelia* and OLINDA desired PHILARIO to favour them with a Song, which command there was no disputing, and therefore he sang the following Stanzas.

I.

Celia's bright Charms my Soul inspire
With ardent Flames; I feel the glowing Fire
  Burn in my Breast, and while in vain
T' extinguish it I strive, the pointed Pain,
  Swift as Jove's *rapid Lightning flies,*
Strikes to my Heart, and in my Bosom lies.
    What beauteous Grace,
    What Charms divine
    Adorn her Face,
    And round her Shine!
She's all Perfection, Heav'n in her appears,
And when she smiles I banish all my Fears.

II.

But oh, I'm drown'd in anxious Grief,
Mourning my Fate, yet dare not ask Relief;
  Passion still smother'd in my Breast
Racks me with Torture and disturbs my rest,
  Labouring for Vent; while o'er my Soul
Black cruel Storms and Waves of Sorrow roll!
    What piercing Smart,
    What hidden Woes
    Afflict my Heart,
    No Mortal knows.
But still the charming Maid smooths all my Cares,
And when she smiles I banish all my Fears.

This

This Song was followed with the Applaufe of all the Company, but OLINDA had the greateft Share of that Pleafure, who knew well enough that he had uttered his own real Thoughts, tho' clothed in the fictitious Habit of a Song. There seemed scarce any Thing now wanting to consummate the Happinefs of all prefent, except the Prefence of *Belinda*, which did not a little damp the Satisfaction, MIRABELL would otherwife have experienced; and tho' he endeavoured to put on an Air of Mirth and Gallantry, yet 'twas evident fomething fat heavy at his Heart. Thofe who were not acquainted with the true Caufe of his Uneafinefs, attributed it to the Wound in his Arm, and therefore advifed him to go to Bed: Upon which all the Company broke up, and it being late, OLINDA was prevailed upon by *Aurelia* to ftay all Night, and fo they all retired to their refpective Apartments. PHILARIO no fooner found himfelf alone, but he began to indulge thofe Thoughts, which fo much Action, and agreeable Converfation had, in a great Meafure, all that Day diverted. And now a tumultuous Crowd of Imaginations prefs'd into his Mind, which was in fo great a Commotion, that I have often heard him fay, if it had been poffible for one to have furvey'd his Breaft at that Time, Heavens, what a Scene of Confufion would he have beheld!—— They fall far fhort of the Mark, who attempt to defcribe a Mind tofs'd with fo many different Paffions, by comparing it to a tempeftuous Sea; which, alas, is all Calmnefs and Serenity to the wild Diforders of the Soul at that Time. Unable any longer to contain the ftruggling Paffion, PHILARIO, with a deep Sigh, uttered thefe Words: " O " fair OLINDA, is it poffible that fo much Divinity

"nity can be ignorant of the Pain I suffer,
"thro' the Wounds of your lovely Eyes! Hea-
"vens, in what a Maze of Uncertainties do I
"wander, the Sport of a thousand Passions!"
He would have gone on in this Manner, had not
his Thoughts reminded him of the Place where
he was, and the Danger of being overheard.

The Disorder of his Mind would not suffer
him to close his Eyes all Night; though Sleep
would have been very seasonable, as well to ease
the Pain of his Shoulder, as a short Relaxation
from that Anxiety that continually haunted him.
In the Morning he found himself extreamly out
of Order: His Pulse beat vehemently, and he
was all over in a burning Fever; so that he was
forced to go to Bed again soon after he rose.
His Distemper increased so violently, that he
was almost in the Grave, before any scarce
thought of his being ill; and many began, not
without Reason, to doubt of his Life. But by
the Blessing of Heaven, the Remedies he took
had a happy Effect, and in about four or five
Days his Fever left him; to which the Presence
of OLINDA, who scarce ever stirr'd from *Neander*'s the whole Time of his being ill, did not a
little conduce. He was pretty well recovered,
when one Morning *Horatio* came into the Room,
and commanding all the Attendants out, addressed him in this Manner:

"My dear Friend, says he, I am not insen-
"sible that the Passion you labour under for
"the beautiful OLINDA, has been the principal
"Cause of your Illness, which now (Thanks to
"all gracious Heaven!) is, I hope, removed;
"and I cannot but think you justly culpable,
"that forgetting your former Vigour and Reso-
"lution, you thus abandon your self to cause-
"less

" less Melancholy. Not that I would advise you
" to dismiss your Love, for that I know were
" vain; besides when the Object is deserving,
" 'tis a noble and godlike Disposition of the
" Soul, and renders us most like the happy Spi-
" rits above: but 'tis weak and unmanly to
" look upon a Cause desperate before we have
" tried all Methods, much more before we have
" attempted one. Are there not favourable
" Opportunities of presenting your Addresses to
" OLINDA, which daily offer themselves to your
" Acceptance? Why then will you not embrace
" them? What can there be to hinder or dis-
" courage you? Is your Birth, or Fortune infe-
" rior, or are you destitute of personal Accom-
" plishments to recommend you to her Esteem?
" Besides, OLINDA's late Carriage (if I have
" any Judgment in the fair Sex) gives me suffi-
" cient Reason to believe, you are no way dis-
" pleasing to her. What else meant the Surprize
" and Disorder she discover'd upon the News of
" your Indisposition, and her constant Attend-
" ance here, ever since you were ill? Let me
" therefore conjure you, dear PHILARIO, to dis-
" sipate those Clouds of Sorrow and Despair,
" that continually dwell on your Mind, and en-
" tertain favourable Expectations of the Success
" of your Passion; and assure your self that so
" much Grace and Sweetness, as OLINDA com-
" mands, cannot be insensible to the moving
" Eloquence of Love."

Horatio had scarce ended, when *Aurelia* and OLINDA entered the Chamber, at Sight of whom PHILARIO felt a secret Joy and Pleasure diffuse it self thro' his whole Soul; so that raising himself up, he received them both in the most obliging

liging Manner, and they being seated near the Bed-side, he thus bespoke Olinda: .

"I cannot, says he, Madam, but esteem my "self infinitely happy in the Honour you now "do me; and assure you it shall be the Busi-"ness of my whole Life to love and praise the "beauteous Authoress of my Happiness." Upon saying this, he gently squeez'd her fair Hand, which he had then hold of, and kiss'd it in so great a Transport, that he seem'd to breathe his Soul at his Lips. Olinda seem'd a little surprised at this Action, and in a kind of a Passion snatch'd away her Hand, which he unwillingly let go, and then proceeded in this Manner:

"The greatest and best good Fortune, Ma-"dam, I can attain to in Life, is to hope my "self the Subject of your kind Concern and gen-"tle Wishes; which Felicity would infinitely "over-balance all the extremest Malice of my "other Fate: for as it is impossible I should "ever be happy without your Favour, so with "that I cannot be miserable; and as there can "be nothing I should wish for comparable to "your Esteem, so that obtained, would suffi-"ciently make Amends for the most rigorous "Fortune." He was going on in this amorous Discourse when *Neander* and *Mirabell* entered the Chamber, upon which the Ladies withdrew, and Philario was hindered from disclosing his Passion to Olinda, which he then determined to have done. The Joy of all present at so happy a Change in Philario's Health, is hardly to be expres'd; for the Presence of Olinda he had just before enjoy'd, had made so sensible an Alteration in him, that he wanted not much of regaining his former Looks and Air.

He

He immediately rose, and after Breakfast walked about half an Hour in the Garden, with the rest of the Company; directing a thousand amorous Glances towards OLINDA, which she, tho' as well acquainted with as he, yet seemed not to understand. A few Days afterwards he visited *Elutherius*, who was still confined to his Chamber; who gave him an Account of the Rise and Progress of their Amour with *Belinda* (the Occasion of all the Quarrels between him and *Mirabell*) almost in the same Manner, as you have already heard. PHILARIO persuaded him to endeavour an Accommodation of the Dispute by some more gentle and moderate Methods, than had hitherto been used; as well to defend her Reputation from the injurious Tongues of the ill-natured Part of Mankind, as for their own Safety and Happiness. He answered, that if *Mirabell* was willing, he would wait his Doom from *Belinda*'s own Mouth: and if she declared her Pleasure, that he should desist from his Addresses, he would for ever banish himself from her Presence, and undergo the Punishment of a perpetual Separation from the Object of his highest Wishes, (than which Hell has not a greater Torment) rather than cause her the least Uneasiness, or deprive her of one Hour's Satisfaction. He spoke these Words with a Pathos, which melted PHILARIO into Sorrow for the ill Success of so pure and ardent a Passion. After some Discourse upon indifferent Subjects, PHILARIO took his Leave of him, debating with himself, whether he had best inform *Mirabell* of *Elutherius*'s Resolution, or keep it Secret; and upon the Result, his Mind declared in Favour of Silence. However he acquainted *Mirabell* of his being with *Elutherius*, and withal, that he desired to speak with

with him along with himself, the next Day. Accordingly they both went, and *Elutherius* spoke thus: "I am very sensible, says he to *Mirabell*, "that you may justly claim a Right to the charm- "ing *Belinda* by the Law of Arms, being Victor "at the Sword, by which I agreed to decide the "Contest. And I cannot but wish Fate had "destined there my Fall; for then you might "have enjoy'd *Belinda* without Molestation, and "I should not outliv'd my Disgrace, and the "Loss of my Love. But since Heaven has de- "creed that I must survive, I think, considering "our antient Friendship, you can hardly deny "leaving it once more to *Belinda*'s Pleasure to "nominate whom she shall best approve of for "her Servant; which done, the other shall im- "mediately desist and enjoin his Passion per- "petual Silence." *Mirabell* readily agreed to this Proposal; and both engaging their Honour to stand to the Agreement, and fixing a Day for waiting on *Belinda*, he and PHILARIO return'd to acquaint *Neander* with the Result of this Interview; who was overjoy'd to hear, that the Dispute was likely to be brought to so fair an Accommodation. In the mean Time *Mirabell*, that he might not give either *Elutherius*, or any of his Friends the least Shadow of Reason to tax his Honour or Generosity, left the Town and retired to *London*, where he waited with Impatience for the Time assigned; which being come, they both met at *Belinda*'s, whom they found to their Wish alone; and after having saluted her with the profoundest Respect, they acquainted her with the Reasons of their Coming. *Belinda* hearing their Resolution, was some Time in Debate with her self what Course to take; but at length after a Pause she reply'd, that the

Person

Person she should make Choice of, was him, who should last after that Time see her. *Mirabell* and *Elutherius* were both surprized at her Answer, and endeavoured by various Arguments to persuade her to alter her Determination; but she remained fix'd, thinking that the only way to prevent all further Quarrels. Wherefore after taking Leave of her in the most passionate Manner, they both withdrew, and the next Morning with only one Servant a-piece, without speaking to any Body, they mounted and rode away to the no small Surprize of *Aurelia* and the whole Family. *Elutherius* went directly and entered himself a Voluntéer under the Earl of *Peterborough*, who was at that Time appointed General of an Army into *Spain*, to assist the Arch-Duke in gaining the Crown of that Kingdom; and *Mirabell* on the other side embark'd for *Flanders*; where we must leave them, and return to PHILARIO and OLINDA, a particular Account of whose Affairs will take up the Second Part of this History.

The End of the First Part.

THE AMOURS OF PHILARIO and OLINDA.

PART II.

PHILARIO being, as I have informed you, recoved from his Illness, he now thought of nothing but revealing his Passion to OLINDA, and the most proper Methods to facilitate, and bring about that Design. There scarce passed a Day in which he did not see and speak to OLINDA, but this was in Company; and therefore he was impatient for an Opportunity to entertain her in private. This was not long before it offer'd; for OLINDA coming one Day when *Aurelia* was engag'd in writing Letters, she desired PHILARIO to keep OLINDA Company till she had done. There needed no Arguments

guments to induce him to so pleasing a Task; and that they might be the more retire, he importuned her to walk into the Garden, which she comply'd with; and after they had taken a Turn or two, talking of indifferent Things, they went into an Arbour by the Side of a pleasant Fountain, where being seated, Philario laying hold on that happy Occasion, began in this Manner:

"The Happiness, Madam, I now enjoy, is
" what I have long sighed for in vain; and since
" kind Fortune has at length put it into my
" Hands, I should be guilty of an unpardonable
" Folly, were I to let it slip without improving
" it. Words, Madam, continued he, tho never so emphatick, are unable to describe, with
" how pure and ardent a Passion I have loved
" you, from the first Moment I beheld those
" charming Eyes. Beauty so attractive cannot
" but kindle a Flame in the Breasts of admiring
" Spectators; and it is almost as impossible to
" see and not adore you, as to approach the Sun
" without feeling the Effects of its Heat. Nor
" can you, fair Olinda, justly blame my Passion; since the Eye, that sees necessarily what
" is presented to it, and thro' which the Fuel
" that feeds this Flame, by unknown Ways is
" conveyed, must be taken with a pleasing Object. If therefore Love be a Fault, it ought
" rather to be attributed to those too lovely
" Eyes that inspire it, than to the Effect which
" they naturally produce. But fain would I
" hope that so much Sweetness as dwells in
" Olinda, will not be deaf to the Pains of an
" unhappy Lover! Yet oh, what Language shall
" I use, or how Address the Soveraign of my
" Soul! Teach me, some propitious Power, that
" soft

"soft perfuasive Eloquence, such as may gently steal upon her Heart, and gain a bless'd Acceptance! O divine OLINDA, can you behold a Lover prostrate at your Feet, in softest Accents breathing out his Vows, and not be touch'd with a reciprocal Tenderness? Methinks it is not possible that so much Beauty and Perfection, as dwells in every Feature of that heavenly Form, can be void of generous Pity and Compassion! No, that's a Temper Heaven detests, nor can it reside where so much Divinity appears! That Frame adorn'd with all that e'er in Heaven or Earth could make it amiable, was sure designed Perfection's brightest Pattern; and it would be an Affront to the Wisdom and Skill of the great Author of Nature, as well as an Injury to you, not to admire a Work, that opens to such a Scene of Wonders. O my Angel, could I but hope you entertained one tender Thought of PHILARIO, that would infinitely over-rate all my former Sufferings! And if a Passion the most sublime and refined, may hope to merit any Thing from so charming an Object, your faithful Admirer may presume he has deserved that Happiness. As soon would I attempt to describe the matchless Perfections you are Mistress of, as tell how much, how ardently I love you. The Sun shall sooner cease to shed his Influence round the World, than I can cease to adore you, or Fate be able to erase the beauteous OLINDA from my Breast. No, while I have Life, I will retain your dear Image nearest to my Heart; and even my latest Breath shall whisper your much lov'd Name."

OLINDA heard all this amorous Discourse with
a great

a great deal of secret Pleasure, and discovered her self not at all displeas'd with the Encomiums he gave her. For Women, tho' they pretend never so strenuously to dislike Flattery, have yet a certain Vanity in their very Constitutions, which, in Spite of all their Dissimulation, will discover it self upon all Occasions of this Nature. However, with an Air between serious and pleasant, she told him; that as to all those Complements of her Beauty, she look'd upon them as Words of Course used by Gentlemen of his Gaiety to her Sex; but notwithstanding he might expect, if faithful, to meet a Reward becoming her Virtue and his Merit. There needed only this to encourage his Addresses; so that imagining his Happiness then in a Manner compleat, in a Rapture pressing her fair Hand and sealing his Vows upon her Lips: "Thus, says he, my charming "Angel, let me ever express my Ecstasy and "Transport, and thus, thus admire the lovely "Cause of all my Joys!

But here the Interview was broke off (to Philario's no small Uneasiness) by *Aurelia*, who having finish'd the Letters they left her about, was come into the Garden to them; whom they joined, and after walking a while, they all went into the Arbour and drank Tea, till *Neander* and *Horatio* came in, who had been to get Intelligence of *Mirabell* and *Elutherius*, but could come at no certain Information of the Matter.

Philario having thus opened the Way to his further Addresses to Olinda, you may be sure pursu'd with the utmost Vigour what he had so happily begun; and Olinda gave so many Remonstrances of her good Esteem both of his Person and his Love, that he at length found her Heart wholly his own; so that there wanted only

Con-

Confummation to make him the happy Man he defired. But fee the ftrange Perverfnefs of Fate, and the Uncertainty of all human Happinefs! For juft as he imagined himfelf entering upon the Blifs he had fo long figh'd for, a Storm from an unexpected Quarter arofe, which drove him fo far back, that almoft any other Perfon, but PHILARIO, would have defpair'd of ever making the defired Port.

Lyfander, his Father, being defirous to fee his Son fix'd in Life, had pitch'd upon a young Lady called *Angelica*, for his Wife; and therefore wrote a Letter to him with ftrict Orders to repair to him at *Launcefton*; for that he had fomething to communicate, upon which both their Happinefs very much depended. PHILARIO was almoft diftracted at this News; not only as it would be a Let to him in his Marriage with OLINDA, which he expected would be foon confummated; but he likewife rightly imagined, that Marriage was the important Bufinefs *Lyfander* had to propofe. He was a long Time in Debate with himfelf, whether to obey Love or Duty; but reflecting upon the certain Difpleafure of his Father, fhould he refufe to comply with his Will, at length the Son prevailed above the Lover. He acquainted *Neander* and *Aurelia* with his Refolution, whofe Concern for his Departure was fomething abated by a Promife of returning, as foon as ever his Affairs with his Favour would permit; but the greateft Difficulty yet remained, which was to work OLINDA to a Compliance, and remove the leaft Doubt that might arife in her Mind of his Truth and Honour. To this End he paid her a Vifit, and after the tendereft Expreffions of Love, and an inviolable Fidelity, he acquainted her with the

fatal

fatal Orders. She discovered a deep Concern at the News, and that not without some Sparks of Jealousy: however Philario having fully satisfied her Fears as to that Point, both by his Father's Letters, and a thousand Remonstrances of his own unalterable Love; assuring her it was absolutely contrary to his own Will, and altogether in Compliance with *Lysander's* Commands that he undertook that Journey; and withal, that he would infallibly return in a very short Time, she seemed, tho' unwilling, to comply.

This Difficulty being surmounted, he prepared with all Expedition to be gone; and all Things being ready, the Night before his Departure he took Leave of Olinda, which Interview had like to have baffled all his former Resolves, and turn'd the Scale in Favour of Love. Olinda could then no longer conceal the Passion she had hitherto smother'd, but notwithstanding all her Art, her Tears betray'd the Sentiments of her Mind. This, as it was the joyfullest Sight to Philario in the World, assuring him of Olinda's Affections; so it went very near influencing him to lay aside his intended Journey. However assuming all the Resolution he was Master of, he comforted her in the best Manner he was able; again repeating the many Vows he had so often swore before, sealing them on her Lips, and giving her the fullest Assurance of a speedy Return. She on the other Side gave him her Hand, plighting with it her Faith never to admit another to the Possession of her Heart, of which she then declared he was the entire Master. Overjoy'd with this Declaration, he at length with the greatest Reluctancy withdrew, and the next Morning with *Horatio*, the constant Companion of his Fortunes, set out for *Launceston*;

ceston; where being arrived, they were received and caressed by *Lysander* and *Amanda*, his Mother, with the highest Demonstrations of Joy.

A few Nights after their Arrival, *Lysander* made a Ball for their Entertainment, as he feigned, but really to promote his Design of PHILARIO's Marriage with *Angelica*. The Company being come, *Lysander* chose out the Lady *Angelica* and presented her to him for a Partner; a Person, as PHILARIO himself confess'd, set off with all the Charms both of Art and Nature; who might very well have captivated the Heart of any other Man but him, whose Mind was already taken up with the Image of his dear OLINDA. Charming as *Angelica* really was, she made no Impression upon his Breast, but rather heighten'd his Love to OLINDA, whose Perfections compared to *Angelica*'s, seemed to him vastly superior. But *Horatio*, the next in Gallantry and Comeliness to PHILARIO, beheld her with other Eyes: To him Fancy never painted any Thing so exquisitely fair; and every Look and Smile she gave, administred fresh Fuel to his struggling Passion.

During the whole Time of the Ball, *Lysander* constantly observ'd PHILARIO's Carriage to *Angelica*, and perceiving that he took all Occasions to entertain her with the utmost Facetiousness and Respect, he imagined that his Plot had more than half succeeded. The Ball being done, PHILARIO and *Horatio* waited on *Angelica* home in her Coach; and upon their Return, *Lysander* took PHILARIO apart, and began to sound his Inclinations, asking him several Questions about *Angelica*; as whether he did not think her a very fine Lady, and how he should like her for a Wife. PHILARIO, who knew well enough his

Meaning,

Meaning, anſwered, that ſhe was indeed a very deſerving Perſon, and he knew ſcarce any that excelled her; but for a Wife, that was a Buſineſs that requir'd mature Conſideration. *Lyſander* proceeded no further at that Time; but tho' this Anſwer of his Son's did not altogether pleaſe him, yet it did not diſcourage him from purſuing his Intent; and therefore a Day or two afterwards he invited *Angelica* and her Brother, *Beaufort*, with a few other Gentlemen and Ladies to a hunting Match; hoping that the ſecond Attack might do more Execution on PHILARIO, than he found the firſt had done. Accordingly at the Time and Place prefixed, the Company all met; but the Splendor of *Angelica*'s Beauty, and PHILARIO's manly Grace and Equipage ſo far out-ſhone all preſent, that they alone drew the Eyes of all upon them. She was array'd in a riding Habit of Silver Tiſſue; a Girdle of the ſame richly ſet with Jewels, contained her ſlender Waſt, and a black Velvet Cap adorned with a fine Plume, and ſtarr'd with Diamonds grac'd her Head; and on the other ſide, PHILARIO was dreſs'd in a Suit of Scarlet Velvet richly embroidered with Gold.

The whole Time they hunted, *Horatio* continually rode by *Angelica*, and endeavoured with the utmoſt Gallantry to fix himſelf in her Eſteem; but tho' ſhe returned it in the moſt graceful Manner, yet her Eyes were ever on PHILARIO, and ſhe ſtill ſeemed to contrive new Occaſions for him to entertain her, which he, as much as Decency would permit, ſtudiouſly avoided, to give his Friend the Pleaſure of her Company, with which he ſaw he was more than ordinarily delighted. The Hunting being over, PHILARIO and *Horatio* preſented what they had killed

killed to *Angelica*, and then each retired to their respective Abodes.

Lisander, not thinking it convenient to let his Son cool, as soon as he was come home, took him into his Closet, and bespoke him in this Manner:

"You cannot, says he, Philario, but be
" very sensible, that your Welfare and Happi-
" ness is what above all other Things I have
" at my Heart; nor has any Thing been want-
" ing that might conduce to so desirable an
" End: and it is with the highest Pleasure that
" I see your Disposition and Behaviour so cor-
" respondent to your Birth and Education. But
" both my Relation to you as a Father, and
" my Experience give me the Liberty to advise
" you in what I think both for your Advantage
" and Satisfaction. The Inconveniences to which
" Persons of your Fortune and Age are expos'd,
" make me, who am now in the Decline of
" Life, very desirous of seeing you fix'd in an
" honourable Marriage; and for this Reason I
" have pitch'd upon a Person whom I would
" commend to your Choice and Esteem; a
" Lady of great Wit and Beauty, as well as il-
" lustrious Birth and Fortune. To be plain, it
" is no other than the Lady *Angelica*, who is
" alone sufficient to recommend her self. She
" is already acquainted with the Reasons of your
" coming hither; and I have very good Cause
" to believe, that neither your Person nor Car-
" riage are any Way disagreeable to her. I
" know it is with great Difficulty that the Ge-
" nerality of young Gentlemen now-adays are
" induced to enter into that State of Slavery
" (as they call it); but I persuade my self that a
" Person of your riper Judgment and Experience
" will

"will not refuse so happy and advantagious a "Match, as this must appear.

This Harrangue only confirm'd Philario in his former Suspicions, and therefore was not near so surprizing to him as it would otherwise have been. And though he would have suffered ten thousand Deaths rather than violate his Faith to Olinda; yet being unwilling to disoblige his Father, he thought it best for the present to seem to comply with his Proposals; and therefore answered that he would yield himself intirely to his Conduct, and he might assure himself he would do nothing contrary to his Pleasure: which Reply gave *Lysander* the greatest Satisfaction.

But Philario's Thoughts were all taken up in contriving how to steer clear of these two dangerous Rocks, so as to preserve his Love with the Favour of his Father; but after all his Study, was as much at a Loss as when he began. As soon as ever he found an Opportunity, he slip'd away from the Company, and retir'd with *Horatio*, to whom he communicated this unlucky Affair. *Horatio* was as much concern'd as he, tho' upon a quite different Account; for all his Care was how to gain the Lady *Angelica*; and the other's how to get rid of her. *Horatio* conjured him by all their Friendship, and the Love he bore Olinda, which he had so often swore never to violate, not to engage at all in this Amour; alledging, that he could not do it without a direct Injury both to his Friend and his Mistress. This Advice, as it was really good in it self, so had it been followed by Philario, would have saved all that Trouble and Uneasiness the Neglect of it involv'd him in; as you will see in the Course of this History. But Philario,

LARIO, fearing the Displeasure of his Father, resolved upon a Method, which in the Sequel proved to be the worst he could have taken; which was this: To visit *Angelica* as his Father had desired, but to show so much Indifference, as might plainly discover his Want of Inclination to marry her, which he imagined would beget the like Indifference in her, and so the Match might be broke off. *Horatio* endeavoured by all Arguments to dissuade him from this Way of Proceeding, easily foreseeing the ill Consequence that would attend it; but he thinking to have thereby a specious Pretence of breaking with *Angelica*, and that she at the same Time seeing her self slighted, would the more readily embrace *Horatio*'s more vigorous and real Addresses, and consent to make him happy, tho' it were only to be revenged on himself, resolv'd to pursue it: little considering, that

Heaven has no Rage like Love to Hatred turn'd,
Nor Hell a Fury like a Woman scorn'd.

Pleas'd with this Project, the next Day PHILARIO paid *Angelica* a Visit, and after he had with a great deal of Indifference prattled to her a little of Love, he left her; and in this Manner their Courtship continued some Time. Mean while *Horatio*'s Addresses met with very cold Reception from *Angelica*; for tho' she plainly saw her self slighted by PHILARIO, yet her Desires (like a rapid Torrent, whose Violence is increased by Opposition) were rather heightened than abated by this Disappointment; and PHILARIO, when too late, found to his no small Concern, that his Words had made a much deeper Impression upon her Mind, than he either de-

designed, or desired they should. He then plainly saw that this Business would involve him in a great deal of Trouble and Uneasiness, and began to repent his neglecting *Horatio*'s Counsel. He fear'd there was no going back without plunging both Families in the utmost Confusion; And how far a jealous Woman's Rage might carry her, he knew not. Besides, *Horatio*'s Passion meeting with such ill Success, he began to suspect some foul Play on his Friend's Side, which PHILARIO perceived; so that he was in the utmost Perplexity. In the midst of these Doubts, he found there was only one Expedient likely to succeed, which was to acquaint *Lysander* with the Business: whereupon he went directly to him, open'd the Case, and begg'd his Assistance. *Lysander* discover'd a great deal of Anger at his Proceedings, and severely reprehended him for abusing both him and *Angelica* in so egregious a Manner; but upon urging his Friend's Passion for *Angelica*, which he was bound by the strictest Ties of Friendship to assist, together with his own Engagements to OLINDA in the Face of Heaven, which he could not break, without a direct Violation of his Honour, and at his Mother *Amanda*'s Intercession, *Lysander* was pretty well pacified, and at length told him that he would endeavour to disengage him from that Affair. And a few Days afterwards, to PHILARIO's no small Satisfaction, he told him the Business was done; but that he was forbid all further Interviews with *Angelica*. PHILARIO immediately flew with this happy News to *Horatio*, who then begg'd his Pardon for the rash Suspicion he had entertained of him, which, he said, was only the Effect of too much Passion. PHILARIO who well knew what it was to

be

be in Love, eafily forgave the little Error of his Friend, glad of the Opportunity to convince him of his Fidelity.

But altho' *Angelica*'s Father was fo eafily perfuaded to break off the Match between PHILARIO and his Daughter, yet fhe her felf being a Lady of a great Spirit, could by no Means brook this Indignity caft upon her Beauty; and her Love being converted into Rage, fhe began to meditate Revenge. To this End fhe apply'd her felf to her Brother *Beaufort*, a Man of a hot ungovernable Temper, conjuring him by the Honour of the Family, and all the Love he ever bore her, not to let this Affront pafs unchaftis'd. Inflamed by thefe Perfuafions of his Sifter, *Beaufort* fent a Meffenger with a Letter to PHILARIO, which he opened and read as follows:

SIR,

I am very forry I am under the Neceffity of demanding Satisfaction of you for the Injury done to my Sifter Angelica, *in bafely deferting her after all your Pretences to Love. And altho' you have efcaped publick Juftice, yet affure your felf there is but one way for you to avoid the Vengeance of a juftly inraged Family, which is a fpeedy Performance of your Promife to marry my Sifter. If you don't think proper to comply with this Demand, I fhall expect to meet you to Morrow Morning between Eight and Nine a Clock in a Meadow at the Weft End of the Town, without any Company but your Sword to decide this Debate: not doubting but that my Succefs will foon convince you of the Juftice of my Caufe.*

BEAUFORT.

PHILARIO,

PHILARIO having read this Letter, immediately wrote an Anſwer in the following Manner;

SIR,

The Satisfaction you demand for the pretended Injury done to your Siſter, I am very ready to give, nor am I, as you may imagine, to be terrify'd with empty Menaces. As to the Charge contained in your Letter, 'tis abſolutely falſe; and therefore I ſhall not fight you upon the Score of a Wrong done to Angelica, whom I never injured, but rather for a falſe Aſperſion thrown upon my Character; nor do I think either you ſo formidable, or my Cauſe ſo bad, that I need avoid meeting you at the Time and Place you have fix'd. But to ſhew you that Honour and not Paſſion engages me in this Quarrel, I am till then your Friend,

PHILARIO.

This Letter he ſealed and delivered to the Meſſenger, who could not avoid being ſeen and known for *Beaufort*'s Man, by *Horatio*; who gueſſing his Buſineſs, as ſoon as he was gone, came to PHILARIO, and aſked him if it was not as he ſuſpected; but he unwilling to ingage his Friend in the Quarrel, there being no Second required, deny'd it.

In the Morning he went out without being obſerv'd, as he thought, by any of the Family; and going directly to the Place aſſigned, he found there *Beaufort* alone waiting for him. As ſoon as PHILARIO came up, *Beaufort* told him he was very ſorry he was obliged to have Recourſe to the Sword for Relief; but ſince he had refuſed to repair the Honour of his Family, ly, which was injured by the Wrong he had done *Angelica*, he muſt thank himſelf for what had happened. PHILARIO reply'd, that he did not come there to excuſe what he had done, but to maintain it, and therefore his Buſineſs was then only to fight. They then drew, and after ſome Paſſes PHILARIO diſarm'd him, upon which he bid him yield; but *Beaufort* ſullenly reply'd, that ſince he was in his Power, he might do as he pleas'd; for though he might kill him, yet he ſhould never conquer him. PHILARIO then generouſly return'd him his Sword, ſaying: "Live " then, *Beaufort*, for I ſhall not uſe my For-" tune againſt one ſo brave." *Beaufort* ſeemed very angry with his ill Fate, and left the Field with all the Symptoms of Rage and Malice. PHILARIO, to prevent all Suſpicion of a Quarrel, return'd home immediately; but was no ſooner out of the Field, than he met *Horatio*, who having ſeen him go out ſo early, imagined he was gone to Fight, and therefore follow'd him at ſome Diſtance unperceiv'd, and was a Spectator of all that had paſs'd; fully reſolv'd if PHILARIO had been ſo unfortunate to fall, either to revenge his Death, or ſhare his Fate.

All that Day PHILARIO had an uncommon Melancholy upon his Spirits, and tho' he had no Reaſon to ſuſpect any, yet was he under a continual Apprehenſions of ſome approaching Diſaſter; and notwithſtanding all his Endeavours to ſtifle it, as thinking it only a groundleſs Fear, yet was he not able entirely to eraſe it, but ſtill ſomething like his good Genius, ſeemed to warn him of ſome Danger towards him. At Night, as they were ſitting in a large Hall up Stairs, *Amanda* deſired *Horatio* and PHILARIO

to

to give them some Musick; upon which a Hautboy and a Flute were brought, and they had scarce play'd one Air, before a Page came into the Room and told PHILARIO, there was a Lady at the Door desired to speak with him. He being the most courteous Gentleman alive, fearing to make the Lady stay, went directly out, without so much as asking who it was; but as soon as he was got out of the Room, two Men seiz'd hold of him, while a third clap'd to the Door, and then came and stab'd him in the Back twice with a Poignard. PHILARIO finding he was wounded, yet unable to draw his Sword, rais'd himself up from the Ground, and by main Force threw himself and the two Assassines quite down Stairs. Being thus disengaged, he got up, and though very faint, yet Rage a while supply'd his Loss of Blood; so that he dispatch'd two of them before any Body came to his Assistance. But the Noise of shutting the Door, together with falling down Stairs, soon alarm'd the Family, who running out to see what was the Matter, and finding the Hall-Door shut, *Horatio* leap'd out of a Window with his drawn Sword; whereupon the other that was left, endeavoured to make off, finding himself overpower'd; but *Horatio* stop'd his Journey by a Wound clear through his Throat. *Lysander* having broke open the Door, found PHILARIO in a Swoon; which Sight was so terrible to *Amanda*, that she imagining him kill'd, fell down by him in a Swoon, and was not without great Difficulty recovered. PHILARIO was immediately carried into Bed, and the Physicians and Surgeons were sent for, who after examining the Wounds gave them some Hope of his Life. It was a Day or two before he recovered his Speech; and when he did, it was so weak, that it was impossible for any who stood but at a small Distance off, to hear a Word he spoke. In the mean Time *Lysander* endeavoured by all Expedients he could think of, tho' in vain, to find out the Authors of this inhuman Action; but many who had heard of PHILARIO's Quarrel with *Beaufort*, imagined him to have been privy to the Assassination; but there being no Proof, none cared to speak openly what they thought. However several Hints were spread about the Town, insomuch that *Beaufort* found his Honour was concern'd in the Business, and therefore gave out that he would fight any Man who should dare to insinuate any Thing to asperse his Character; which coming to *Horatio*'s Ears, he presently challenged him, and after an obstinate Duel for some Time, they were both carried out of the Field dangerously wounded. But *Lysander* and PHILARIO both blamed *Horatio*'s Conduct in this Affair, because this would still the more incense *Angelica* against him.

Soon as PHILARIO was permitted to speak, he sent his Man with a Letter to OLINDA, and in it a Ring of great Value, which he used to wear. Upon opening the Letter, she found as follows:

My dear OLINDA,

The Wounds I now labour under are nothing to those I receiv'd from your lovely Eyes; and when I consider that they are the Effects of my Truth and Fidelity to OLINDA, *they rather give me Pleasure, than Pain. You only are capable of conceiving*

ceiving my Impatience for the happy Hour that shall make you mine; and the only Uneasiness I now suffer, is that of being kept from the dear Object of all my Wishes. I have a thousand tender Things to say, but am forbid to speak much for Fear of a Fever. My Man will inform you of the Particulars, and in the mean Time wear the inclosed as a Pledge of the inviolable Love of your faithful Admirer

PHILARIO.

OLINDA was ready to swoon at the News of his being so dangerously wounded, but hearing that he was in a happy Way of Recovery, her Grief was something abated: nay notwithstanding all her Concern for his Safety, she found a secret Pleasure in knowing it was for her Sake he was in Danger. Mean while *Angelica* finding her Revenge had miscarry'd, was in the greatest Perplexity; she was loth to desist, and yet afraid to pursue her Resentments. *Horatio*'s Person, Courage and Address began to be much more agreeable to her than formerly, and had it not been for what happened soon after, I am apt to believe she had forgone her Anger, and consented to his Happiness. But PHILARIO and *Horatio* being both recovered from their Wounds, PHILARIO determined to return speedily to *London*; and accordingly had fix'd the Day for his Departure, imagining then the End of all his Wishes near. This coming to *Angelica*'s Ears, her Passion knew no Bounds; but transported with Rage, Jealousy, and Shame for her slighted Beauty, she vow'd Revenge, tho' at the Expence of her Life. Her Brother *Beaufort* having been twice foil'd in her Cause, was very unwilling to undertake

undertake it a third Time; but overcome by her repeated Tears and Sollicitations, he was at laſt prevail'd with, tho' much againſt his Inclination. Accordingly about three or four Days before PHILARIO intended to ſet out for *London*, as he was going home to Dinner, a Gentlewoman came up to him, and preſenting him a Letter, he preſently knew the Hand to be *Beaufort's*, and opening read as follows:

SIR,

The Advantage Fortune lately gave you over me at the Sword, might probably make you think I ſhould not attempt any further Satisfaction; but I aſſure you an Indignity of ſo high a Nature caſt upon my Siſter, ſhall not paſs unpuniſh'd while I have Power to revenge it; nor can the Diſpute ever end but with one of our Lives. Beſides, there is not only Angelica's, *but my own Honour to be defended againſt a ſcandalous Imputation of hiring Perſons to aſſaſſinate you; the Odium of which Fact you have, without the leaſt Reaſon, thrown upon me. If therefore you dare juſtify theſe Proceedings, this Meſſenger, who is a Page diſguis'd to prevent Suſpicion, will conduct you where I expect you with my Sword, to put a final End to this Controverſy, either by* Conqueſt *or* Death.

BEAUFORT.

PHILARIO having read this Letter, ordered the diſguiſed Page to follow him Home, and while Dinner was preparing, he retired into his Chamber and wrote the following Anſwer:

SIR,

SIR,

I was indeed in Hopes that the Difference between us had been e'er this concluded, being for several Reasons desirous rather to make you my Friend, than my Enemy. But since you seem resolv'd to maintain a causeless Enmity against me, to convince you that whatever I once dare act, I dare justify, if you please to send a Gentleman upon whose Honour I may depend, I am ready to meet you at whatever Time and Place you shall think proper; but having once narrowly escaped with my Life by only stepping out of Doors, I should think my self very imprudent to go out of Town under the Conduct of a disguis'd Page.

PHILARIO.

This Letter he seal'd and deliver'd to the Page, and then ordered his Man to stand at the Door to bring whoever should ask for him directly to him. All that Day he heard no farther News from him; but pretty early in the Morning a Gentleman was conducted into his Chamber, whom as soon as he saw, he knew to be a brave Knight call'd *Pamphilo*, who addressing him, said: "I suppose, Sir, you are already acquainted with the Reasons of my coming by the Letter you receiv'd yesterday from *Beaufort*. It is indeed with some Unwillingness that I have engaged in this Affair, but my Intimacy with him left no Room for a Denial. I beg you therefore to choose some Friend, who may with me not only be a Witness of the Action, but also share in the common Fate." To which PHILARIO reply'd, ply'd, that as to a Second he would take none, but to satisfy his Defire of not being an idle Spectator of the Combat, he promis'd him that if *Beaufort* left him with Life, he would give him fome Exercife. " If you are fo refolv'd, " fays *Pamphilo*, then let us go, for he has al- " ready waited fome Time." Philario immediately ordered his Horfe to be got ready, and fo mounting, with only his Man he went out with *Pamphilo*, who led him to a Field about a Mile diftant from the Town. As foon as *Pamphilo* faw *Beaufort*: " Yonder, fays he, is my " Friend: if you pleafe I will fpeak with him " firft, if not I will leave you both to Fate." Philario reply'd, he might do what he pleas'd: whereupon he rode up to him, and taking Leave of him, he retired fome Diftance off to view the Combat. As foon as the Combatants approach'd each other, *Beaufort* told Philario, that he was ftill willing to compofe the Difference upon peaceable Terms, if he thought proper; but Philario reply'd, that he did not come there to capitulate, and therefore he muft refolve either to fight, or die, fince he refufed to live in Friendfhip with one who, tho' injur'd, had fought it at his Hands. " Then be it as it " may, reply'd *Beaufort*:" and fo without fpeaking any more, they turn'd their Horfes, and began to move towards each other with the utmoft Violence. But Philario perceiving that *Beaufort*'s Horfe was much fwifter than his, tho' not fo ftrong, refolv'd to fhock him with his Horfe, as well as ftrike with his Sword; which *Beaufort* obferving, turn'd his Horfe fwiftly to fhun the Force of Philario's; but could not move fo nimbly, but that Philario join'd in with

him

him with incredible Speed, and ran him clear through. *Pamphilo* seeing his Friend fall, turn'd his Horse toward PHILARIO, who rode with great Fury to receive him; but as soon as he came near, *Pamphilo*'s Horse rais'd himself up upon his hinder Feet, which PHILARIO very narrowly escaped, and taking that Opportunity thrust the Sword up to the Hilt in his Belly, which made him bound and fling in such a Manner, that *Pamphilo*, tho' an excellent Horseman, was soon thrown off; which PHILARIO seeing, nimbly leap'd from his, and claping his Sword to his Breast, bid him surrender. But he reply'd, that since Fortune had declared for him, he might use his Victory as he pleas'd; but he would not owe his Life to the Man that had slain his Friend. " Since you are so resolved, " says PHILARIO, I once more give you the Op-" portunity of revenging your Friend's Death:" And so saying, he gave him his Sword; upon which there began an obstinate Duel between them, insomuch that Victory stood a while in doubt which Side to take. But *Pamphilo* fighting with more Rage than Judgment, it was not long before PHILARIO gained an Advantage over him; for he thinking to put an End to the Combat at one Blow, made a violent Thrust at PHILARIO, which if he had not put by would have certainly revenged *Beaufort*; but before he could recover himself, PHILARIO closed with him, and ran him thro' the Lungs. PHILARIO immediately mounting, with his Man rode out of the Field, not so much glad of the Victory, as sorry that he had bought it at the Expence of so much Blood.

In the mean Time *Horatio* being told that

PHILARIO was gone out with *Pamphilo*, went directly after them; but not knowing the Place where they were met, he fought a long Time in vain; but at length he found *Pamphilo*, who was juft at the Point of Death, and with him a Gentleman call'd *Philander*, a Friend of his, who had been likewife fearching for them, imagining they were gone to fight. *Horatio* took him by the Hand, and beg'd him to relate the Caufe of this Difafter: " The Circumftances, fays he, " of the Combat are too long to tell, but both " *Beaufort* and my felf fell nobly by PHILARIO's " Hand, and *Beaufort* alone is to blame. This " I think my felf obliged to declare before my " Death, which will be in a few Moments, to " clear the Honour of the braveft Gentleman " in the World from any Imputation that may " be thrown upon him. *Philander* knows the " reft, but I can no more:" —— and at that Word he fainted, and in a few Minutes afterwards expired; leaving *Horatio* and *Philander* in the higheft Admiration of PHILARIO's Valour and Fortune. They both returned to Town, but could hear no News of PHILARIO; for he was retired to a fmall Village at fome Diftance, where difguifing himfelf, as foon as it was dark, he return'd Home to confult what was to be done. They all agreed that he muft immediately leave *England*, before the News of this Accident fhould fpread far; and that *Lyfander* in the mean Time fhould make ufe of all his Intereft to obtain his Pardon of the Queen. Nothing troubled him but his being obliged to leave all his Affairs with OLINDA unfinifhed; whom he refolved however to fee, tho' at the Hazard of his Life. Accordingly after taking

Leave

Leave of *Lyfander*, *Amanda* and *Horatio*, in the moſt affectionate Manner, about ſix a Clock, he ſet out, ſcarce ever ſtoping his Horſe till he came to *London*; where being arrived, he again difguis'd himſelf, and went to *Neander's*, who did not know him; but he ſoon difcovered himſelf, and inform'd them of what had happened. Great was their Trouble and Concern for this unfortunate Accident: but the melancholy Scene is yet to come. OLINDA had ſoon Notice of his being there, and came on all the Wings of Love to meet him, imagining then all her Fears were at an End; but alas, how ſadly was ſhe miſtaken! and to deſcribe her Grief at the fatal News, is beyond the Force of Language. But there was no avoiding this Separation, without manifeſt Hazard of his Life, upon which all her Happineſs depended; and therefore ſhe was obliged, hard as it was, to ſubmit to her Fate.

All that Day, which had it been an Age, would have been too little, they ſpent in exchanging their mutual Vows; but when Night came, and they muſt part, what Tongue can paint their Woe? Sure never was there a Separation ſo full of Sorrow! What did he not ſay to calm her ſwelling Paſſion? For while he held her in his Arms: "By all thoſe Fires, ſays he, that "ſhine above our Heads, and by thoſe bright "Eyes that are the Light and Joy of my Soul, "I ſwear, to keep thy lov'd adored Image in "my Heart; and ſooner, thou deareſt, ſweeteſt "Creature Heaven e'er form'd, to part with "my Life, than my Fidelity to OLINDA." She would have reply'd, but Grief fettered her Tongue; yet what that denied, her Sighs and Tears expreſs'd. At length with a Kiſs he made

a Shift

a Shift to take a laſt Adieu; and taking Leave of *Neander*, *Aurelia* and *Belinda*, he ſet out, and the next Day arrived at *Dover*, where by good Fortune he found a Ship bound for *Calais*, in which he immediately embark'd.

But to return to *London*. The Day after PHILARIO's Departure, *Cleon*, *Beaufort*'s Father, took Coach for *London*, and coming to the Court acquainted the Friends of *Pamphilo* of what had happened; conjuring them to join with him in revenging their Deaths. Accordingly they all went to the Queen, and intreated her Juſtice againſt PHILARIO, the Author of this Diſaſter. But by good Fortune, *Lyſander* had been there before them, and throwing himſelf at the Queen's Feet, implored her Royal Clemency toward his Son; ſo that the adverſe Party did not meet with altogether ſuch a Reception as they expected. However the Queen iſſued out a Proclamation commanding PHILARIO to appear, and anſwer to the Charge brought againſt him; which, had he been in *England*, he would hardly have obey'd, well knowing that notwithſtanding *Lyſander*'s Services might claim ſome Conſideration, yet ſo great was the Reſpect the Queen and the whole Court bore *Pamphilo*, that the moſt favourable Sentence he could have expected at that Time, would have been Baniſhment.

PHILARIO therefore not coming within the Time limited in the Proclamation, the Queen was highly incens'd; and one *Dorimant*, a Nephew of *Pamphilo*'s, a great Favourite then at Court, inſinuated, that it was plain from his not appearing upon that Summons, that he was guilty of ſome foul Action in their Death, which he

he was afraid fhould be difcovered. This coming to *Lyfander*'s Ears, he with *Horatio* and *Neander* went in Perfon to confront them; and *Horatio* inform'd her Majefty, that he faw and fpoke with *Pamphilo* before his Death, who told him and *Philander*, that after PHILARIO had flain *Beaufort*, he was attacked by *Pamphilo*, who was foon unhorfed; and after his Life was in his Hands, he generoufly return'd him his Sword, and *Pamphilo* renew'd the Combat with him on Foot, in which it was his Fortune to fall. " This, fays *Horatio*, I had part from *Pam-*
" *philo*'s own Mouth, and part from *Philander*,
" a Friend of his, whom I found talking with
" *Pamphilo* in the Field, to whom he had re-
" lated the Particulars of the Combat, as he
" can atteft." The Queen then difmifs'd them, commanding them to attend her Pleafure another Time, and bring *Philander* along with them, to confirm what *Horatio* had faid. But great was the Confternation of all PHILARIO's Friends, when after the ftricteft Enquiry had been made in all Parts, no News could be got of *Philander*.

Notwithftanding this Difappointment, they all prepared to wait upon the Queen at the Time fhe had ordered; and well knowing the Power of Beauty, they requefted OLINDA, *Aurelia*, and *Belinda* to attend them, if poffible to move the Queen to Clemency. When her Majefty was ready to give them Audience, they were conducted into the Prefence, and at another Door the Accufers were ufhered in, with whom came *Angelica*; whom when OLINDA knew to be *Beaufort*'s Sifter, fhe could not help admiring PHILARIO's Conftancy, who could refift fo many

Charms,

Charms, as she was Mistress of. The Splendor of this Company was perhaps never equalled on the like Occasion, but OLINDA's incomparable Beauty, which as the Sun in its Meridian Glory, eclipsed all present, alone drew the Eyes and Admiration of all upon her; and even *Angelica* her self confess'd she could not blame PHILARIO's Fidelity to one so fair. But to our Business.

The Accusers were first heard, and *Cleon* pleaded strenuously for Justice on the Murderer of his Son, as did likewise *Dorimant* for the Death of *Pamphilo*. After this *Lysander* threw himself at the Queen's Feet, and in the most moving Language entreated her Royal Goodness towards PHILARIO; in which he was seconded by *Neander*, *Horatio*, and all the rest of that fair Company. But when OLINDA went to kneel in his Behalf, her Majesty, as a Mark of her Favour, with her own Hand lifted her from the Ground; and in fine, their Intercessions had such Influence on the Queen, that she granted PHILARIO's Pardon, on Condition he appeared in three Months to justify his Honour. I need not tell you that the Joy of all his Friends was great, for it was unspeakable; and after they had return'd the Queen their most humble Thanks, they were dismiss'd.

Lysander sent a Gentleman directly with an Express to PHILARIO, whom we left crossing the Sea to *Calais*, where he made no long Stay, but set out for *Paris*, resolving to go by the Way of *Brussels*; where finding several *English* Prisoners of War, he stay'd some Time, and got acquainted with several Gentlemen he had formerly known in *England*. Going one Night to sup

sup with some Officers and Persons of Figure; he no sooner entered the Room, but he saw at the Table a Gentleman whose Countenance he had been well acquainted with; but advancing nearer, how was he surprized to find it indeed no other than his Friend *Mirabell*, the only Man in the World he most wish'd, and least expected to meet. *Mirabell*'s Surprize was equal to his, and he could hardly at first believe his own Eyes; but finding that it was really PHILARIO; they embraced each other with the utmost Joy. PHILARIO then inform'd him of the Reasons of his coming to *France*, which Accident he no longer thought unfortunate, since he had been so happy to meet the Person whose Absence alone, even in the Enjoyment of OLINDA, would have given an Allay to his Felicity.

Mirabell in Return told him, that as soon as he left *England*, he went to the Duke of *Marlborough*'s Camp, whom he knew very well, and was received by him as a Volunteer; and some Time after in an Engagement, seeing the Colours of his Company in the Enemy's Hand, he leap'd over an Hedge to redeem them, which he did with the Loss of his own Liberty, and the Life of him that held them. Being thus made a Prisoner of War, he was removed to *Brussels*, where he had remain'd ever since. Not long after this they both set out for *Paris*, where *Mirabell* obtained his Freedom, and PHILARIO waited with Impatience to hear News from his Father.

The Messenger *Lysander* had sent, was on his Way to *Paris*; but passing by the Side of a Wood, three Villains attack'd him, and upon his making some Resistance, he was unfortunately shot

shot thro' the Head: by which unhappy Accident PHILARIO miss'd of the Intelligence, which had like to have involv'd them in fresh Troubles.

During their stay at *Paris*, they recived Information, that *Elutherius*, who I before told you went a Volunteer under the Earl of *Peterborough*, was, at the storming of *Monjouick*, a strong Fortification of *Barcelona*, slain by a Shot from the Fort, as he was bravely fighting by the Prince of *Hesse*, who fell soon afterwards. They were both deeply concerned at the Death of this unfortunate Gentlemen: and tho' *Mirabell* was by that Means rid of the only Man, that hindred his Happiness with *Belinda*; yet when he considered that intimate Friendship that had been for several Years between them, which was now thus fatally dissolved, he could hardly avoid thinking himself unhappy in gaining a Mistress with the Loss of his Friend.

The Time fix'd for PHILARIO's Appearance drawing pretty near, and no News coming either of him or the Messenger *Lysander* had sent; no Body knew what to think; and OLINDA, who before thought she held Fortune in her Hand, began now to fear some new Disaster. In the midst of this Perplexity, *Horatio* himself embarqued for *Paris*, resolving to find out PHILARIO and bring him along with him; but the Day before he arrived at *Paris*, PHILARIO was gone to *Fontain-Bleau*. It was just dark when he came to the Edge of the Forest, and he had not rode long before he found by the Report of five or six Pistols, that fighting was near; spurring his Horse toward the Place, where he heard the Noise, he could discern by
the

the Moon, which cast a glimmering Light thro' the Shades, a Gentleman bravely defending himself against six or seven Thieves, who had already unhors'd his Man, and wounded himself. PHILARIO with his Sword in one Hand, and a Pistol in the other, rush'd like Lightning to his Assistance; and letting fly, he shot two of them dead upon the Spot, and almost the same Moment ran another clear through from Side to Side; and all this with such incredible Speed, that any one would have almost judged it a single Action: so that the Villains were beaten off with the Loss of four of their Company, before they were well apprehensive of any Resistance; and the Gentleman found himself reliev'd, e'er he could scarce think of any Succour. The three that escaped, being fled, he found among the slain, the Stranger's Man still alive, tho' very much wounded, whom they seated on Horseback, and then rode forward. Upon PHILARIO's asking the Gentleman how he came to be thus engaged, he reply'd; that they had followed him a good while, but he not thinking them Highway-men, kept on his Way; and when he was got into the Wood, they came up to him and demanded his Money, which he refusing to give them, there began an obstinate Battle: "In which, said he, I must "have inevitably perish'd, had not Heaven sent "you to my Assistance. But pray, Sir, conti- "nued he, may I not know to whom I am in- "debted for my Life?" Upon PHILARIO's telling him his Name: "Heavens, cry'd he, "am I then thus infinitely obliged to the only "Man in the World I ever injured!" PHILARIO was as much surprized as he, not knowing

ing what he meant: but he continued in this Manner: "My Name, says he, is *Philander*: "I was an intimate Acquaintance of *Pamphilo*, "who fell by your Hand in *England*. *Horatio* "and I were the only Persons who saw and "spoke to *Pamphilo* before he expired, who "gave us as particular Account of the Combat, "as his Circumstances would permit, conclu- "ding with the highest Encomiums on your "Virtue and Courage, and charging me to ju- "stify your Fame against any Imputations of "Dishonour that might be thrown upon it. This "*Dorimant*, *Pamphilo*'s Nephew, your greatest "Foe, well knew; and therefore overcome by "his Sollicitations, and the Love I bore my "deceased Friend, I left *England* on Purpose to "avoid declaring the Truth of that Action, "which I was certain would be required. The "Event proved as we expected; for *Horatio*, "little thinking that I was absent, cited me as "a Witness of the Truth of what he had at- "tested. But see the Hand of Heaven, in "first bringing my own Life into Danger, as "a Punishment of the Crime (for I can now "call it by no other Name) I had committed "against you, and then sending you to my De- "liverance!"

PHILARIO could not but be glad of this Dis- covery, since he had laid an Obligation on *Phi- lander* to vindicate his Reputation to the World; and therefore told him, that all the Re- turn he desired was, that he would maintain, whenever it was necessary, what he had related to him about that Combat: which *Philander* engaged his Honour to perform.

Being

Being come to *Fontain Bleau*, they all took in, and the next Morning *Philander*, having Business about three Leagues further, left PHILARIO waiting his Return, which was in about two Days, and then they came both together to *Paris*. In the mean Time *Horatio* having found out PHILARIO's Lodgings, the first Person he saw there was *Mirabell*, who after their mutual Expressions of Joy at so happy and unexpected a Meeting, told him that PHILARIO was gone to *Fontain Bleau*, from whence he expected him back in two or three Days; for which Reason *Horatio* resolved to wait at *Paris* till he came, He was much surprized when *Mirabell* told him they had neither seen, nor heard any Thing either of the Express, or Messenger *Lysander* had sent; and they both concluded, that some Accident had befallen him.

When PHILARIO return'd, both *Horatio* and *Mirabell* were gone out; but it was not long before they came in to PHILARIO's no small Amazement, seeing *Horatio*; but he quickly informed him of the happy News he had brought, and that he must directly prepare for *England*. PHILARIO in Return acquainted them with his Meeting with *Philander*, and the whole Adventure in the Forest of *Fontain Bleau*. Two Days afterwards they all left *Paris*, and in a little Time were all landed in *England*.

Lysander remained all this Time at *Neander's*, longing for the Arrival of *Horatio* and his Son; and as OLINDA and they were all sitting together in a Parlour, a Page came into the Room, and told them there was one at the Door had brought News of PHILARIO. OLINDA was the first that started from her Chair to receive this welcome

welcome Meſſenger; but inſtead of that, PHILARIO himſelf came in, and running to embrace her, ſhe with Exceſs of Joy and Surprize fell down in a Swoon; but being recovered, it was a good while before he diſengaged himſelf from her, to do Reverence to *Lyſander* and *Amanda*. But to deſcribe the Joy of all this Company, eſpecially upon the News of *Philander*'s being found, will require a Pen much more florid and elegant than mine. Afterwards PHILARIO going to *Belinda*, ſpoke thus:

"There is a Pleaſure, Madam, ſays he, yet
" to come, in which you will be the greateſt
" Sharer of any yet preſent, tho' we ſhall all
" be Partakers. You may remember, Madam,
" when laſt *Mirabell* and *Elutherius* viſited you,
" you told them you would chuſe him for
" your Servant, who ſhould come laſt to you;
" but by the unhappy Death of *Elutherius* in
" *Spain*, that Sentence is now no longer of
" Force, and therefore I will to mine add the
" Interceſſion of all this Company, that *Mira-*
" *bell*, who now waits your Pleaſure, may be
" admitted to that Happineſs, he has ſo long
" and ſo well deſerved."

There needed not much Perſuaſion to a Thing ſhe was already ſo well inclined to, and therefore ſhe deſired he would come in. Upon her ſaying this, *Mirabell*, who had overheard all that had paſs'd, entered the Room, and kneeling to *Belinda*: "Behold, Madam, ſays he, at
" your Feet once more your faithful *Mirabell*,
" to receive his Doom from your fair Lips!"
She immediately deſired him to riſe, and giving him her Hand, reply'd: "Since then *Elutherius* is dead, whoſe Fate I cannot help mourn-
" ing,

"ing, and you have proved your self faithful, I will for once dispence with my Resolution, and consent to be none but yours." *Mirabell* receiv'd it with an Ecstasy of Love; and then embraced *Aurelia* and the rest of the Company, which till then he had not Time to do.

The News of Philario's Arrival was soon spread over the Court, and there was scarce any Thing the Subject of Discourse but this Affair; which every one, as is usual, spoke of according as they affected or disliked the Party. But the Friends of *Cleon* and *Dorimant* were in a strange Confusion when they heard of *Philander*'s Arrival, who, they knew, was the only Person that could justify Pihlario's Honour. And accordingly a few Days after his Arrival, *Philander* was introduced into her Majesty's Presence; and reciting all that you have already heard relating to the Combat between Philario, *Beaufort* and *Pamphilo*, fully confirm'd *Horatio*'s Testimony, and satisfied the Queen of the Justice of the Action; upon which Philario's Pardon was signed, and he had afterwards the Honour to kiss her Majesty's Hand.

There wanted only one Thing more to compleat the Satisfaction of this whole Assembly, which was *Angelica*'s Consent to make *Horatio* happy. To this End Philario paid her a Visit; and after he had in the most graceful Manner beg'd her Pardon for the Injury he had done her Beauty, to which he could never have been just without violating his Faith to Olinda, he conjured her, since she had so generously forgiven the Death of her Brother, that she would give one more Proof of her Goodness by crowning his Friend's Wishes. This Request

quest she a while opposed, but at length overcome by his repeated Sollicitations, she yielded to *Horatio*'s Happiness, and the next Morning the joyful Nuptials were all consummated.

The Day concluded with a fine Ball, and every Thing else that spoke Delight and Transport; and at Night they retired to the full Fruition of all those Joys, to which after so many Storms and Dangers they were happily arrived.

Thus Fate may wish'd Success awhile retard,
But virtuous Deeds still find a sure Reward.

F I N I S.

The Forced Virgin

Anonymous

Bibliographical note:

This facsimile has been made from a copy in the British Museum (1093.i.18)

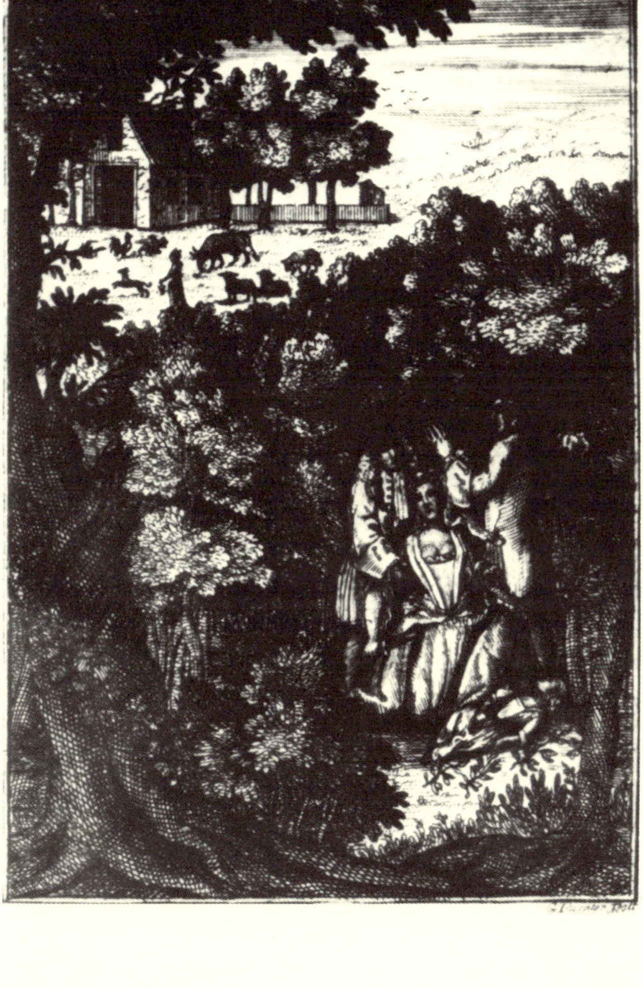

THE
FORCED VIRGIN;
OR, THE
Unnatural Mother.
A TRUE
SECRET HISTORY.

―――*How strange a Riddle Virtue is!*
They never miss it, who possess it not,
And they who have it ever find a Want.
　　　　　　　　　　Rochester's Valent.

LONDON:
Printed for W. TROTT, at the *Seven Stars* in
Russel-Court, Drury-Lane. MDCCXXX.

[Price One Shilling.]

TO

Mrs. *JANE BLACHFORD.*

MADAM,

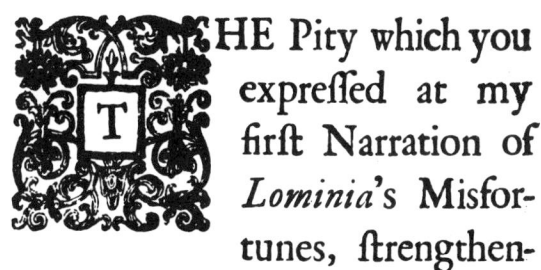

THE Pity which you expressed at my first Narration of *Lominia*'s Misfortunes, strengthened my Desire of it's appearing in Print; and I have now accordingly ushered it on a Satyrical World under your Protection.

Dedication.

tection. Though unlicenced by You, Madam, I have made this publick Dedication; I hope the Rigour of my Transgressions will merit some Abatement, when I declare, the chief Inducements were, that *Lominia*'s Failings required the Illustration of a Patroness, highly blessed with that Portion of Virtue, under which she fell. So that in relating the Woes of the One, I bring, at the same time, the exceeding Beauties of another's Mind to retrieve that Female Fair-ones Weaknesses.

Heaven, Madam, hath blessed You with a distinguishing Mind

Dedication.

Mind and Judgment. Neither fond of condemning or praising, Free from the Prude or Coquette, yet by a pleasing Mixture placed in the middle of each. Who then could be so proper as the Person I have chose?——It is your never-failing Conduct can make us wink at *Lominia*'s Deeds, and give her Misfortunes, Pity. Pardon the Acts she committed, and view in your Person, what her Virtues first were.

Love, when opposed in its directive Way, swells like a rapid Torrent over all little Bounds, and Deluge-like sweeps
wide

Dedication.

wide Destruction round. — Such were the first Accidents of the lost *Lominia!* — And, now, if the Trouble I have taken, should meet with your Liking, and warn those, (if any) Guilty, from the rash Actions she committed, my Endeavours will obtain their Ends, and your Approbation crown the weak Attempts of,

MADAM,

Your most Obliged,

most Obedient and

most humble Servant.

THE
Forced *VIRGIN*;
OR,
The Unnatural MOTHER.

OF all those Passions, which Human Nature is liable to, none have a stronger Effect on the Soul than Love; To this, the Prince, the Courtier, All from the lofty Palace to the humble Cottage bend, 'tis This alone which makes the Tyrant bow, and consent to Mercy, to pardon those he but lately condemned, and give them a Length of unexpected Joy: The Prude, and Coquer, when only warmed by the first glowing Symptoms of this delightful Pain, forget their former Pleasures, and accept the ready Thrall. Like a rapid Stream it sweeps a yielding Current, and drives the World at Random; even Virtue's-self submits to the Yoak, and draggs the welcome Chain.

[2]

And yet of so unsteady and changeable a Nature, that, instead of its producing an End agreeable to its first Grounds, Rapes, Treachery and Murder supply the late melting and dying Ecstasies.

Lominia, the unfortunate Subject of the ensuing Pages, was the Daughter of a wealthy Merchant in the Northern Part of this Kingdom; a Maid by Nature formed so exactly Lovely, that no Eye could gaze on her Beauty without Admiration; to this was added both an Harmony of Voice, and a discerning Judgment, so addicted to Learning, which, attended with a ready Wit, made her the Wonder of her own Sex, and the Desire of the other: Among the Multitude of those who sought her for their Wife, none was so signally respected by the Fair, as *Arastes*; this young Gentleman made it his constant Assiduity to be ever present with her, his Wit charmed, his Form ravished, and his Gallantry pleased; In return, her every Accomplishment shone to his transported Soul, all transparent; nothing was more entertaining than her Company, and nothing seemed obstructive to compleat the utmost Summit of his aspiring Wishes. Approv'd, and admitted as a Lover, by the Consent of *Lominia*, and her Parents, who indulged the happy Choice of their Daughter, He made his Visits more open, and bold;—— One plenteous Round of Joy delighted each transported Heart, and tun'd each Soul to Rest:—— Noise and Discord knew no Residence, but with smiling Transport the Hours danced away:—— Each revolving Day was scarce distinguish'd; the Night abandon'd, and

glim-

glimmering Dawn receiv'd with Melody and Mirth.

Thus pleasing, and pleased; the equally loving, equally beloved Pair pass'd the Hours of Delight in the Infancy of their Loves; till fickle Fortune, never steady, perceived an unguarded Hour: *Arastes's* happy Success had created him many Rivals; But above the Rest, the implacable Hatred of *Lysanor*, a Man so universally feared, that scarce any Ear was a Stranger to his Villanies; He had for a long time loved the fair *Lovinia*, but with small Success; the frequent Repulses which he met with, he fancied were occasioned by his too happy Rival's welcome Reception. Which Thought still gaining greater Root, swelled his Soul with such Vexation, that he intended nothing more than the Death of *Arastes*. To compleat which, he immediately executed every Purpose that seem'd inclinable to his End. But so happy was the ardent Lover, that without the least Danger, he escaped every Snare: *Lysanor*, vexed to the Soul at the many Disappointments he had received, was thinking to give over his Attempts; when one Day it fell out, that *Arastes* being with his much-desired Fair in her Room, and the Garden's Situation opposite to his View, he thought something of Pleasure seem'd therein so inviting to his Eye, and the Motives of his Soul at the same time instigating his Desires with more Ardency, he craved his fair *Lovinia* to accompany him in the expected Pleasure. The Weather being pleasant and serene, she attended his Will; every Wish sympathized to a Compleation of his

B 2

his Felicity, and nothing of so soft and inticing a Demand could receive a Denial. She gave him her Hand to lead her on, secure in his Admiration, despised the Stings of the World's invenomed Malice.

The Way into the Garden was by an easy Descent from the House, made with Steps of the finest Marble, bounding on a beauteous Green enamell'd with Flowers of various Hue, whose opening Buds cast a delightful Odour round. 'Twas now the God of Love, with Tyrant Sway, play'd with recruited Force on the Soul-enamour'd Youth; in *Lominia*'s Eyes the little Ruler fixed his Seat, where with resistless Strength, and smiling Pride, he shot *Arastes* with every golden Dart.

The Garden of *Orontes* (by which Name I shall distinguish the Maiden's Father) was a true Perfection of Nature, and Art. Here, to the ravish'd View appeared the Ever-Greens, which cut by the curious Hand of the diligent Gardiner, created a Wonder to the Beholder's Eyes. There, by a cooling Fountain fix'd in a pleasant Vale, the verdant Shades of the Art-wrought Avenues butted in divers Forms. In the Trees, the tender Birds chose their delightful Seats, and with melodious Notes sung forth the Summer's Glory. While, with regardless Care the Soul-enamour'd Youth trode heedless on the flowery Plain; A Piece of Nature's brighter Boast charm'd his admiring Sight, and required the darling use of every Faculty.

'Twas now, the tender Pair had reach'd the Fountain's Brink; When *Arastes* turning his Eyes espied a curious Arbour, where the Sun-

Beams

Beams unresisted Force could scarcely shine. ——A Place so accidentally fitted to the Purpose of his Soul, that unheard, and unobserv'd, he could breath forth the Complaints, and Fondness of his Love; thither the manly Youth led on the tender Maid, the Entrance of which seem'd rather a deluding Vision than a real Arbour, whose friendly Darkness made by the thick spreading Boughs, warmed his Mind with unusual Transport:—— A Darkness not horrid or terrible; but such as an eager Lover desires with his glorious Prize, when, all-transporting, gazing, dying in raptur'd Bliss, each eager Wish partakes an unbounded Spring! 'Twas thus he lay, retired, and secret from the Eyes of the gazing Vulgar, when his Joy-compleated Soul struggling with the present Ecstasy, thus disclos'd his already too discernable Passion, "O "my fair *Lominia!* (cryed he), Thou tender "Maid, let me never taste a Bliss, less, than I now "enjoy; but, with consenting Eyes, and open "Ears, receive my unchanging Passion; and "soothing tell my raptur'd Soul the pleasing "Grant, which Love, like thine, obtained, will "ever create; — Let me, Oh! Let me, thus "gently welcome meet my Fair; when, a Pa- "rents Consent, —— Heaven's regarded Bles- "sing! smiles on my Hopes, and helps on an "Amour, so exquisitely good, so yielding to "every Wish; —— Crown me with thy Con- "sent, which once obtained, will repel the "Doubts now struggling in my distracted "Soul."—— Here he stop'd, swell'd with unendless Pleasure, his Tongue now lost its Utterance; his Spirits retreated, and gently down

his

his drooping Head fell on her snowy Bosom; Her panting Breasts, before unacquainted with so pleasing a Burthen, seem'd now with swelling Heaves to resist, and now with gentle Falls to be still more desirous of the pleasing Weight, ⸺ The unexpressible Transport of her Mind!

So passionate a Declaration proclaimed his utmost Fondness; and the raptur'd Maid, now, a little recover'd from the pleasing Trance, his amorous Addresses had occasioned, opened her Mind in the following Words. ⸺ "Love is a
" Passion so little known unto me, that no one
" ought to wonder if I misconstrue its Significa-
" tion: You say my Parents consent to your De-
" sires; if it be so, which I doubt not, when
" testified by the worthy *Arastes*, the Duty of a
" Child shall not be wanting, or the Obedience
" of *Leminia* questioned by her Relations:⸺
" No:⸺I will receive thee with all the Testi-
" monies of my Father's Friendship, but hope,
" though my perhaps too forward Heart hath
" made me thus openly confirm my Love, your
" generous Soul will not triumph over my Weak-
" ness." No, my sweet Angel! (replied he) tran-
sported beyond the Bounds of Reason at her Words; "*Arastes* can never blaspheme the Deity,
" that thus pleasing drops the healing Balm to
" his scorching burning Wound: No, should
" numberless Woes withstand our Loves, and stop
" the Way to Bliss; my Strength, my Life, my
" All should stand the fatal Shock, and show how
" far, as Life, I love the heavenly-kind *Leminia*:"
⸺ To show how far thou injurest the Soul-afflicted *Lysanor*, (cried a Voice, which, accompanied with a Rustling in the Bushes, foretold
some

[7]

some Treachery at hand;) when immediately, to their great Surprize, appeared four Men, each in a disguised Habit; who rushing with a sudden Speed on the tender Couple, obtained with a faint Resistance the Purport of their Intent. Two of them bore away the long-wish'd-for Prize, who with piercing Cries proclaimed to Heaven the hidden Villany; while the others were busy in binding *Arastes* to the sturdy Bole of an adjacent Oak. When the doleful Shrieks of the violated Maid reached his Ears, he strove with his utmost force to break the corded Bands; Agitated by the open Wrongs he saw preparing before his Face, with more than human Strength he snap'd the Cords, and set his imprison'd Body free. When arising from the Ground, he perceived a Sword, which one of the Villains had been so careless as to neglect; this with a wonderful Alacrity he seiz'd, a Treasure more welcome to his distracted Soul than Food to a starving Wretch; Armed thus unexpectedly with so pleasing a Companion, he flew on the Wings of Love to a Revenge the most glorious in its Nature; to *Leminia*'s Relief, his speedy Steps with hasty Flight bent their resistless Course.

But Oh! into what unthought-of Ruin doth Love, that justly blinded Deity, involve his inconsiderate Subjects! The injured Youth had no Eyes, but what were fastened on the flying Coursers; 'twas there his Sight lay intranced, and there alone he fancied Danger. When, to his Destruction, the two Villains who had bound him, and only retired a small Distance to observe his Attempts, rushed from behind
their

their bushy Retreats, and set on the noble Youth. Each with their drawn Swords assaulted him with unequalled Violence, whose thickening Blows, like hasty Showers of stormy Hail, fell so fast, that *Arastes* was quite confused; at length recovering from the fierce Insult, and preparing to put himself in a Posture of Defence, one of the Traitors stealing unobservedly behind him, thrust his Sword with so powerful a Force into *Arastes*'s Back, that he fell prostrate on the Earth; which seconded with other Blows, they left him in all Appearance dead; and making their best Way to the Garden Gate, where their Horses stood, mounted thereon and rode immediately after their Companions.

Orontes, wondering at their Stay, sent his Servants into the Garden to acquaint them, that Dinner waited for them; one of whom went directly to the Place where *Arastes* lay bleeding; the ghastly Sight astonish'd the Man, he stood like one bereft of Motion. At length the Blood relaxed, and warmed again each beating Fibre, creating new Life in his stiffen'd Carcass; recover'd now from his late Surprize, he called to the rest of his Companions, who had dispersed themselves in different Parts of the Garden on the same account; every one at the Summons directed themselves to the dreadful Place; where, when arrived, they saw (alike astonished) their Fellow-Servant, busy in binding up the Wounds of the bleeding Youth. *Arastes* was so well beloved, that each one with streaming Eyes bemoaned his savage Fate. Each was willing to assist the other, and carefully

lifting

lifting the Body on their Shoulders, conveyed it to their expecting Master.

When *Orontes* and his Wife beheld their Servants with the Coarse of *Arastes*, a cold Sweat seized every Limb, and chilling Fear spread every Sense with raw convulsive Shakings: the last bitter painful Agonies of Death, by their outward Deportments, seem'd to sway their inward Souls, but soon the returning Senses gave new Pain to Thought. The Servants related to them, where, and how, in this present Condition, they had found *Arastes*; but on the most diligent Search, they were unable to learn where *Lominia* was.

This second Thunder-bolt shook their still-disordered Senses with a greater Force and deeper Despair than the former. But *Orontes* recalling his sicken'd Soul to Thought, ordered a Surgeon to be immediately sent for. A Gentleman of that Profession happening at that Instant to pass the Door, whom the Servants knew to be such, they intreated him in, who immediately ordered a warm Bed to be prepared, wherein he laid the languid Lover. In a short Space the heaving Pulse began to move, and discover, to the almost dead Spectators round, some hopes of remaining Life. Having dressed the Wounds, and prescribed proper Medicines, he took his Leave for that Day, not without a welcome Assurance, that none of the Wounds were Mortal.

The Loss of so much Blood had weaken'd his Spirits, and lull'd his Eyes to soft Repose. Sufficient Attendants being ordered to watch him, the sorrowful Father dispatched into every Road his Men and Horses, to endeavour to learn an Account of the lost *Lominia*. On which

C requisite

requisite Search let us leave them, and now see what became of the Beautiful Fair.

The Villains thus beyond Expectation having succeeded in their Attempts, made the nearest Road to the intended Hold. Vain was all Resistance; by hurtful Pressures they confin'd the tender Captive.——Her piercing Shrieks were needless too, the swift-footed Coursers had bore her beyond hopes of Assistance. They quitted now the publick Road, and alighted in a Forest; where taking the trembling Maid from off the Horse, they forc'd Her towards the Place they intended. Not far had they directed their Way in the whispering Grove, but they came to a Place, which naturally seem'd to interrupt their Design, and stop their plotted Mischief——The Spraiey Briars and prickly Thorns were strongly wove together, and made a just Defence:——No verdant Feilds or flowery Meads blest their Eyes with a refreshing View, but all appeared an horrid Scene of Woe:——A Place so detestable in Appearance filled the Maiden's Mind with a thousand boding Fears; she thought, that now they would, by some brutal Act, display the most savage Falshood of their blotted Souls——And now she thought *Arastes*'s Life had paid its dreadful Tribute:——When sinking, dying in the perplexed Wildness of her Thoughts, a sudden Stop recall'd her stroling Senses back to Knowledge.

They were now arrived on a verdant Plain, wherein Nature had formed a secret Cave; which these Ruffians chose for their Residence: At the Door or Entrance of which stood a Man habited, as costly as Riches could supply him; This was *Lysanor*, the cursed, dread Promoter

moter of all the woeful Mischief. With all the Transports of a Soul-ravished Ecstasy, he flew to the Maid, snatched in his Arms the long-desired Prize, and clasp'd her to his throbbing Breast, vowing an Happiness he never tasted of before:——— *Lominia* filled the Air again with peircing Shrieks,——— she tore her Hair,——— she raved; beating her snowy Breasts, and showering out Curses on the Heads of her brutal Ravishers; but vain was every Cry, and each Blow created to herself a direful Pain:——— Force was used, when Perswasions failed; for finding what they named Kindness incensed her Hatred more against them, they threw aside all Regard to Virtue, or Respect to her Sex's Modesty, and used a crueler Method; some seizing her by the Hair, others laying hold of her Ivory Limbs, forced her by strength to their secret Hold:——— Thus they dragg'd the beautiful Innocent in; forcing her thro' many dark Turnings to a Room, in Appearance, more like a Palace, than a Place of so villainous a Retreat; where she again saw, seated on a Purple Couch, the hated *Lysanor*.

At her Entrance he arose, and with all the Submission of a virtuous Lover, addressed the distracted Maid; he threw himself at her Feet, and utter'd a thousand passionate Declarations of the most violent Love.——" But Oh!, con-
" tinued he, I sue in vain; the fair *Lominia* hath
" fixed her Throne within my bleeding Heart,
" and like a Queen with Sovereign Force tri-
" umphs over her dying Subject." To this she returned no Answer; her boyling Griefs now wanted room to flow; and the briny Tears, which rowled in gushing Streams down her Crimson Cheeks, denyed her Speech a Vent.

In this desperate Agony, big with unutterable Woe, she threw herself on the Floor, and discovered her dreadful Affliction by the following Words——" O ye just Powers, why have I
" lived to know this fatal Minute? how much
" better would it have been, had I never seen the
" Light?—— What an Affliction of Fate am I
" now arrived to? torn from my Father's House,
" from every Friend, and born to this detested
" Hell —— A Place of Torment worse than
" the Damn'd endure.—— But hold, (said she,
" returning again to Sense,) am I not to blame,
" to rave thus against the Power which framed
" me? cannot his tender and forgiving Mercy
" relieve me from this detested Scene? surely it
" will; I'll therefore wait with Patience the
" happy Moment."—— While she was in this Tumult, *Lysanor* left the Room, and the distress'd Fair spent the remaining Time in desperate Grief; 'till Sleep, that gentle Balm to uneasy Minds, spread his leaden Wings on her gathering Sorrows, and closed her Eyes to soft Repose.

Assoon as the Morning's Rosy Blushes proclaimed the Approach of Day, and *Phœbus* with his Golden Beams darted his Glory round the Earth, the Grief-swolen Maid arising from her Bed of Repose took a deliberate Walk around the Room, and with searching Eyes endeavoured to find an Avenue, whereout she might escape; but vain were all Attempts, too strictly guarded was every Pass. While she was busy on this Purpose, and ruminating on the Distress and Misery which she was thrown under, *Lysanor* entred; whom when she beheld, the Lovely Fair with swift Rapidity fell at his Feet, and with uplifted Hands and streaming Eyes craved

his

his Confent to depart:—" Turn me (faid fhe)
" into the open Foreft.—Bear me to Beafts of
" Prey, which range the Woods for Hunger;—
" lead me far diftant from any humble Cottage,
" do any thing, that flighted Love can dictate,
"—Spare but my Virtue." *Lyfanor*'s Soul,
however before hardened to her Speeches, now
melted; he could not indure to fee the Defire
of his Wifhes in fo fore an Extremity; whenever fhe pray'd, his Heart bid him to forgive;
he could not fee her weep without accompanying her Tears. Her Intreaties were of fuch
Force, and fo powerful her Interceffions, that
he would again have carried her to her Father,
would it not have ftrengthen'd his already too
powerful Rival.—Love and Diftraction poffeffed his Soul by turns, and each found an equal
Sway; he loved her with too difcernable a
Paffion, but then the Thoughts of a Rival, one
that had a Parent's Licence for his Addreffes,
rived his Lion-Heart with Agonies; to reftore
her to her Father, was putting *Araftes* in too
great a Felicity:—" But *Araftes* (fays he, with
" namelefs Joy) is Dead, my Bravoes never leave
" a Work but half performed: then, what need
" I fear? I'll give her again to the Arms of her
" longing Parents; when fhe finds him dead, per-
" haps, after the wily Woman's Tears are fpent,
" my Services and Generofity may fet me dear in
" her Efteem; and fhould fhe refufe, the fame
" Ways as before are open to my Hopes; Force
" and Ravifhment fhall bring her here again."

Having thus reafon'd with himfelf, and
turn'd to *Lominia*, (who in her Tears appeared
ftill more beautiful) he began to harden again,
and raifing his Voice in an angry Tone, " Come,
" (faid he,) you defire to go home, which you
" fhall.

"shall. But first, swear both by Heaven, and
" Hell; by every Being or Power which rule
" over Us, that to no one but me you will be
" Wife."——A Proposition of so dreadful a
Nature frightened the weeping Maid; she had
fresh Recourse to her Prayers, but now his Heart
was Stone, and deaf to all Intreaties. " Away,
" (said he) nor strive again to move me with
" your Tears; consent to what I propose, or
" open Force shall yield me your Beauties."——
" Here, (continued he, calling to his Compa-
" nions) lead this coy and fickle Fair to my
" Chamber, prepare the stately Bed to receive
" my throbbing Love, and dress the Bridal
" Fair in gaudy Pomp". *Lominia*, dreadfully lost
in Amazement, was again hauled away by the
brutish Attendants.

The Chamber intended for the Sacrifice of
this Beautiful Fair was lined with Cedar;
Pictures of the finest Pencils appeared all ex-
celling; Pleasures, which at any other time
would have engrossed her every Faculty, now
pass'd unregarded: Sighs and Groans ecchoed
out their dreadful Sounds; and one reigning
Terror shook her tender Frame: In Tears she
spent the heavy Minutes: Thus passed away the
few remaining Moments of her Peace, few indeed! for with speedy steps the dreadful time
approach'd, when Ease should find no more a
Residence, but Distraction possess her every
Thought.

No sooner had the Salvages executed their
Tyrant Lord's Command, and left the distracted Fair alone; but *Lysanor*, impatient of Delay,
already prepared for the direful Act, came hasty
in; from forth his burning Orbs the destructive
Light'ning flew;—— His whole Frame shook

with

with boiling Joy; Luſt, not Love, ſway'd his Soul, and nothing leſs than *Lominia*'s Ruin poſſeſſed his Brain. The Door at his firſt Entrance he ſecured, when with a ſudden Turn he ſeized the trembling Maid;——The beauteous Fair, preſs'd in his rough and harden'd Arms, by more than manly Force he bore with Pleaſure to his ſtately Bed: in vain ſhe prayed, his Luſt had ſhut his Ears to ſuch Intreaties.——In vain ſhe ſtrove to ſtay his raging Flames; Regard to her Virtue, or Fear of future Puniſhment, could make no room for a Moment's Delay; he had her now in full Poſſeſſion, and was reſolved to uſe the wiſhed-for Hour; with one Hand intangled in her Hair, he held the Maiden down; while the other furthered him to compleat his helliſh Purpoſe.

Mad at the Approach of ſo villainous an Act, ſometime a fixed Frenzy ruled her Mind, anon Reaſon regained her Throne, and harrowed all her Brain: In one of theſe Intervals of Thought, her Voice, ſweet as the *Syren*'s Song, ſtrictly charged him to think of Heaven, and quit the filthy Deed; " Though ſecret (ſaid ſhe) from
" the Eyes of Men, an Almighty Power ſees
" your Actions, and will too ſoon juſtly puniſh
" the Offender:—Oh! then defiſt, nor let my
" unſpotted Virginity be thus proſtrated.——
" Nor Heaven, nor Hell, (cryed he) ſhall ſhare
" my Joy, or participate with me in my good
" Fortune.——I'll make one continual Riot
" of the much-deſired Feaſt, nor ſhall fear of
" any Puniſhment rob my ſwelling Love.——
" My Soul's on the Wing! O Enjoyment! un-
" able for Expreſſion,——I melt,——I die,
" ——I live,——I feel your Charms; the
" balmy Bliſs revives my drooping Soul, and
" I'm

"I'm all Ecstasy!——O glorious Scene of such enchanting Substance! my Soul shall ravage every secret Avenue.——Love's Torch shall flame transparent o'er our Beds, and light us to new Joys. No more I'll treat thee ill; Thou art, from hence, my Wife, my Love, my Wish, the Center of every Hope, Sustainer of my Life; forget the Force I used to make you mine; the Road to Bliss was all a Sea of Love, which cleans'd my Raptures, and supplyed new Force to my coward Nerves:——I'll restore you to your longing Parents Arms, whose kind Consents shall make me ever happy. Thee, Traitor! (replied the Soul-distracted Maid;) What! shall the Ruiner of my Peace, the most detested Fiend of Fiends, triumph o'er my Fall, and in my Parents view? No, thou damned Monster, thou more than Devil, meet there the Justice due to thy Merit."——At these Words, she snatched up a Dagger, which lay on an adjacent Table, and struck it in his Breast——" Fly (continued she) and let thy blacken'd Soul seek out a Retreat, suting its Deserts, among the dark Residers of the Infernal Regions." The Blow was given with too willing an Hand to fail in the design; it pierced his Heart, and felled him to the Earth, where, in the convulsive Agonies of Death, he threw out impious Curses on his Murderess. The Blood sallied apace from the Crimson Wound, and the heavy Wings of Death sealed down his lustful Eye-lids.

Now, in the room of the base *Lysanor*, appeared a clayey Lump:——" O! (cryed the distressed Damsel) had you been thus but one hour agone, my Virtue had been saved,

"and

" and *Lominia* fled unpolluted to the Arms of
" her *Arastes*. But it cannot be! *Lominia's*
" ruined, her Virtue loft.———— O diftracting
" Thought! How fhall I fee my Parents, how
" meet my Friends, after fo deteftable an Act?
" ———— To die, now, would be a Bleffing; I
" have the Means to free my Soul, but want the
" Power to do;———— Religion and Reafon for-
" bid the happy Eafe;———— What then remains
" to do? return to my Parents? yes, the Road
" for my Efcape lyes open to my View, nor
" will I let flip fo kind an Opportunity."————
At this fhe threw by the decent Coverings of
her Sex, and ftripping the dead Carcafs, habited her felf in the very Drefs which *Lyfanor*
wore.

 Big with the Expectation of the happy Succefs of her Defign, fhe left the fad and difmal
Place, where her Ruin had been compleated,
and pafs'd undifcover'd through the Cave: The
Joys of Liberty diverted her Soul, and took up
every Senfe: She was now in an open Wild,
unattended, and knew not the way to any
ready Road. But fear of being purfued, added
Speed to her Steps; and after much Fatigue,
fhe wandered into the High Way, which led
to her Father's Houfe. So delightful a View,
charm'd her every Thought; Grief and Defpair
were awhile banifh'd, and nothing more than
the hoped-for Protection of fo beautiful a Man-
fion filled her Mind. 'Twas much about the
Evening's Dusk, when fhe arrived at the Gate,
and being admitted into the Houfe, ordered the
Servants to acquaint their Mafter, that a Stranger, who waited below, had a particular Secret to relate him, concerning his Daughter.
Every one ftrove to be the Bearer of this defired

fired News, and soon the longing Father knew the welcome Tale; their Bufinefs delivered, they returned to the unknown *Lominia,* and conducting her into the Parlour, left her to wait the coming of her Father; the Sight, which here appear'd before her, began to awaken in her Mind the foft Hours often fpent in *Araftes*'s Embraces, "O! (faid fhe, with ftreaming "Eyes) how various now is *Lominia*'s Peace of "Mind, to that, when fhe laft refided here; O "*Araftes!* O my Soul's better Part! how fhall I "meet again thy Embraces?" Thus fhe fighed out her many Griefs; which, when a little difperfed, gave fome leifure to her hafty Soul, to obferve the Difference now, and a few Hours agone, of the Houfe of *Orontes.* —— No Mufical Inftruments charmed, as ufual, the hearkening Senfes, but all around was fpread a profound Silence: Grief and Sorrow appeared in every Vifage. — *Lominia* was gone! — The Sun of *Orontes*'s Horizon was fet, and Darknefs ruled the Day.

Her Parents being now come into the Room, *Lominia* perceived the outward Havock her Lofs had created: The big-dropping Tears hung on their Eye-lids, a fad and defponding Care appeared in their dejected Countenances. Every thing which can be thought of the utmoft Defpair, and Grief, feemed to deprefs their Minds. *Lominia*'s Heart was pierced at the firft View; all the Maiden's Softnefs fhone through her manly Habit; Duty to her Parents forbad her to encreafe their Diftraction, by a purpofed Narration of her Misfortunes; but with all the hafte of an inexpreffible Duty, fhe threw herfelf on the Floor, clafp'd her aged Parents Knees, and bathed their Hands with gufhing

Tears,

Tears, which flow'd so fast, that they denied her Tongue the Power of Speech. The old People, suprized to see again their Daughter, stood likewise mute; 'till at length, *Orontes* mastering the Tide of Passion, which flowed with a rapid Current; cried out, with an unbounded Joy; " My Daughter! My *Lo-*
" *minia!* My *Arastes*'s Love returned! be
" great, my joyful Soul, and bid an ever-
" lasting Adieu to Grief! Arise, my Child:
" Thou Fondling of my Heart! dishabit your
" self from this different Dress, and fly to your
" Lover; distill in *Arastes*'s Soul, the welcome
" Drops of a new-returning Life.—O, my dear
" Father! (cryed the lovely Maid) *Arastes* hath
" all my fond Love can wish, but see him, I
" must not; his Sight (desirable as it is) will tear
" my Heart, and give me endless Torment:—
" O I am ruined, undone, and here, O here, in
" the Face of Heaven I vow, never to meet his
" Arms, polluted as I am; and robbed of the
" Glory which blesses a Bridal-Bed; he has my
" utmost Wishes, and must ask no more."

Such unexpected Exclamations from one so usually tender and loving, struck her Parents with a second Wonder, far greater than the first: But the awhile-lost Sense returning, they desired her fully to relate her Sufferings, since her Absence; to which she consented: and after she had made way for her Tale, in wiping off her Tears, began the dreadful Story from her Rape in the Garden, to her present Arrival at her Father's House; not in the least diminishing one Tittle.

At the Relation of her never-to-be-recovered Ruin, inexpressible Grief stop'd the Motion of their Words, choaked the rising Speech, and Horror seized every Thought; but, at the Relation of *Lysanor's* Death, a blooming Redness screamed the late wan and death-like Countenances, spreading new Life in every Wish. "—So glorious, so noble, and so godlike a "Revenge! (cried the distracted *Orontes*) ought "to be recorded to future Ages.—O my *Lo-* "*minia!* (continued he) though thy Ruin in "one Point cannot be retrieved; yet thou art "my Daughter still.—Haste then to *Arastes*; "if thy Spirit is too great to condescend to "be his Wife, yet let your Presence give his "strugling Life a Subsistance."

Lominia was too much engaged in the Sufferings of *Arastes*, to deny the Request desired by her Parents; she wanted to see him, her fond Soul coveted an Interview with the Subject of her constant Wishes. Different Agitations at sundry times divided her Breast, her Mind was in a continual Variance; now she was resolved, and now she would not go; the changing Winds seem'd more true than her Intentions. But whilst she was in this extravagant Dilemma, *Arastes*, hearing of the Return of his Charmer, rush'd into the Room wherein were at present the Wishes of his Soul; with all the transporting shocks of a Soul-dissolving Love, he flew to the Maid, clasped her in his eager Arms, and with impatient Haste devoured the burning Kisses from her Coral Lips. The uncommon Joy, which now possess'd his Breast, was too great to find Restraint; that *Lominia* was living, and in his View, created in him too strong a Fire to be long concealed; his present Hopes, his Desires, his wild and gnawing Wishes writhed his Frame with ungovernable Passion; his whole Body was at War,

War, and every Sinew swelled with unendless Strength. These sudden Agitations of his wild and sweeping Flights, caused such a strong and fervent Motion of the Blood, that the Bandage burst from off his yet-green Wound, the Blood sallied apace; every Artery, every Vein flowed to the widened Stream, and issued with an uncommon Spring; so terrible a Scene occasion'd *Lominia* to swoon; *Arastes*, scarce able to be accounted with the Living, yet used his utmost Skill to recover the dying Maid, heedless of himself; but so far as Strength, or Power admitted, careful of her, on whose Life depended his; he loved, admired, nor could he bear now a Separation of a Minute's durance. Proper Medicines being applied, *Lominia* recovered from her late Trance; *Arastes*'s Wounds were bound up afresh, and nothing but a plain and open View appeared to Joy.

Some few Days being past, and *Arastes*'s Wounds healed, he now began to partake of the Delights and rural Sports, which Persons of his Rank are able to maintain; he could now embrace again the Charmer of his Soul: Every Wish had its full Completion, nor could Thought request more than at present he possessed: He was now at the aspiring Summit of earthly Felicity: But Oh! how fleet and various are the Chances of this Mortal Life! Love, now of some Duration, increased Desire, and nothing but Marriage could quench the Flames of his lawful Passion; to compleat which, he intreated *Lominia* to bless his Bed, and take on her that most happy Title; a Wife. A Proposal of this Nature, he thought, would have found no Denial; it's true, she wished it, but had it not in her Breast to grant; the false *Lysanor*'s

sanor's detested Embraces rose fresh in her Mind, and created a new Power of Resistance; though the little God of Love softened her Soul to all Impressions of *Arastes*'s Behaviour, and his everready Wit could bear down all Obstacles, still she withstood his Request; and now a second Difficulty arose to his Wishes, she began to feel the weighty Burthen of *Lysanor*'s filthy Embraces, the dreadful Product of her destructive Ravishment! This was a Woe beyond Comparison, hideous to Thought, and ruinous to her everlasting Peace. Instead of her late sweet, and affable Disposition, now continual Sadness seated it self on every Air; one reigning Sorrow composed her fading Visage. Love and Pleasure, the former Delights of her Soul, were lost, gone, and never to be retrieved. Wild with her crowding Fancies, and fearful of a blasted Fame, Reason had left her Throne, and grinding Thoughts possessed her aking Brain: In this dreadful Confusion of her Mind, with a sudden Joy, she had straightway recourse to the Attempt of a thing, even detested by Nature; and with wild Exclamations which strengthen'd her former Resolve, thus broke out the Anguish of her Soul. " If the
" *Fœtus*, (cried she) now ripening in my pol-
" luted Womb, should ever see the Light;
" my Name, my Reputation, will be lost for
" ever; the only Blessing known to Mankind;
" nor will the censorious World give them-
" selves time to examine into the Foundation,
" and original Cause of this my Woe; but
" with inconsiderate Speeches blast my Fame,
" ridicule the clouded Carriage of the much-
" thought-prudent *Lominia*, with the Serpent-
" Tongue of Woman's utmost Malice.—What,

(con-

"(continued she) shall I be made the Jest of
" the World? O dismal Scene of approaching
" Scorn! No; avert it every Power! The
" Means of Relief croud in my receiving
" Brain, and I will use the welcome Offer."
At this, with some small Trouble, she obtained
those Herbs which promote Abortion, in which
dreadful Act, she trusted no one but herself;
the material Ruins being prepared, she drank
the fatal Juice; but ignorant of her Constitution, took too much: The Liquor operated
with such Violence, that she expected nothing
but Death: she wished for the welcome Messenger, yet feared to undergo the painful Journey.
Her Parents finding her in such Pain, used all
possible Means for her Relief; but stubborn in
her Will, she refused to have any Advice, judging that Men of proper Education, would soon
discover the real Cause of her Illness.

Arasles, whose Soul was fixed in hers, attended her Bed, watched every Sigh, and enjoined her to admit of their Prescriptions, for the
Safety of that Life, whereon his eternal Felicity depended; but every Request was spent in
vain, her Ears were deaf to his Intreaties, nor
could her Parents joined Tears and Intercessions
move her fixed Resolves. The time for Rest
approaching, Decency required every one to
depart, nor would the distracted Fair admit of
any Company, whose pleasing Conversation
might divert the cankering Grief, she so fondly seem'd to indulge. Her Commands being
obeyed, she began to think on her late Rashness. Now at any Hazard would she have
bought that Station of Life, wherein the former Day had seen her! but vain was any such
Hope, that Time was pass'd, and Fate itself
could

could not obscure the next Day's Dawn. Having obtained a little Respite from her Pains, she began to think the dreadful Deed was passed; when on a sudden, quick piercing Heats raged through her Frame, and set the Blood on fire: Next, chilling Bolts of Ice freezed the hot Blood, and filled the Nerves with shivering Anguish; thus was her Body at War, offended Heaven supplied the vengeful Torments, and scattered dreadful Grief thro' every secret Recess of her Soul. In these distracted Starts of Punishment, she had straight recourse to Prayers, like an offending Sinner, required Heaven's Forgiveness, and vow'd an entire Obedience to the Almighty Will: her constant Intercessions were serious from her Soul, and favourably received by the Divine Power, for on a sudden she felt recruited Strength to swell in every Nerve, and her former state of Health had resumed the Seat of the beauteous Life.

Early the next Morning, *Arastes*, guided by the God of Love, came flying to the Chamber of the Oppressed, and with an impatient haste, inquired after the Health of the Goddess of his Soul. The welcome News of so sudden a Recovery, revived his drooping Heart; the late residing Grief and Terror, which ruled his every Thought, were banished, and nothing now but Joy and Gladness appeared in every little Motive. One continual Mirth possessed the Souls of all, and shortly after *Lominia* began to shine in her former Lustre. She refreshed her late decaying Spirits with her usual Pastimes, which, with the Breathings of the healthy Air, added a strong Recruit to Life.

Nothing remained to compleat the longing Hopes of the Soul-enamoured Youth, but tying of the sacred Knot; again he sollicited her Consent, that the Sanctity of the Church might make them One; that his lov'd *Lominia* would be the Bride of his Joys, and sweet Companion of his approaching Days; every thing, that craving Love could desire, or Eloquence and Wit inform his half-distracted Soul, he utter'd; but vain was all Address: the beauteous Fair, mournful for her lost Virtue, shun'd the Offer, she once would have received with Transport; her cold and obstinate Sedateness became Mistress of her looser Wishes, and her late dreadful Act made her fear to feel a Mother's bitter Pangs. *Arastes* too deeply experienced the Maiden's open Conduct to indulge any Hope of obtaining his Ends by the Methods afore proposed; his Love was a Passion of so strong a Vehemence, that it carried him to Actions even desperate to his Peace; he urged her Parents to grant him their Daughter's Person; they endeavoured with her as much as could be, but fruitless were all Requests.

Arastes had loved her long, but never enjoyed the Partner of his Soul; 'twas that whetted the Edge of Desire, and made him sollicit her with double Force. One Day returning from Hunting, a Pastime *Lominia* very much delighted in, she refreshed herself as usual at *Arastes*'s House. The Day being now far spent, and the Evening Clouds eclipsing *Phœbus*'s transparent Rays; *Lominia*, by the Importunities of her Lover, consented to stay Supper, and partake of his House for that Night's Retirement. A very rich Collation was served up, of which they feasted themselves very heartily. Supper being ended, *Arastes* began to execute his Intentions, by such a Stratagem, which he thought his

Good,

Good, but Evil Genius had put in his Brain. The sparkling Wine enliven'd their tired Spirits, when an opportunity offering most desireable to his Wishes, he threw into her Glass the Juice of some bruised Poppies; which secret Design, or any other, the Innocent Maid no way dreaded: she thought herself, in this House, as secure, as in her Father's; she drank the prepared Liquor, which being seconded with other Opiates, began shortly to make their long-wish'd-for Operation. Now heavy Sleep press'd down the starry Lights, and seated it self on her clasping Eye-lids;— A sudden Numbness possessed every little Motion, and she appeared a Coarse senseless, and unmoveable. *Arastes*, overjoyed at the Success of his Design, snatched up the Captivated Fair, laid her on an adjacent Bed, and there performed the Act his Desires had long urged him to. Again, the tender Unfortunate was Enjoyed, though to herself unknown; the Liquors were of so strong a Mixture, that they still retained her every Faculty in the fleecy Folds of Sleep. The next Day she awaked, Innocent and thoughtless of her compleated Ruin; and arising from the Bed, whereon she thought she had securely reposed, prepared her Departure for her Father's House, wherein she residing passed her Hours with an undisturbed Felicity.

Arastes still continued to visit her, and daily pressed her to consent to the Performance of their Nuptials; but instead of a willing Answer, he received a cold Denyal; that holy Sanction! that ever to be adored and sacred Tye was waved by the Maid with an indifferent Neglect!

Some

Some Months being now paſſed, and *Araſtes* not ſpeeding in his Deſires; the daily conſuming Pains which attend neglected Love began to ſway his Soul. He was a Man ſo far different from the reſt of his changing Sex, that the Enjoyment he had lately obtained, did not in the leaſt cloy his Appetite, ſtill he admired her, wiſhed her his Wife; which ſweet ſounding Title, whenever repeated, filled his Ears with Soul-tranſporting Accents. His Flame was pure Love; nor branded in the leaſt with Man's brutal Luſt. 'Twas now, a Point ſeemed to offer to his Wiſhes moſt acceptable, moſt deſired; the pregnant Maid daily began to feel the weighty Burden of the teeming Womb, ſhe perceived herſelf with Child, but how or by whom ſeemed Myſterious; 'twas not in her Power to unriddle the dark *Ænigma*; ſhe found the growing Miſchief to be hourly ripening, which by the Uſe and Means of her Dreſs ſhe perfectly well concealed from the Eyes of the gazing Multitude. None but *Clarina*, a young Lady, her particular Friend and Confident, knew of this approaching Danger; 'twas to her ſhe related every miſerable Fact of her former Unhappineſs; created as ſhe thought by *Lyſanor*, and her inhuman Proceedings for an Abortive Birth; and now, with her, ſhe conſulted every Action, and would not without her Conſent follow any of her own Dictations, in ſo unhappy and unforeſeen a Viciſſitude of waving Fortune.

The Time of her Delivery now approached; each Minute her Pains increaſed, nor would the Infant be any longer reſtrained in his darkſome Cave;—— A beauteous Boy was born, to the Conſternation of both the Ladies; for no one but the new-made Mother and *Clarina* were in the Room; the latter of which affifted her Dear Friend with all Neceffaries befitting a Perfon in her Condition: when *Lominia* was a little recovered, fhe confulted *Clarina* about difpofing of the Babe, tho' her Reafons were little regarded; the diftracted Mother, fearing the Shame and Blemifh of her Reputation, ordered *Clarina* to hafte with it into the Garden, and conceal it among fome large Flaggs which grew at the lower End, 'till a better Opportunity fhould offer. *Clarina*, with an aking Heart, obeyed the cruel Dictates of the ftedfaft Mother; fhe conveyed it into her Lap, and unbolting the Garden Door, hafted to the Place which *Lominia* had ordered; when fhe came there, fhe immediately disburthened herfelf, and laying the Child in its flaggy Cradle, gave it a parting Kifs, and pofted to *Lominia* to acquaint her of the Proceeding.

Araftes, in his Vifits, continually kept a conftant Eye on *Lominia*'s Actions; and perceiving her Endeavours to conceal the growing Birth from all Eyes, made him fear fome defperate Deed might attend her Delivery; in order for fuch Difcovery, by the help of a Key to the Garden-Gate of *Orontes*, which he had, when he firft made his Addreffes to her, (becaufe thro' that Gate a Path-way led directly to his own Houfe, which faved a great fpace of Ground in his Vifits to, and his Returns from thence) he pofted himfelf fome Nights before under her Window, partly gueffing the time of the expected Birth; nor was abfent at this Juncture; for obferving a Light and hearing a Noife in *Lominia*'s Chamber, he doubled his Diligence, and fhortly after beheld *Clarina* open

the

the Garden Door, and retire to the Place, where she had left the Babe. Soon as she was departed he went to the Place where the Child lay, and by its tender Cries he soon found out his Son; with an eager Joy he snatched up the Babe, and eagerly kissed the welcome Product of his happy Enjoyment; then nursing it from the cold Winds and unhealthy Dews, carried it to an old Widow-Woman, who lived about a Mile from thence, and on whom he daily bestowed his Bounty; commanding her at the same time to bring him up, as careful, as her Diligence could compleat; After these Admonitions, he left his dear-loved Child, and giving the Woman a Purse of Gold towards its Maintenance, he retired to his own House to ruminate on that Night's Adventure.

When the Night's sable Glooms were vanished, and *Aurora* with rosy Blushes brought on the glorious Day; *Arastes*, as usual, paid his first Visit at *Orontes*'s House; but took no Notice of the past Accident. Enquiring for *Lominia*, he was told that at present she was a little indisposed, and desired to see no Company. He was too far concerned in her Disease, to make any Objections to her Commands, but recommending to her his best Wishes, took his leave, and departed. No sooner was he from the House, but he posted away to the humble Cottage of the Ancient Matron, there to divert himself with the Product of his Love.

Lominia was acquainted by *Clarina* of the loss of the Babe, that no Remains of the Child appeared to her searching Eyes, but that some of the Flaggs were torn: the cruel Mother now thought she was discovered, but her Friend assured her, that no one saw her conceal the Babe;

Babe; nor on the strictest Hearkening, could she learn any Rumour of this Loss, spread in the House. This welcome Assurance in some nature pacified the astonished Mother; the loss of the Child was, even, what she desired, and the happy Report cost her not a falling Tear; the Mother's Pains were over, but none of the Mother's Fondness succeeded. *Lominia* hearing no Account of the Child grew perfectly regardless; and increasing daily again in Strength, received Visits as usual; among the rest, *Arastes* still addressed her, as a Lover, and at the same time bred up the Babe with all the Care of an indulgent Father. Oftentimes he would retire to his lovely Boy, and then again visit the beauteous Mother; in which nature he spent most part of his Time.

Nothing of any Occurrence happened, 'till one Day, *Arastes* and his still beloved *Lominia* walking in the adjacent Fields; as was often their Custom, to take the Benefit of the Spring's delightful Product; on a sudden the late clear and azure Sky was darken'd by black hastening Clouds big with heavy Rain; the certain Assurance of a sudden Storm, obliged them to house in the first seeming Shelter, which offered; no other Cottage was at hand, but the Hospitable Nurse's rural Hut. The Thatched Buildings, and Storm-bearing Elmes which grew round, gave an exact View of a contented rustic Life; 'twas here they retreated from the Shower, and being seared, in came the tender Prattling of their forced Embraces. The Child had grown much in Strength, and now attained the Age of three Years; the too cruelly-guilty Mother, ignorant of its near Affinity, yet expressed a Regard, so kind, and obliging to the

lovely

lovely Infant, that *Arastes* began to hope all Things would terminate in an happy End; she kissed, and embraced the Babe with all the Fondness of a loving Mother; when *Arastes* addressing her with his usual Freedom, began to display the Felicity they might arrive to, would the Desire of his Soul consent to bless his Bed; "Who knows, (continued he,) but "that All-seeing Heaven may bless our "Loves with as fair an Offspring as now ap-"pears beore us" *Lominia* carried off his Proposal with a smart Gallantry, and the Storm being abated, they directed their Journey homeward.

On their Way to her Father's House, *Arastes* told her, that being one Evening in the Garden, examining his uneasy Thoughts, he accidentally roved to the most unfrequented Part, where to his Astonishment he heard a tender Infant's Cry, moved with Compassion, he took it from its cold Cradle and conveyed it to this Woman's, who by his Order had brought it to this Maturity; yet notwithstanding his private Endeavours, he could never learn out the Parents of this beauteous Orphan, and as he had brought it up to this Age was resolved still to keep it, 'till some happy Event should clear the now cloudy Mystery. At this Account, Anger, Revenge, and Hate filled her Soul! To think that any Part of *Lysanor* was in Being, revived obliviated Woes. Yet, in this extravagant Point, was she so far Mistress of her Thoughts, that *Arastes* could not see any Variation in the tormented Maid; though her Griefs were highly swell'd, she curb'd the rising Passions, and parted with him in appearance as usual. Assoon as he was gone, she hasted to her Chamber,
inten-

intentively to ruminate on the many Misfortunes, into which her anxious Fate had cast her.

It was now, her crouding Thoughts came too fast for a strict Examination; nothing but Revenge and Murther filled her once virtuous Soul; to take away from the Child that Life he but borrowed from her, she thought would be the only Means to secure her former Ease, and shun the Arms of *Arastes*; whom now she began to loath with as great a Remorse, as before she received his Addresses with Pleasure. All that can be thought of the most rigid Hate, swelled her every Intent; 'twas now she would have rejoiced at the welcome News of the Death of that Person, whom once she adored as Life it self; so wavering is the human Soul, that, once injured, especially in such a Point as this, it can scarce forgive. In the wildest Flights of Thought, and intent on Murder, she spent the few remaining Hours of Night; nor did the next Day's early Dawn produce the least Abatement or Delay of the rigid Execution; she went secretly from her Father's House, with a fixed Resolution to sacrifice the innocent Product of her severe Virtue; soon as she reached the humble Cottage of the ancient Matron (the sight of which seem'd a Delight to her pregnant Fancy) the little Babe, fond of its unknown Parent, came running with a Smile on his Brow, to the Arms of the more than brutish Mother. *Lominia*, with soothing Words and trifling Toys, prevailed so far on the Child, that unperceived, she seduced him to an adjacent Wood; a Place befitting the most detested Rapes or Murders; where, with an uncommon Vengeance, she struck the lovely Boy three

or

or four desperate Blows on his snowy Bosom, with a Ponyard, which she had taken out with her, and concealed till then in her Breast; the Lamb-like Babe sunk under the heavy Strokes, in the folds of Death, where, extended at its Length, the lovely Offspring lay exposed to the open Wild.

Cruel as she was, yet Decency, she thought, required a Covering for the Babe; and immediately tore a few green Twigs from off the neighbouring Trees, and spread them around the Child; the tender Spriggs hung down their drooping Heads, and seem'd to mourn over and naturally entwine the lovely Coarse; while the unfortunate *Lominia*, having compleated her late Design, retired out of the Wood, and directed her Way home.

In the mean time, *Arastes* had been at the old Woman's Hut; and enquiring as usual after the Child, she told him, that the Lady, who with him had sheltered herself the precedent Day from the sudden Storm at her Cottage, had taken the Child, and was walking with him in the adjacent Wood. This News refreshed his Soul, and speeded his hasty Steps with quicker Flight; it was now he thought all would end well, and *Lominia* own her pictured Product; " It is I (cried he) am made the hap-
" py Father, she, the alike blessed Mother;
" now dawns the Day of Joy, a welcome Cer-
" tainty of eternal Bliss. Happy, happy *Arastes!*
'Twas at this Instant he reached the Out-skirts of the Grove, where to his ecstatic Soul appeared the darling Maid. Eager with a burning Impatience to press the Fair, he flew with out-stretched Arms, and clasp'd his Joy; ten thousand Raptures glided in every Sense, and

F strong

strong Embraces swell'd each little Artery e'en to bursting.——His Eyes shot forth all-piercing Brightness, and wildly rowled about;——his Frame with an aspiring Transport shook, and every supporting string of Life was wound to its highest Pitch——The wildness of his Joy a little abated, and *Lominia* hasting home with an unusual Speed, created in him some Astonishment, and looking round now missed the Babe. Inquiring of *Lominia* for it, she told him, "that "having appointed some Company to see her "at home, she had overstaid her time, and there- "fore sent her Maid back with the Child to "its pleasant Mansion. And (continued she) I "really think the Babe more beatiful than "Fancy can paint. Alas! cried *Arastes*, how "could it be otherwise, when so sweet and "beautiful a Lady as my *Lominia* gave it Birth." At these Words, all the agonizing Pangs that attend a guilty Thought, possessed her every Part, and reigned triumphant on her blushing Cheeks. "Surely, (replied she, in the utmost "Amazement) you bear your Jesting too far, "thus endeavouring to cast a Blemish on my "Virtue. Ungrateful Man! whom I particu- "larly respected; how dare you thus utter so "base, so vile a Subject: My Virtue is too "well known, to be in this Nature spotted "with so much Infamy.——If I offend, (an- "swered he) in relating Truth, henceforth my "Tongue is dumb.——No, Traitor, (cried she) "I dare your utmost Malice, combined as you "are, to rob me of my Reputation: Relate, I "charge you, every Occurrence which your "pretended Brain would know. When *Lo-* "*minia* commands, what Tyrant can deny; "(replied he:) No, be Witness every Power, I
"will

"will relate the whole Adventure; nor swerve one Tittle from Truth!" At this, he opened unto her every Transaction he knew; from his Enjoyment obtained by the prepared Liquor, to the present Moment. Terrified as she was before, now unspeakable Horror ingrossed her every Thought. But now, and happy to her own Mind, she had reached her Father's House, which obliged *Arastes* to forsake mentioning any more Words on so hateful a Subject. Thus released as she was from so wracking a Discourse, she soon found Means to retire to her Chamber, and resolved immediately to see again the murdered Innocent. Scarce had *Arastes* departed the House, but the guilty *Lominia* hasted to the bloody Scene; his unexpected Discovery had so alarmed her Mind, that she could not be easy, till she had taken a second View of the dismal Spectacle. Arrived now on the fatal Spot, the weeping Maid threw, with an impatient Eagerness, the leafy Coverings about; she took a just Survey of the murdered Babe, and thought each Sight strengthen'd her Opinion in *Arastes*'s Relation: Speechless awhile she stood, ignorant of the Power of Utterance; the briny Tears swelled o'er their Fountain-brims, and flowed with a swift Rapidity, and tumultuous Sorrow swelled her Breast with weighty Anguish. Assoon as her Thoughts were free from this Delirium, she, kneeling on the Earth, bowed down and kissed the Babe, dreadfully mourning her past Action.—Now she would call on Heaven for Forgiveness, and now pour out Curses on her wretched Head; one Moment she would pray, the next rave, and tear herself in such a manner, that the most rigid Executioner must have melted at her Complaints. It

It was in this woeful Position, two Men passing the Road saw the distracted Fair; and striking out of the Path, came up to her Relief, just, in that very Instant, when the cruel Mother was going to sheath the fatal Weapon, already stained with the Blood of the lovely Babe, in her own savage Heart; and interposing themselves, wrested the Dagger from her Death-dealing Hands. So sudden a Stop, struck *Lominia* with Wonder; awhile she appeared cold, and motionless: But when the returning Springs of Life flowed to her frozen Heart, and thawed the dying Spirits, she found two Persons by her, and, in all appearance, the fatal Witnesses of this savage Deed: Wild with the dreadful Apprehension, she burst out in the following Exclamations. " Seize me, ye base Avengers " of Fate! I ought to suffer for the cruel Act. " It's true, the languid Babe was my own " Child. I have committed this most detestable " Sin: —— Bear me to Justice! Let the inno- " cent Boy have Restitution, for the Brutality " of a Parent's Action." At this, she surrendred herself to the Passengers, and by them was conveyed to a Magistrate, who knowing the Family of *Lominia*, appeared like a Man Thunder-struck at the dismal Narration; he immediately sent for her Parents, who little thought of such an unforeseen Malignity. At the dreadful Tale, the pearly Dew drop'd down their aged Cheeks;—— Mourning and Horror possessed each attending Soul. Recognizance being entred into, by *Orontes*, and a Friend, the too culpable *Lominia* was taken home to her Father's House; where, ever and anon, the Soul-stinging Jaws of Conscience goaded her turbulent Breast. Apace the fearful Time drew

on,

on, when the unhappy *Leminia* was to be tried for her foul and guilty Murder; the Judges were seated, Spectators thronged the Court, and every Tongue was pitying or condemning the too savage Fair. The Hour being now come, the sorrowful Father went to the Room of his Captive Daughter, with intent for her taking her Trial; when to his weeping Eyes appeared the once-darling Fair of his pristine Hours, weltring in her purple Gore; her Breast flashed with two or three Wounds, to lose her hated Life, and on an adjacent Table, two Letters; the one directed to her Father, and the other to *Arastes*. The Substance of the first, confessed the guilty Act, and that her Death, though contrary to Religion, or Reason's Law, must be compleated by her own Hands, which, as they had not trembled to do a Deed, so much unbecoming Nature, would not fail to end her hapless and unfortunate Life.

The other, which was sent as directed to *Arastes*, when opened, struck in him the greatest Consternation imaginable; when plainly, to his unexpecting Eyes, appeared the following Words.

To the too dear Ruiner of my Peace of Mind.

"IF my Destruction, when I last saw you, was as you related, why did you, O *Arastes*, discover the fraudulent Deed? Better it had been, as I was to have been led on in Ignorance.—— Deceitful as thou wert, I could still love you, would Life permit: But alas! that brutish Act which I have committed,
" requires

" requires an Attendant Sin. The Reason of
" my shunning your Bed, will surely be ad-
" mitted juſt, when I tell you, that by Force
" my Virtue was proſtrated by *Lyſanor*'s de-
" teſted Embraces; it was he that tore me
" from you, my once Haven of Felicity!
" when on the enamell'd Bank I liſtened to
" your boundleſs Love. Could I then meet
" my *Araſtes*'s Embraces, thus polluted? No:
" Rigid to my own Deſtruction, I coyfully
" ſhunned your Love. Yet, you ſhould not
" thus have deceived me, when I gave you my
" Company, my Converſation; every thing
" which I lawfully could; or when (as it now
" is evident) you could not; yet you ſhould
" have endeavoured to have ſpared the ſad Re-
" lation of the loathed Birth;——O! then I
" ſhould have died ſomething leſs Sinful;—I
" thought the Child *Lyſanor*'s, not Yours; for
" how could I otherwiſe, ignorant of the Deed
" you committed. The Time of my Pregnancy
" might have diſcloſs'd that Secret, but alas!
" I thought no other but that filthy Villain
" had known Me; forgive me, my Dear *Ara-*
" *ſtes*, and blot from out your Memory the un-
" fortunate *Lominia*. The ſmall Remainder of
" Life which I now poſſeſs, I ask of you and
" Heaven Forgiveneſs, both for the paſt and
" future Sin; for conclude e're this the loſt
" *Lominia* Slain.

Wild with this terrible Account, he ran immediately to the Houſe of *Orontes*; whoſe outward Countenances of the alike affrighted Family ſpoke the Deed too true; in the fatal Room he found the once-darling Pleaſure of his Soul, ſmeared with the Crimſon Stream, her Parents weeping over her with deſponding Heads.

Diſtracted

Distracted with this mournful Sight, he stooped to kiss the breathless Coarse; her clayey Lips now warmed his beating Heart no more, and cold as Stone would admit of no Impression; big with the gathering Grief, arising from the Maid, his Feet struck the Ponyard which had committed the hideous Act, so far before, that the glittering Point shone through the gushing Tears to his weeping Eyes; with a sudden Spring he snatched the glittering Weapon from off the Ground, and stretched his Arm to give the desired Blow; when some of the Servants perceiving his Intent, intercepted themselves, and wrenched the Dagger from him, without any further Damage than a slight Wound in his Breast. He was carried to his own House, and a Surgeon sent for to examine his Wound; which not being very deep, yet obliged him to keep his Room, about eight or ten Days; in which time, *Lominia* was interred, greatly lamented by every One.

Arastes was now recovered, but much different from the Man he once had been; a sullen cloudy Aspect reigned on his once-cheerful Brow, and constant Grief possessed his Heart; *Lominia* was gone, and nothing worthy Regard remained on Earth, nor was Life itself desireable. To make what Amends lay in his Power, he sent for an eminent Lawyer, and ordered him to draw a Conveyance of his Estate to *Orontes*'s Family, which was acordingly done and executed; then taking his everlasting Leave, secretly departed from out the Country, unable to live any longer in a Place, where his inadvertent Act had been the Occasion of the Deaths of two Persons, both so dearly admired by him. The next Day he took Shipping, and is thought by by every one to be dead; the Ship nor any of its Crew being since heard of.——*Orontes* and his Wife not long survived their Daughter; the Loss of so amiable a Child set so heavy on their aged Hearts, that Death soon ended their Days. Their Estate, with that also which *Arastes* conveyed to them, descended to their only remaining Child, a beautiful Boy, then about eight Years of Age, who is since arrived to Manhood, and blest with a Wife rich in every Female Virtue.

Thus ended the Amours of *Arastes* and *Lominia*, more unhappy than their first Days of Courtship promised; but Fate cannot be revoked, and the lovely Unfortunate, through her sad Calamities, committed those Actions which once she contemned.

From hence, ye Fair, learn to detest the Deed,
Which made this Guilty Maid as Guilty Bleed.

F I N I S.

Narzanes

Anonymous

Bibliographical note:

This facsimile has been made from a copy in the British Museum (101.f.64)

NARZANES:

Or, the injur'd

STATESMAN

Containing the moſt important

Negotiations, *and* Tranſactions

Of that great

MINISTER,

Whilſt HE preſided over

AFFAIRS of *PERSIA*.

———————— *Behold, ungrateful Men,*
Behold my Boſom naked to your Swords,
And let the Man that's injur'd ſtrike the Blow,
Which of you all ſuſpects that he is wrong'd,
Or thinks he ſuffers greater Ills than Cato?
Am I diſtinguiſh'd from you but by Toils,
Superior Toils, and heavier Weight of Cares!
Painful Pre-eminence!   CATO.

LONDON

Printed for, and Sold by *T. Payne*, at the
Crown in *Pater-noſter Row*. (Price 1 s. 6 d.)

MDCCXXXI.

DEDICATION.

TO ALL Sincere Lovers OF THEIR COUNTRY,

The following Sheets are, with the utmost Deference, inscrib'd by

The Editor.

THE PREFACE.

THE following Memoirs concerning Narzanes, were extracted from the Manuscript of an English Gentleman, who resided several Years at Ispahan; and, being very intimate with some of the principal Grandees of the Persian Court, he had an Opportunity of discovering the most remarkable Transactions of that Empire: And as the Author wrote this

PREFACE.

this for the Information of his Countrymen, he thought proper to cloath it in an European Dress.

The Design of publishing these Papers, is to shew that Men who have made the greatest Figure in the Administration of State Affairs, and were favour'd by their Sovereign, have always been expos'd to the Malice and Envy of ambitious Competitors; who have constantly endeavour'd to promote their Downfal, even at the Hazard of involving their Country in Ruin. Such were

PREFACE.

were Euryphax *and his two Associates* Salem *and* Alharzaman, *whose detestable Arts are related in the following Piece. This* Triumvirate *being Men of the most corrupt Principles, and animated by a restless and factious Spirit, had for many Years labour'd at the Destruction of* Narzanes, *which at last prov'd fatal to themselves.*

It may perhaps seem strange to find here several Particulars relating to the Amours *of this great* Statesman, *intermix'd with his* political *Tran-*

PREFACE.

Transactions: But as that Part of his Story was previous to his Administration; and attended with extraordinary Circumstances, which afterwards were of Service to it: And as the Lady who was the Object of his Love, possess'd all the Perfections which can grace a female Character, and even several, worthy the greatest Heroes; *it is to be hop'd, that the Incidents attending it, will be entertaining to the polite Reader.*

PREFACE.

Some People will possibly imagine, that under the Character of Narzanes, a particular Minister of these Times may be shadow'd: But with Respect to this, I shall only observe, that as every Man is free to think as he pleases; so they may draw the Parallel, or make the Application, in whatever Manner they shall judge proper.

NARZANES:

Or, the injur'd

STATESMAN.

THE Kingdom of *Perſia* had been for many Years involved in a vexatious War with the *Saracens* and *Arabians*, when by the wiſe and prudent Conduct of the *Miniſter* who was then at the Helm, the *Perſians* obtain'd an advantageous Peace, and were ſoon reſtor'd to their former Grandeur. He was a Man of extraordinary Talents, and had given many Inſtances of his Ability in the Adminiſtration of Affairs both at Home and Abroad; for which, he juſtly deſerv'd the Favour of his *Prince*, who diſtinguiſh'd him with peculiar Eſteem and Affection.

This *Nobleman* had a Son whofe Name was *Narzanes*. He was in the twentieth Year of his Age when he made his firſt Appearance at Court, where he was receiv'd with the greateſt Marks of Diſtinction; not only on his Father's Account, but for his own perſonal Merit, being a young Gentleman of a graceful Preſence, with fine natural Parts, and Maſter of all the *Eaſtern* Learning; for which he ſeem'd to have a much ſtronger Inclination than is generally obſerv'd in young Noblemen, who, for the moſt Part, prefer their Pleaſures to the Study of thoſe Sciences which in Time would redound more to their Credit. His good Senſe, genteel Behaviour, Affability and Politeneſs, ſoon gain'd him the Affection of all who convers'd with him; yet in the midſt of a gallant and magnificent Court; he never ſhew'd the leaſt Deſire to contract an Intimacy with any of the Courtiers, whoſe Sincerity he very much ſuſpected, and therefore judg'd them incapable of Friendſhip. Nor was he forward in recommending himſelf to the Favour of the *Fair*, who are ever jealous of the Tribute that is due to their Charms. In ſhort as he was a Youth of great Sagacity and Penetration, he ſoon

diſ-

discover'd the Characters of the Courtiers of both Sexes; and was therefore resolv'd within himself, not to spend much Time in their Conversation.

It is probable, that as at his Years, he could be no great Politician, he was somewhat too free in declaring his Sentiments; therefore his Father who view'd all his Actions with a watchful Eye, began soon to read the Disposition of his Mind; and told him one Day that he had observ'd his Averseness to the Diversions of Courts; and that he was often absent, when the rest of the Nobility were endeavouring to rival each other, in distinguishing themselves by a splendid Appearance, and paying an assiduous Court to their Prince; that he himself, being principal *Minister* of State, his Son had as great a Right as any one to make a handsome Figure; that besides it might in Time be of great Advantage to him to be well known to his *Sovereign*; who made it his constant Care to prefer Men of Merit, and reward the Services of such of his Subjects as distinguish'd themselves.

Narzanes, without being in the least affected with his Father's Discourse, told him ingenuously, that far from having the least Inclination to be a Courtier, he had so great a Dislike to the Character, that he chose to live a private Life; and enjoy the Pleasure of Independence, rather than be possess'd of the highest Employments in a Court, where he had already discover'd too much Falshood and Dissimulation; and that he esteem'd those Men unhappy, who, to make themselves great, were under the Necessity, either of being subservient to a Sett of designing Men; or becoming obnoxious to the Malice and Envy of others, who would contend with him for Authority.

This Answer from one of his Years, surpriz'd his Father, who at that Time was in great Power, and could easily raise his Son's Fortune, without apprehending that any one would presume to oppose him. He represented to *Narzanes* the Services he had done his King and Country, which entitl'd him to ask any Favour of his *Sovereign*; and told him, that if there was any Employment in the Government agreable to him,

he

he himself could place him in it without applying to any other Person.

An Offer of this Kind, would have been a strong Temptation to any young Nobleman, who propos'd to ascend the Stage of Life early, and act an eminent Part in so illustrious a Court: But all that his Father could say to persuade him was ineffectual. He persisted in his first Resolution of making no Steps towards his Preferment; and the more his Father us'd Means to inspire him with Notions of Grandeur the more he declar'd his Reluctance to it; till at last declining all Company, and chusing a solitary Life, he apply'd himself entirely to the Study of the Mathematicks and polite Literature, in which he had already made a considerable Progress.

This he made his Pretence for not attending often at Court; and when he did appear there, it was with so great an Air of Indifference, that every one obsery'd his Behaviour, which some ascrib'd to Indolence; while others who were not so good-natur'd, imputed it to Pride. The King himself took Notice of it, and would have div'd into the Cause, when the Father of *Narzanes*, who was well acquainted with the Genius of the Court, thought of an expedient which might in time wear out any ill Impreſſion the Courtiers had conceiv'd of his Son, and by Degrees give a new Turn to his Sentiments. This was to ſend him a travelling, by which Means he would acquire a more perfect Knowledge of the World, and be better qualify'd for whatever Employment Fortune ſhou'd deſign him.

Soon after, his Father took an Opportunity of communicating his Intentions to him, which *Narzanes* receiv'd with Joy; and as he was independant and unambitious; being the only Son of a Father whoſe Riches were immenſe; he propos'd an inexpreſſible Satisfaction to himſelf, in being ſome Years abſent from a Court, for which at that time he could have no Reliſh.

About this time a young *Nobleman*, Son to the Treaſurer-General of *Perſia*, was preparing for his Travels; and hearing that *Narzanes* intended to take a Tour into *Africa*, he was very deſirous to accompany him, which their Fathers having agreed to, theſe two young Noblemen

blemen embrac'd the Opportunity with Pleasure.

The Treasurer's Son, whose Name was *Euryphax*, had a most ardent Passion for *Almazaida*, who was a celebrated Beauty at the *Persian* Court, and a Lady of an illustrious Family: But her Father not approving of the Match, was determin'd to use all possible Means to prevent it, which created some Enmity between the two Families; and the Treasurer, being but too well inform'd of the violent Inclinations of his Son, thought that his Absence from Court would also divert him from a Passion, which if pursu'd, might prove fatal to him.

This young *Nobleman* was of a quite opposite Character to *Narzanes*; for tho' his Person was beautiful, the Disposition of his Mind was no ways answerable. He was ambitious, insolent, and imperious; a great Master of Dissimulation, and lov'd his Pleasure too much to be qualify'd for Business. He had Courage enough to fight when Occasion offer'd; but was not so great a Slave to Honour, as to refrain from doing the worst Actions, when they tended to gratify his Passions.

All Things being prepar'd for the Departure of the two Noblemen, they both set out from the Court of *Persia* with a Retinue suitable to their Quality and Fortune; and having travell'd thro' many Kingdoms of *Asia*, they at last came into *Africa*, where they took a View of every thing that was most remarkable in that Part of the World; residing some time in every great City, where they met with a splendid Reception from all the *African* Princes, whose Courts they visited.

Narzanes, whose Design in travelling, was not so much to ramble from Court to Court, as to improve his Mind in the Study of all curious Knowledge, resolv'd to fix in some Country where he might reside a few Years; and having chosen the *Abyssinian* Empire for that Purpose, he communicated his Design to *Euryphax*, who not being of a Disposition to continue long in any Place, agreed to accompany him thither, till Variety and his inconstant Temper might invite him elsewhere.

They

THEY were, when this was propos'd, at the Court of *Morocco*, from whence they set out on this tedious Journey, and after having travell'd for several Weeks through the Desert of *Zaara*, the Kingdom of *Nubia*, and other *African* Countries, they at last reach'd *Ethiopia*, the Dominions of the famous Emperor of the *Abyssins*. *Narzanes* and *Euryphax* had not been long arriv'd there, but they made their Appearance at Court, where they were honour'd with the same obliging Reception, which they had met with at those of the other *African* Princes. The Splendor and Magnificence of the Emperor's Court, was for some Days the Subject of their Admiration; and as Foreigners, they were continually entertain'd with new Diversions according to the Customs of that Country; till *Narzanes*, beginning to reflect on the Time he had spent in those Amusements, thought it might be employ'd to better Purpose; and therefore having resolv'd to apply himself seriously to study, he insensibly declin'd seeing any Company, as was his Custom at the Court of *Persia*: However, as it was not equally in his Power to absent himself from a Court, where he was treated with great Distinction;

in

in return to their obliging Politeneſs, he was often forc'd, tho' contrary to his Inclinations, to partake in their Diverſions.

Euryphax had a quite different Notion of Life, being a Man who would have ſacrific'd all Things to his Pleaſures. He omitted no Opportunity of diſtinguiſhing himſelf in all Companies without Exception; and was particularly fond of ſuch Entertainments as were intermix'd with looſe and criminal Diverſions, which he was very deſirous of promoting: In what Company ſoever he was admitted, his firſt Scheme was to form an amorous Intrigue, without which Life was to him a Burden; ſo that he had but little Time left for Converſations of a learned and ſerious Turn. Beſides, what will yet appear more blamable in his Conduct, is, that when ever he was ſuccesful in his voluptuous Adventures, he would be ſure to make the fair Captive the only Subject of his Diſcourſe in all Companies; and could not be at reſt, till by his repeated Hints and Intimations he had pointed out the unhappy Lady; the vile Effect of his intolerable Pride and Vanity.

T H I S

This vicious Difpofition of Mind involv'd him often in troublefome Broils, out of which, he could not eafily extricate himfelf, without cafting a Blemifh on his Reputation, and frequently drawing his Friends and Acquaintance into many Difficulties; for which Reafon, fo foon as he began to be known in any Court, he not only was treated with Indifference, but alfo defpis'd by all Men of Honour; and he himfelf was fo fenfible of his indifcrete Conduct, that he therefore made but very little Stay in any Place.

Narzanes on the contrary, having diftinguifh'd himfelf by his inimitable Deportment on all Occafions, was highly efteem'd by all that convers'd with him; even the Emperor's *Minifters*, who were Men of the fineft Underftanding, did not think themfelves above courting his Friendfhip; his penetrating Judgment, and fublime Manner of expreffing himfelf on all Subjects where it was natural, made the wifeft Politicians fond of his Company; and as a more particular Inftance of Difcretion which is feldom feen in Perfons of his Years; he was never known to contract, unthinkingly, too great a Freedom with any one; a Circumſtance which recommended him ſtrongly to the Affection of the greateſt Men.

Yet with all theſe noble Endowments, his Actions were generally attended with a certain Melancholy, which gave his intimate Friends ſome Uneaſineſs: But as good Manners forbid their enquiring into the Cauſe of it, they therefore were cautious of intruding ſo far, as it might perhaps be diſagreable to him. He us'd to retire every Day for ſome Hours, to ſtudy the Languages; and in a ſhort Time he made ſo great an Improvement in them, that he had the Advantage of converſing with Perſons of all Nations, by which Means he acquir'd an univerſal Knowledge; and it may be ſaid without Partiality, that where ſo many Perfections center'd, there was juſt room to expect, that his Abilities would, in a few Years, entitle him to the higheſt Employments.

However, ſo various is the Viciſſitude of all ſublunary Things, that notwithſtanding the prudent Meaſures this young *Nobleman* was taking to preſerve his Innocence; we yet ſhall ſoon ſee him
in

in the deepeſt Diſtreſs, and even his Life in Danger, before he is rais'd to that exalted Grandeur which Fortune had deſign'd him. All the Wiſdom and Virtue he poſſeſt, could not yet ſecure him from the Charms of powerful Love; a Paſſion inſeperable from brave Spirits, and which has reduc'd the greateſt Conquerers to a State of Captivity.

Narzanes, who was us'd to chuſe the moſt ſolitary Places for his Meditations, ſet out one Morning early, in order to walk in the Emperor's Gardens, which were the fineſt in *Africa*; and having taken ſeveral Turns in ſome of the remoteſt Alleys, he on a ſudden found himſelf almoſt fainting, which he imputed to the exceſſive Heat of the Weather, it being then the middle of Summer. This oblig'd him to retire to a little Eminence, heightned by a moſt pleaſing Verdure, where he laid himſelf down; but inſtead of receiving any Benefit by it, his Spirits fail'd him, and in an Inſtant all his Faculties were ſuſpended. Thus he continu'd ſome Time, when to his great Surpriſe he found himſelf recovering from his Swoon, by the Help of an agreeable Odour

which

which was adminifter'd to him; and opening his Eyes, he beheld with Admiration, a moft beautiful young Lady near him, with feveral Women who feem'd to be her Attendants. This unexpected Incident caus'd a furprizing Emotion in *Narzanes*, who had hardly Power to exprefs his Gratitude for fo much Goodnefs. He arofe from the Place where he lay, and with his Eyes fix'd on the divine Object, he endeavour'd to fpeak, but his Voice was loft, fo great was his Diforder; which the young Lady perceiving, fhe immediately retir'd, before he could know the Perfon to whom he was fo highly indebted.

Here it would be difficult to reprefent juftly the State of a Man, who, from a perfect Indifference for the fair Sex, and an uncommon Application to the moft ferious Studies, finds his Breaft glowing with a Paffion, which muft neceffarily difcompofe the whole Frame of his Mind, and create Anxieties in him, to which he had, till then, been an entire Stranger. This was the Cafe of *Narzanes*, who was now defperately in Love with the unknown Lady abovemention'd. He return'd to his Apartment

ment penfive, dejected, and full of the Object which had made fo deep an Impreffion on his Breaft, when he apply'd to his Books for Relief, but to no Purpofe; he was reftlefs, and could find nothing in them to alleviate his Pain.

He continu'd fome Time in this Anxiety, going daily to that Part of the Emperor's Gardens, where he had firft beheld the beauteous Creature, in Hopes of meeting her again, or finding fome Means to difcover who fhe was; but all his Endeavours prov'd fruitlefs: His Hopes were now chang'd into the blackeft Defpair; and his raging Paffion increafing every Inftant, very much heightned the Melancholy which was natural to him. He often call'd Reafon to his Aid, but the Wound was too deep, to admit of an immediate Cure; fo that he began to think that Time and Abfence were the only Remedies he could apply to fo violent a Difeafe, which made him refolve to leave a Place where he could no longer enjoy the leaft Peace of Mind.

This fudden Refolution being known at Court, created fome Surprize in all who had an Affection for him, and to whom

whom he had not long before communicated his Intention of ſtaying in this Place ſome Years. Amongſt the reſt, there was a Perſon of great Credit and Diſtinction in that Empire, to whom the Father of *Narzanes* had formerly done conſiderable Services, during his Reſidence at the Court of *Perſia*. This Nobleman being inform'd that *Narzanes* propos'd to leave *Abyſſinia* ſoon, came to pay him a Viſit, and was deſirous of knowing the Cauſe of it: But *Narzanes* could not well gratify the Curioſity of his Friend, without revealing a Secret to him, which he had vow'd never to diſcloſe, but to the dear Idol of his Affections; in Caſe he ſhould be ſo happy, as to be once more bleſt with the Sight of her. He only told him, that ſome Affairs of Moment call'd him home; but that he would not ſet out from Court, till he had firſt paid his Acknowledgments to the many Noble Perſons, to whom he was ſo greatly indebted for all the Favours they had indulg'd him ſince his Arrival, which he ſaid would take up ſome time.

Narzanes utter'd theſe Words with an Air of the deepeſt Melancholy, which very

very much affected the Noble *Abyssinian*, who, in order to divert it, gave him an Invitation to spend a few Days with him at one of his Country Seats, not many Miles distant from Court. This the young Nobleman would have declin'd, but the other insisting upon it, *Narzanes* could not well refuse so obliging an Offer, without being guilty of the greatest Rudeness; he therefore at last consented to it, and the *Nobleman* agreed to call on him the next Morning, in order to carry him into the Country. The Sequel of this extraordinary Adventure will manifestly shew that *Narzanes* could not fly from his Destiny.

EARLY the next Morning, a Servant was sent to acquaint *Narzanes*, that his Master would wait upon him in an Hour's Time, and accordingly he came in his Coach, attended with a handsome Retinue; but with what Astonishment was *Narzanes* seiz'd, when he saw the inchanting Creature in his Friend's Coach, who had administred Relief to him in the *Emperor's* Gardens, and had rais'd such a Tempest in his Soul! Words can never paint the Disorder he was in at this unexpected Meeting, which was too visible not to be perceiv'd by the young Lady, who was

C   Daugh-

Daughter to this Noble *Abyſſinian*. As for her Father, he had no Room to ſuſpect any Thing of this Kind, not knowing that *Narzanes* had ever ſeen her before.

They travell'd on for ſome Hours, and about Noon arrived at this *Nobleman*'s Seat, which for Splendor and Magnificence was ſcarce inferior to any of the *Emperor*'s Palaces. It was a ſtately Edifice, erected on the Side of a Hill, which afforded a moſt delightful Proſpect; and the Beauty and Regularity of its Architecture, ſhewed it the Maſter-Piece of a great Artiſt. The Gardens alſo were laid out after ſo beautiful a Manner, which was chiefly owing to the natural Situation of the Ground; that the Whole repreſented the Palace of a *Sovereign* rather than the Country-Seat of a Subject.

In this delightful Retirement, *Narzanes* was entertain'd after a moſt elegant Manner by this Noble *Abyſſinian*, who daily invented ſome new Scene of Diverſion; and having prevail'd on him to ſtay ſome Time there, *Narzanes* found frequent Opportunities of paying his Devotion to the beauteous *Elphamira*,

mira, for that was the Name of this excellent *Lady*, who in their first private Conversation, mentioned, with an Air of the sweetest Innocence, something relating to what had pass'd in the *Emperor*'s Gardens; but at the same Time gave him to understand, that what she had then done, was meerly out of Compassion to a Stranger, who seem'd to be suddenly taken ill, and had no Person near at Hand to give him any Assistance; but that after she had left him, she never expected to see him more. Amongst other Particulars she told him, that having lately lost her Mother, whose Memory would be ever dear to her; she therefore had not appeared at Court since her Death; but chose to lead a retired Life, in order to indulge her Melancholy; that she had one only Brother whom she lov'd intirely, and that he was then on his Travels in Foreign Countries, from whence she waited his Return with the utmost Impatience.

It were needless to mention here the Transports of Joy which possessed the whole Soul of *Narzanes*, during his Stay in the Country: We may naturally suppose, that he thought himself completely ly bleſt, in thus enjoying the Company of a virtuous and lovely Lady, who had inflamed his Breaſt with a moſt violent Paſſion. So far as Modeſty would admit, he was flatter'd with the Hopes of recommending himſelf to her Favour; which ſoon made him determine not to purſue the Reſolution he had ſome Time before taken of leaving *Abyſſinia*. But Mankind are too apt to perſwade themſelves, that whatever Deſign they are ſtrongly bent upon, muſt of Courſe meet with Succeſs, when once they ſet about it.

Narzanes was indeed a Gentleman of excellent Talents, as was before obſerved; and ſo handſome, that few Ladies could receive his Addreſſes with Indifference: But being not ſo well vers'd in the Myſteries of Love as in the Sciences, he therefore could have but a very imperfect Idea of the Nature of that Paſſion; and thought that if he could but once make his Addreſſes agreeable to *Elphamira*, nothing more would be wanting to complete his Felicity. He did not conſider the oppoſite Intereſts of the *Perſian* and *Abyſſinian* Nations, who were ſometimes Friends but oftner Enemies; and

and how jealous both were of marrying with Foreigners, which by their Laws was a great Crime in Noblemen, unless they first obtain'd the Consent and Approbation of their *Prince.* These, with many other Things of the like Nature, had escap'd his Observation, at a Time when his Thoughts were confin'd wholly to the Object of his Love; and the more he indulg'd his Passion, the less he was capable of pursuing his first glorious Design.

THEY had now spent a few Days in the Country, when some Affairs of Moment call'd *Elphamira*'s Father back to Court; and as he was exceedingly delighted with *Narzane*'s Conversation, he told him at his Return thither, that he hop'd he wanted no further Invitation to his House; that so long as he continued in *Abyssinia*, he insisted obligingly on the Favour of his Company, so often as his Leisure would permit; and heightned the whole with many other polite Expressions, which were no Ways disagreeable to *Narzanes*, whose Hopes increas'd Daily with his Passion. Yet all this While his Discretion would not permit him to make any rash Overtures; for as
he

he had often found Opportunies of conversing in private with the beauteous *Elphamira*, he had obferv'd that when ever he introduc'd any Thing relating to Love, she assum'd an Air of Severity, which soon oblig'd him to change the Subject. However, he visited her Father constantly, who always receiv'd him not only after a Friendly Manner, but even treated him like a Son, which often procur'd him the Satisfaction of seeing *Elphamira* when other Visiters were refus'd Admittance.

IN the mean Time *Euryphax* was entertain'd with new Adventures of every Kind. He had now got acquainted with most of the young Noblemen at the *Emperor's* Court, and had contracted an Intimacy with such as he fancy'd to be of the same Turn of Mind with himself; by which Means he was Daily introduc'd into Parties of Pleasure, and enjoyed all the Variety he could wish for: But as he put no Manner of Restraint to his loose Appetites, he was soon forsaken by his dearest Companions; who, tho' they were Men of like Passions with himself, had yet the Caution not to engage too far in his riotous Proceedings, for Fear of
incur-

incurring the *Emperor's* Difpleafure, in cafe it fhould come to his Ear; or lofe the Favour of their Relations at Court, on whofe Intereſt they depended wholly for Preferment.

'T WOULD have been happy for *Narzanes*, had he never known *Euryphax*, or at leaſt that they had not fet out together from the *Perfian* Court; for, tho' he would never confent to join with him in his diffolute Parties of Pleaſure; he yet could not avoid feeing him almoſt every Day, during his Stay in *Abyffinia*, they living in the fame Houfe, and defraying their travelling Expences in common. This created a ſtill greater Familiarity between them, which often gave *Narzanes* an Opportunity of adviſing his Friend, and reproving him for the diforderly Life he led, which was now become fo fcandalous, that no Man of Honour would keep him Company. Remonſtrances of this Kind, from one who was not much older than *Euryphax*, were very grating to a Man of his imperious Temper; which undoudtedly he would have refented, had he not been afraid that a Difference, between him and *Narzanes*, whilſt they were at the *Abyffinian* Court, would

would turn to his own Prejudice. However, 'twill soon appear, of what fatal Confequence it is to be acquainted with Men of bafe Principles, fince they feldom fail of involving their Friends in the Evils which they themfelves promote. But let us now return to the charming *Elphamira*.

THIS young *Lady* was diftinguifhed from the reft of her Sex, for fome Superior Excellencies which are not always rank'd among the Female Virtues. Her Perfon indeed was adorned with all the Charms which a Woman could boaft; but the Beauties of her Mind, to which a Pre-Eminence ought always to be allowed, were fuch as attracted the higheft Admiration. Her Magnanimity, Generofity and Compaffion, and a large Share of Prudence and Difcretion made the leaft Part of her Endowments; fo that from what was before obferved, we may eafily conclude that fhe was not to be amufed with the fond Prattle, which young *Votaries* generally employ when they addrefs the *Fair*. Her Time was fpent in Converfations of a more fublime Nature, which often check'd the Tranfports of the Paffionate *Narzanes*: And as he him-

himself plainly discover'd her Sentiments, by her Behaviour towards him; he used the utmost Circumspection, lest, by any wrong Step, he might happen to incur her Displeasure.

ONE Evening, as *Narzanes* and *Elphamira* were walking in a solitary Part of her Father's Gardens, they heard a prodigious Roaring; and soon after perceiv'd, to their great Surprize, a Leopard that had broke loose from his Den, and was engag'd with a young Tyger, which being no longer able to make any Resistance, was forc'd to yield to the Conqueror. But how much greater was their Astonishment, when they saw the Leopard leave his Prey, and make up towards the Place where they stood, without any Possibility of their flying the Danger.

Narzanes, who, till then, had never met with the like Occasion of putting his Valour to the Tryal, but had always discover'd a Greatness of Soul in every Action, resolv'd at once to encounter this fierce Animal; when addressing himself to *Elphamira*, he beg'd her to retire, and make the best of her Way towards

towards her Father's Houſe, during which he would keep the Leopard in Play: But this excellent Woman who did not expreſs the leaſt Fear for her own Sake, could not be prevail'd upon to leave him expos'd alone to the Fury of a fierce Beaſt, who was now at Hand, and made a Motion as tho' he intended to attack her firſt: Whereupon *Narzanes* run at him with his drawn Sabre, and ſtruck it into his Jaws; but the Leopard ſtruggling furiouſly, broke the Weapon, and having diſengag'd himſelf, made a ſecond Attempt upon *Elphamira*, which *Narzanes* likewiſe oppoſed with wonderful Activity and Courage; and making Uſe of the remaining Part of his Sabre, he ruſhed in upon the Leopard, and ſheathing it in his Stomach, kept him down; till, by good Fortune, ſome of the Keepers being alarmed at the hideous Roaring of this Animal, came to *Narzanes*'s Aſſiſtance; and thus put an End to the Fight, by the Death of the Leopard, *Narzanes* having received but a very ſlight Wound in one of his Hands.

This Adventure, may, in the Opinion of ſome People, ſeem in a Romantic Strain;

Strain; and indeed there would be Reafon enough for it, were it not that both the *Afiaticks* and *Africans* are Daily expos'd to Dangers of this Kind, and are very dexterous in combating fierce Animals. However, the Intrepidity of *Narzanes* on this Occafion, recommended him highly, not only to *Elphamira*'s Favour, who was under the greater Dread upon his Account; but alfo acquired him the Reputation of a brave and gallant Man, amongft thofe of the firft Rank, both at Court and in the *Emperor's* Army.

Euryphax was the only Perfon that could not relifh the mighty Applaufes which were beftow'd univerfally on his Friend: And as he himfelf was now become odious, and fcarcely taken Notice of at the *Abyffinian* Court; whilft *Narzanes* was treated by all with the greateft Marks of Diftinction, it created fo much invidious Rancour in him, that he refolved on fome defperate Attempt, by which he might retrieve his own vile Character, or blaft the unfpotted Reputation of his Friend.

THIS

This ungenerous Resolution, would in all Appearance, prove fatal to one of them: But as *Euryphax* was deeply skilled in the Arts of Dissimulation, he acted the Politician with *Narzanes*, and carried himself as fair as usual, till an Opportunity might offer to put his Design in Execution.

The Father of *Elphamira*, on the other Hand, who justly thought he owed his Daughter's Life to *Narzanes*, express'd all the Gratitude imaginable for it; and made it his chief Study how to return so signal a Service. But the Favour of *Elphamira*, which was the farthest from her Father's Thoughts, was the only Reward *Narzanes* desir'd. And as this Adventure had created a more intimate Familiarity between the young *Lady* and him, he look'd upon this as a favourable Juncture for the disclosing of his Sentiments. And accordingly, in their next private Conversation he breath'd his Passion; and address'd her in so soft, so tender a Manner, that notwithstanding her great Presence of Mind, she at first could not help shewing some Disorder; which he readily interpreted in his own Favour. But he was

too

too foon convinc'd of his Error; for, recovering from her firft Surprize, and affuming an awful and fevere Countenance, fhe told him that fhe was infinitely indebted to him for the Service he had done her, and thought that her Friendfhip and Efteem, fhew'd the deep Senfe fhe had of her Obligations to him; but that in cafe he requir'd any Thing more, fhe fhould be under a Neceffity of never admitting him into her Company. Here *Narzanes* would fain have repeated his Vows, and pleaded in Behalf of his Paffion; but *Elphamira* refolving not to hear him, rofe up inftantly and retired into another Apartment, leaving her difconfolate Lover to bemoan his unhappy Fate.

When *Narzanes*, who had always dreaded the Confequence of fuch a Declaration, began to confider the Overture he had made; he accus'd himfelf of the higheft Indifcretion, and was determined to reftore himfelf to *Elphamira's* Favour, at any Rate, fhould he even be forced to ftifle a Paffion which had already depriv'd him of his Peace. But inftead of giving him an Opportunity of juftifying his Conduct; fhe ever after

after endeavour'd to shun him; and would not admit him into her Company, unless her Father or some other Person were present, which was a cruel Restraint to a Man who had so long enjoy'd the Conversation of so amiable and virtuous a Lady, in whom he had Daily discover'd some new Perfection, which only made the Flame rage with greater Violence: But as she made it her chief Care to avoid seeing him in Private, many Days pass'd before he could take any Steps towards a Reconciliation.

About this Time, it happen'd that *Elphamira*'s Father was oblig'd to go into the Country; and as it was not convenient to take his Daughter with him, she stay'd in Town, in order to receive her Brother, who was hourly expected at the Court of *Abyssinia*. *Narzanes*, who hitherto had been allow'd the Privilege of visiting *Elphamira*, was exceedingly pleas'd to reflect, that he should now, as her Father would be absent, find some Opportunity of making his Peace; and therefore, went as usual to pay his Devoirs but was not admitted, upon Pretence of her being indispos'd. He repeated his Visits, and for a long Time
met

met with the same indifferent Reception, which fill'd him with the deepest Anguish, till at last, being resolv'd to see her, he one Day sent a Message, that he had some Affairs of the highest Importance to communicate to her, and therefore beg'd to be heard. *Elphamira* might easily guess the Cause of his Importunity; and as she had observ'd for some Time that he abandon'd himself a Prey to the blackest Melancholy, she thought it would be but prudent and generous to inform him of her Sentiments; and to this End she condescended to see him, with a Resolution to banish him her Presence for ever. At his first Approach he fell at her Feet, and said all that Love, heightned by Respect could suggest, in order to obtain her Pardon for his rash Attempt; and at the same Time discover'd so much Despair in his Countenance and his Gestures, as would have melted the most obdurate Heart.

Now, whether *Elphamira* was affected with the Condition *Narzanes* was in, or dreaded the Consequence of so violent a Passion, I shall not pretend to determine: But with a graceful Air she bid him rise up, when she said that
she

she had once more admitted him into her Presence, in order to declare her Intentions, with which she hop'd he would acquiesce, as being the greatest Favour she could possibly indulge him. Just as she had ended these Words, a Messenger brought Word that her Brother was arrived, upon which addressing herself to *Narzanes*, she told him, that in Consideration of so agreeable a Piece of News, she would forgive him what was past, but upon Condition that he would never be so indiscreet for the future.

These Words gave new Life to *Narzanes*, who was enraptur'd at the pleasing Thoughts of being restor'd to *Elphamira*'s Favour; and was just going to thank her for so singular an Instance of her Goodness, when a second Message was brought, by which she was inform'd that her Brother was in her Father's Apartment, and was coming to salute her. *Elphamira*, who was very impatient to see her Brother after so long an Absence, and thought it would not be proper for *Narzanes* to be seen with her at that Juncture, desir'd him to withdraw; nor indeed was he himself desirous of being then introduc'd to a Stranger, who very possibly

possibly might perceive the Disorder he was in; and form such Suspicions as would create some Uneasiness between the Brother and Sister; and therefore he took an Opportunity of retiring, unperceiv'd by *Elphamira*'s Brother.

But that very Evening, a fatal Accident happen'd, which destroy'd all *Narzaens*'s Hopes, and threw the whole Court into the utmost Confusion. He had not been long in his own Apartment, where he propos'd to be alone for the rest of the Evening, when *Euryphax* came to interrupt his solitary Meditations; and after a few Words had past between them, he began to banter him upon his retir'd Way of living, and in so ill natur'd a Manner, as tho' he really intended to provoke him to quarrel. *Narzanes* knowing that *Euryphax* was very much given to Raillery, and often spoke without thinking, took but little Notice of what he said; but at the same Time, would have been very glad to get rid of his Company. However, *Euryphax* not being inclin'd to leave him, prest him earnestly to take a Walk in the *Emperor*'s Gardens, which *Narzanes* was very unwilling to do; and would have excus'd

D him-

himself, had not the other been vastly urgent, so that at last he chose to comply with his Request, rather than be troubled with his Impertinence.

The Evening was somewhat gloomy at their setting out, and they had not taken many Turns in the Gardens, when Night seem'd to come on apace, which occasion'd most of the Company to retire. *Narzanes* and *Euryphax* had struck down a long and narrow Walk, when they heard some People talking and coming up toward them. *Euryphax*, by the Sound of the Voice, immediately took it to be a Person who had insulted him some Nights before, but had been prevented fighting him by the rest of the Company, so resolv'd not to lose this Opportunity of being reveng'd. By this Time they perceiv'd two Men at a little Distance from them; upon which *Euryphax* made a Stand, and first address'd one of the Gentlemen in the insulting Tone which was natural to him, who having no Knowledge of him, told him he certainly was mistaken in the Person, but that he was not afraid of any Man living. This abrupt, tho' just Answer, made *Euryphax* persist in his Error; when,

when, without any farther Explanation, they both drew, and made several vigorous Attacks at each other, till at last *Euryphax* gave him a mortal Wound, which fell'd him dead on the Place.

In the mean Time, the other unknown Person seeing his Friend extended on the Ground, came up to *Narzanes* with his drawn Sabre, and vow'd he would revenge the Death of his Friend upon him, *Euryphax* having made off: But *Narzanes* looking upon this as a very unwarrantable Quarrel, would willingly have declin'd engaging in it, had not the other upbraided him with Cowardice, which oblig'd him to draw; and thus he fought for some Time in his own Defence, having no Design to wound his Antagonist, who thinking he had the Advantage of *Narzanes*, clos'd in with him, in order to disarm him; but missing his Aim, he run directly upon the Point of his Sabre, by which he receiv'd a Wound that laid him at *Narzanes*'s Feet.

The Company were not yet all retired from the *Emperor*'s Gardens, so that some People who were in the adjacent

jacent Walks, being alarm'd at the clashing of Swords, ran to this fatal Alley, where they found two Gentlemen weltring in their Gore, and *Narzanes* standing by them; which rais'd such a Scene of Horror in the Minds of the Spectators that they knew not what to think. But seeing *Narzanes* with his drawn Sabre in his Hand, they immediately secur'd him, and carried him before a Magistrate; whilst, by the Light of the Torches, they soon discover'd who the other two unfortunate Gentlemen were; the one being Son to the chief *General* of the *Emperor*'s Forces, and the other, Brother to *Elphamira*. The former was already dead; but the latter having some Signs of Life remaining, was carried to his Father's House, where it was not expected that he could live an Hour.

This sad Catastrophe made a great Noise in the *Emperor*'s Court; and as there were no Witnesses to be examin'd, it was universally suppos'd that *Narzanes* was guilty of the Murder; and finally resolv'd that he should be prosecuted with the utmost Severity. By his Examination, and the Account he gave

of

of the whole Affair, it manifeftly appear'd that *Euryphax* had been the chief Promoter of this unlucky Quarrel; and therefore an Order was immediately iffu'd out for the apprehending of him living or dead, but he was out of their reach; for being confcious of his own Guilt, and dreading the Confequences of fo barbarous an Action, he had abandon'd his Friend, and made off that very Night; purfuing his Journey with the utmoft Speed, till he had got out of the *Emperor*'s Dominions.

Narzanes was now confin'd under a ftrong Guard, and being inform'd who the unhappy Gentlemen were who were faid to have loft their Lives in this unfortunate Rencounter, he abandon'd himfelf intirely to Defpair; not fo much for his own Sake, as for that of his dear *Elphamira*, who, as he fuppos'd, had loft her darling Brother, for it was reported that he was dead: And when he came to reflect that his Sabre had, tho' innocently, been the fatal Weapon which had robb'd him of his Life, his only Defire was to die. But it may not be improper to mention here what paft between *Elphamira* and her Brother before he breath'd his laft.

The Night he was brought home, the great Quantity of Blood he had loſt depriv'd him of his Speech, and he continu'd in fainting Fits till the next Morning, when his Spirits began to revive, and recovering his Voice a little, he had juſt Life enough to give *Elphamira* a ſhort Account of what had paſs'd the Night before; and he told her withall, that he could not in any Manner lay his Death to the Perſon with whom he had fought; for that he himſelf had been the Aggreſſor, and had haſtned his unhappy End, by making too raſh an Attempt to diſarm him; That he was ſatisfy'd the Wound he had receiv'd was not given willfully, and therefore deſir'd, as he had not many Hours to live, that ſhe would declare his dying Words to the World; in order that a Stop might be put to *Narzanes*'s Proſecution, whoſe Innocence, he ſaid, he thought himſelf in Honour oblig'd to defend. Here his Speech fail'd him, and ſoon after he dy'd in *Elphamira*'s Arms, whoſe Grief on this Occaſion was inexpreſſible.

By this time, the News of this young Nobleman's ſad Fate had reach'd his Father's Ears, who immediately return'd

from

from the Country, but did not come time enough to find his Son alive; and when he was inform'd of the whole Affair, no Diſtraction of Mind could be equal to his. The Death of ſo amiable a Son, who was dear to him as Life it ſelf; and the Preſence of a Daughter in the deepeſt Affliction for the Loſs of her Brother, were daily preſent to his Imagination; whilſt on the other Hand, he could not but look with Compaſſion on the diſtreſt State of *Narzanes*, whoſe involuntary Crime, now expos'd him to the ſevereſt Puniſhment: For tho' *Elphamira*'s Father had no Intention to concern himſelf in his Proſecution, he knew very well that the *chief General*, whoſe Son had been kill'd by *Euryphax* had taken the Affair in Hand; and being a Man of a fiery Temper, and of abſolute Power; was reſolv'd to make an Example of the one, ſince the other had made his Eſcape and could not be brought to Juſtice.

EVERY one almoſt who had been acquainted with *Narzanes*, ſhew'd a real Concern for his Misfortune, and employ'd all their Intereſt to ſave him; but as he was to be try'd by the *Emperor's* peror's Council, who were all influenc'd by the chief *General*, there was little Hopes of his being clear'd. The *Emperor* had been apply'd to by several Persons of Distinction in *Narzanes*'s Behalf, and even by *Elphamira*'s Father, who found his *Sovereign* inclin'd to shew Mercy; tho' he never would determine any Affair of Consequence without advising with the chief *General*, in whom he confided solely, and whose Voice always govern'd the rest.

MATTERS standing thus, *Narzanes*'s Case was thought desperate; and indeed, he himself was no ways sollicitous about saving his Life; for when his Trial came on, he appear'd with the greatest Unconcern imaginable; and instead of pleading for himself, and extenuating his suppos'd Guilt, he neglected his own Cause, to lament the deplorable Death of the two young Noblemen; and express'd himself in so tender, so pathetic a Manner on this Occasion, that he mov'd the whole Audience to Pity, mix'd with Astonishment, who could not but admire his Greatness of Soul; so that even the *Emperor*'s Council were inclin'd to save him. But the incens'd *General* perceiving

ing the Difpofition they were in to favour him, made a fevere Speech, in which he heightned the whole with the moft aggrevating Circumftances; and withal reprefented to them, how dangerous it might prove, even to the *Emperor*'s Perfon, in cafe a Murder of this Nature were to go unpunifh'd in a Foreigner, who had prefum'd to draw his Sabre in the Verge of his Imperial Palace; a Crime that fingly was made Death by the Laws of their Nation. Thefe, with many other Arguments to the fame Purpofe, gave a fudden Turn to *Narzanes*'s Caufe, who after a fhort Deliberation was condemn'd by a majority of the Council to lofe his Head; and accordingly a Day was fix'd for his Execution.

But Virtue often proves a powerful Advocate to the unjuftly wretched. The generous *Elphamira* could not think of *Narzanes*'s Doom without being grievoufly affected; fhe faw no Profpect of faving his Life by any Intereft that could be made at Court; and as fhe was convinc'd of his Innocence, fhe thought it wou'd be cruel to let him fuffer Death, in cafe there was any Poffibility of faving him.

him. She therefore thought how she might assist him in making his Escape; but this she found would be very difficult, because of the Impossibility of bribing his Guards, it being as much as their Lives were worth.

NEVERTHELESS, after having well weigh'd the Affair, she call'd to Mind that a young Gentlewoman, who was one of her meanest Attendants, was about the Size of *Narzanes*, and not very unlike him in Features. To this Person she disclos'd her Intention, and told her, that in case she would consent to go with her to the Place where *Narzanes* was confin'd, and change Cloaths with him, he might make his Escape in this Disguise; which the other, in order to oblige her Lady, who had sav'd her Father's Life, and to whom she was entirely devoted, immediately agreed to. Upon this, *Elphamira*, attended by the young Woman, came to the Castle where he was close Prisoner; and being admitted to his Chamber, she addres'd him as follows. " Think
" not *Narzanes* that I am come hither
" to upbraid you, or charge you with
" the Death of my unfortunate Brother;
" so far from it, that I am satisfy'd you
" are

"are innocent; and therefore in Obedi-
"ence to his dying Words, have endea-
"vour'd to juſtify your fatal, tho' in-
"nocent Action. But alas! All my
"Efforts have prov'd fruitleſs; the *Em-*
"*peror*'s Council is ſway'd by the Autho-
"rity of the chief *General*, who is of a
"moſt cruel Nature, and abſolutely bent
"to revenge the Death of his Son upon
"ſome-body: Now as *Euryphax* has
"made his Eſcape, the Puniſhment of
"his Guilt would inevitably fall upon
"you only. To morrow ſays ſhe, is
"appointed for that Purpoſe; you ſee
"the time is ſhort, and the only Expe-
"dient I can think on to ſave your
"Life, is for you to dreſs your ſelf im-
"mediately in Woman's Apparel and fol-
"low me. I have now brought a Per-
"ſon with me whoſe Cloaths you ſhall
"take; I having prevail'd with her to
"ſtay in your Room.

Narzanes, whoſe Amazement was beyond Expreſſion, could ſcarce believe his
own Eyes; his Thoughts were too con-
fus'd to make a ſuitable Anſwer to ſo
much Generoſity: But after a Moment's
Silence, he flung himſelf at *Elphamira*'s
Feet, and told her, that ſince what he
had

had done had put her to so much Anguish, he did not desire to live; that he was sure his Crime, how innocent soever it might be, must have render'd him odious to her; that nothing less than Death could attone for the Loss of a Brother, who had been so dear to her; and therefore, he was ready to submit to whatever the Council should think fit to inflict.

Here the Tears stole down *Elphamira*'s Cheeks, when her tender Sorrow yielding to her generous Compassion, she interrupted him with these Words. "I am
" perswaded *Narzanes*, that the sad
" Scene in which you was so unhappily
" engag'd, must have fill'd your Soul
" with the most gloomy Ideas: But
" alas! no Attonement can ever call
" back the Dead to Life. As I always
" took you for a Man of Honour, and
" was inform'd by my Brother in his ex-
" piring Moments, how handsome you
" behav'd on that fatal Occasion, I have
" not the least Room to suspect your In-
" nocence; nor am I insensible of the
" Passion you had for me, even from the
" Beginning of our Acquaintance: But
" as it was not in my Power to gratify
" it,

"it, I endeavour'd to procure a Remedy to your Distemper before it grew too violent; all which you yourself must undoubtedly have discover'd, by my Behaviour: And the dangerous Step I now take, is a convincing Testimony of the real Esteem I have for you. Therefore lose no Time: Let us retire instantly from this dismal Mansion; and as a stronger Proof of the Value I have for you, the Moment I receive the News of your being in a a Place of Safety, I'll set out after you, and unite my Destiny with yours."

Such kind and unexpected Expressions gave new Life to *Narzanes*, who thought the best Return he could then make to so generous an Offer, was immediately to obey her Commands; upon which he huddled on his Disguise, and went out of Prison undiscover'd with *Elphamira*. This generous Lady had also taken Care to supply him with every Thing necessary for his Journey; and thus he set out, attended only by a Servant whom *Elphamira* had appointed to be ready for that Purpose; and having rode with prodigious Speed the remaining Part of of that Day and all the Night following, they arrived at *Mombaza*, a Sea Port Town out of the Dominions of the *Emperor* of *Abyssinia*, and the Place where *Elphamira* had promis'd to meet him.

During this Interval great Preparations were making at Court for *Narzanes*'s Execution, which, by the *General*'s Order, was to have been perform'd in a public and most solemn Manner. There was a large Scaffold erected in one of the Outward Courts of the *Emperor*'s Palace, and a Kind of Amphi-Theatre built round it for the Spectators. The *Emperor*'s Guards were drawn up in Battalia, and every Thing being ready for this tragical Scene, News was brought, that the Person in Custody had declar'd to some of the Keepers that she was a Woman, and that *Narzanes* was gone off the Day before. The *General* being inform'd of this, fell into such a Rage that nothing could pacify him; and so excessive was it, that he would have had the young Woman executed in *Narzanes*'s Stead, had not all the Ladies at Court interceeded for her. Every one, him-

himself excepted, was overjoy'd at this lucky Disappointment.

Elphamira was exceedingly pleas'd to find her Project succesful; and as she had sav'd the Life of a Man, whom she was persuaded deserv'd it; she did not value what Constructions the ill-natur'd Part of the World might put upon her Conduct. Her Father was the only Person whose Displeasure she dreaded. But as he knew his Daughter's Virtue, and *Narzanes*'s Merit; he was fully satisfied that she had been prompted to act this Part meerly out of Compassion to a Stranger, who had been doom'd a Sacrifice to the chief *General*'s Inhumanity.

But now the Person whom *Elphamira* had ordered to attend *Narzanes*, till he had got safe out of the *Emperor*'s Territories, returned with the following Letter.

Narzanes *to* Elphamira.

*A*FTER *so singular an Instance of your Generosity, nothing more is*
want-

wanting to complete my Felicity but the Presence of the excellent Elphamira. *To you, Madam, I am indebted for a Life which I shall ever devote to your Service; and tho' so small a Tribute be infinitely inferior to the Obligation you have conferr'd on me; yet as you alone have a Right to dispose of it, I hope you will not disdain the grateful, tho' mean Offering. My future Happiness depends wholly on the Performance of your Promise to me when I left you. And as no Pleasure can be equal to that of enjoying the Company of my inchanting* Elphamira, *I shall wait her Arrival here with the utmost Impatience.*

WHEN this Letter was deliver'd to *Elphamira*, she express'd the utmost Satisfaction, finding that *Narzanes* was out of Danger, and could now provide for his own Safety. The Messenger who brought it, inform'd her that *Euryphax* had taken the same Road; and was seen at *Mombaza* disguis'd in a Sailor's Habit, from whence he had set out for the Court of *Persia*.

THE

THE Reader is to be inform'd, that when *Elphamira* promis'd to follow *Narzanes*, she had done it meerly because she knew it would be the most powerful Argument she could use, to persuade him to make his Escape. For at that Time he seem'd to almost disregard Life, and was very unwilling to take any Steps towards saving it. The Letter which she wrote to him, will discover evidently the generous Intentions of this incomparable *Lady*; who was induc'd to serve him from no other Motive but that of a sincere and most generous Friendship. 'Twas as follows.

ELPHAMIRA *to* NARZANES.

IT was no small Pleasure to me, to receive with your Letter the welcome News of your being out of the Reach of your mercilefs Profecutors. The Diftrefs you were in under your Confinement, gave me a real Concern ; and my Thoughts were wholly employ'd how to avert the Danger which threatned you. I obferv'd your Defpair, and being no Stranger to the Caufe of it; I contriv'd a Project, which, thank Heavens, has

E   *met*

met with *Succefs*. But Narzanes, *forgive me, if I tell you, that when I made you the Promife, to which you now lay Claim, I did it purely to deceive you. For my chief and only Intent at that Time, was, to fave a Life which you feem'd not to value, tho' dear to your Friends; and I could not think on a more powerful Expedient to urge your Departure, than to affure you that I would follow you. Now my Wifhes are completed; and therefore, it would be a fruitlefs Attempt in you, to entertain me with a Paffion, which, oh! I cannot return. Yet, if you are inclin'd to correfpond with me as a Friend, but not a Lover, your Letters will always be acceptable. The Poffeffion of what we fondly admire, may foon or late prove indifferent; but the Endearments of Friendfhip are folid and lafting. Confider this* Narzanes, *and hafte to the Court of* Perfia, *where Fortune only waits your Return, to crown your Days with Profperity and Glory.*

THIS Letter, we may fuppofe, was far from being agreeable to *Narzanes,* who had been waiting with Impatience for

for *Elphamira*'s Arrival. During his Stay at *Mombaza* he wrote several Letters to her, in which, he in the most tender Words, insisted on her Promise; and said all that Love and Honour could suggest to persuade her into a Complyance; but nothing could prevail on this generous *Lady*, who, in her Answers, always referr'd him to the Contents of her first Letter; which, at last, quite damp'd all his Hopes, tho' not without many grievous Conflicts betwixt Reason and the violent Impulses of his Passion.

Things were in this State, when he received an Express from his Father, to whom *Euryphax*, who was then arrived at the Court of *Persia*, had related the whole Misfortune of his Son; with the melancholy Circumstance of his being condemn'd to die, which he affirm'd was inevitable. In his Father's Packet were several Letters from the King of *Persia*, directed to the *Emperor* of *Abyssinia*, and the principal Members of his Council, which now being of no manner of Service to *Narzanes*, he took little Notice of them; but when he came to peruse his Father's Letter to him,

him, which was drawn up in the moſt pathetic Terms, it gave a ſtrange Turn to the paſſionate Sentiments, he, till then, had ſo raſhly indulg'd in Favour of *Elphamira*. He tax'd himſelf with the higheſt Ingratitude towards a Parent, who, from his Infancy, had given him the moſt convincing Proofs of his Paternal Affection and Tenderneſs; and particularly on this Occaſion, when he acquainted him in his Letter, that the News of his Diſtreſs had like to have kill'd him; and that if Fate had decreed his untimely End, it would be impoſſible for him to ſurvive his Loſs. Theſe and many other Expreſſions of the like Nature, having affected *Narzanes* in a moſt ſenſible Manner, he reſolv'd to ſet out with the utmoſt Diligence for the Court of *Perſia*: But before he did this, he thought proper to communicate his Deſign to *Elphamira*, who being inform'd of his Reſolution approv'd it very much, as being the only Thing ſhe aim'd at; and was exceedingly pleas'd, to find, that among other Motives which had induc'd him to take this Step, her good Advice had made ſome Impreſſion on his Mind.

WHILST

Whilst these Things past, *Euryphax* who began to envy *Narzanes*, could not reflect on the Misfortune he was under, without feeling a secret Pleasure, tho' he himself had been the chief Occasion of it. He was no Stranger to his personal Merit; and knowing likewise the great Interest he had at Court, he propos'd no small Advantage to himself by his Death; he being the only young Nobleman that could stand in Competition with him for Power and Superiority. As he was fully inform'd at *Mombaza* that *Narzanes* had been sentenc'd to die, he look'd upon his Death as certain; and took the utmost Pains to persuade the whole Court of *Persia*, that far from believing there was any Possibility of saving his Life, he was sure the *Emperor*'s Decree must, by that Time, have been put in Execution. He had even prepossess'd *Narzanes*'s Father with so strong a Notion of his Son's fatal End, that he fell ill upon it, and continued so without any Hopes of his Recovery.

Such was the melancholy News *Narzanes* receiv'd by a second Express, with whom he immediately set out for *Persia*, and in a few Days arriv'd at Court,

Court, to the great Joy and Surprize of all his Acquaintance, *Euryphax* excepted, whose Astonishment and Perplexity on this Occasion were inexpressible. The Father of *Narzanes*, as has been observ'd, was now extremely ill and scarcely able to speak. However, at the Sight of his Son, whom he never expected to see again, his fainting Spirits began to revive, and he felt a Pleasure within him, which, in the weak Condition he then was in, he could not well express: But reaching out his Hand, he utter'd these Words in a faint and expiring Tone of Voice. " You are come too late *Narzanes*; " and your Presence, which I have so " long, so earnestly wish'd for, has not, " alas! now the Power to restore me to " a Life, which the News of your sad, " sad Fate has brought to its Period. " Yet I die with Comfort, since you " have found an Asylum; and as I " have not many Hours to live, I conjure you to consider my dying Words " with the deepest Attention. Above all " Things, have a strict Regard to Religion. Love and Honour your *Prince* " who is a Father to his People; and " remember what you owe to your " Country, which ought ever to be dear
" to

"to you: Sacrifice your Life and Fortune to both in cafe it be neceſſary; and never ſuffer Adverſity to depreſs your Courage; let all your Actions be the Reſult of Judgment." *Narzanes* was ſo oppreſs'd with Grief to ſee a fond Parent in this Extremity, that he was not able to once open his Lips, which his Father perceiving, he continued as follows. " Don't afflict your ſelf, deareſt Son, ſince it is a Tribute we muſt all, one Day or other, pay to Nature. I am going to leave you for a Time; but if any Thing relating to this World can give me Pleaſure, after I am remov'd from it, 'twill be to know that you ſpend your Days in the Practice of Virtue and Honour, without which no Man can be ſaid to be truly great." He had no ſooner utter'd theſe Words, but his Speech fail'd him; when preſſing his Son to his Boſom, he expir'd in his Arms.

The News of this great Man's Death was receiv'd with univerſal Concern throughout all *Perſia*; but the *King* was particularly affected at the Loſs of a Miniſter, of whoſe Merit and Abilities he was ſo ſenſible, that he had always repos'd pos'd an intire Confidence in him. 'Twas thought at firſt that *Euryphax*'s Father, who at that Time was the next great Man in the Empire, would have been made principal *Miniſter*: And *Narzanes* himſelf was of the ſame Opinion, when a few Days after the *King* ſent to acquaint him, that he could not give a ſtronger Proof of the high Value he ever had for his deceas'd Father, than by calling him to all his Employments. *Narzanes*, who was now left independent, with a conſiderable Fortune; and was far from entertaining ſo high an Idea of his own Capacity, as to think himſelf qualified for the great Truſt which his *Maſter* intended to honour him with, would fain have declin'd the Offer; but the *Emperor* inſiſted on his Compliance, and order'd him immediately to take the Adminiſtration of Affairs into his own Hands.

This young *Nobleman* being inveſted with all the Power and Authority, which his Father had before poſſeſt, ſoon convinc'd his *Sovereign*, that he was not unworthy of the Dignity to which he had rais'd him. He now began to ſhine in a Court, which had been prejudic'd againſt him by a falſe Notion
they

they had imbib'd of his being a very proud and indolent Man; and he had not been long at the Helm, before he acquir'd the Love and Esteem of all. He was liberal and compassionate; ever ready to redress the Grievances of the oppress, and relieve such as appeal'd to him for Justice. In a Word, his Virtues, like the Sun, diffus'd their Benevolence universally; and cou'd scarce be parallel'd in the wisest and most experienc'd *Ministers*. He trod directly in his Father's Steps, with Regard to the Government of home Affairs; but what will appear wonderful at his Years, is, that he was already so well skill'd in all foreign Negotiations, that when any Affair of Moment was debated in the *Emperor*'s Council, concerning either neighbouring *Princes* or foreign *Nations*, he was chiefly consulted; and his Opinion was generally approv'd, and usually attended with Success.

So peculiar a Talent join'd to his excellent Qualities, had entitled him to the Favour and Confidence of his *Prince*; who daily retriev'd in the Son, what he suffer'd by the Death of the Father; and by this time, *Narzanes* had ingratiated himself

himself so much into his Favour, that he resolv'd to recommend a Wife to him, whose Virtue and Riches wou'd heighten considerably his Grandeur. The young *Lady* whom the *King* design'd him, and who indeed was endow'd with many Perfections, besides a very plentiful Fortune was the same beauteous *Almazaida*, with whom, as was before observ'd *Euryphax* was distractedly in Love, which had been the Occasion of his being sent on his Travels.

THIS Match being propos'd by the *Emperor* himself to *Narzanes*, as a thing agreeable to him; 'twas reasonable to presume the *Minister* would have agreed readily to so advantageous an Alliance: But whether it were that he had no Inclination to a wedded Life, or that he still harbour'd some secret Hopes of being one Day united to *Elphamira*, with whom he still carry'd on a Correspondence; whatever I say, might be his Thoughts on this Subject, he seem'd to decline the Proposal, and desir'd his *Master* to allow him some time to consider of it. The *Emperor* was willing to oblige his Favourite; but being impatient to know his Intentions, he would not indulge him a long Deliberation; and therefore soon after took an Opportunity of asking him his Opinion with Regard to *Almazaida*, and whether he did not think she surpafs'd all the Court Ladies in Beauty. *Narzanes* perceiv'd plainly by the manner in which the *Emperor* exprefs'd himself, that he requir'd a positive Answer to his first Proposal; and therefore, tho' he was not in Love with this charming Woman, in whose Eyes he already appear'd amiable; yet when he consider'd the numberless Obligations he ow'd his *Master*, who could have no other View in this, but the promoting his *Minister*'s Interest, he was determin'd, (after some Struggles to think of forgetting the generous *Elphamira*,) to marry her, in order to convince his *Sovereign* that he approv'd of the Choice he was pleas'd to make for him, and that in all Things he was ready to submit to his Will and Pleasure,

Accordingly the Nuptials were solemniz'd some Days after, with the utmost Splendor, to the intire Satisfaction of all except *Euryphax*. The Prosperity of his Rival fting him with Envy; and the Thoughts of losing the Object of his Passion plung'd him almost into Despair.

'Tis

'Tis very probable that had he then been able to contend with *Narzanes*, he poſſibly would have ſhewn his Reſentments: But not being equal to him in any Degree, he thought fit to have Recourſe to Diſſimulation, till ſuch Time as he might find an Opportunity of revenging himſelf, which he thought would be a Work of ſome Years.

But in the mean Time, as his Malice to *Narzanes* increas'd continually upon other Accounts, he propos'd a ſecret Pleaſure to himſelf, in privately contriving ſome Method by which he might diſturb his inward Peace, ſince it was not in his Power to hurt his Perſon; and in order to ſucceed in his black Artifice, he thought that in caſe he could, by ſome Means or other, inſtill Notions of Jealouſy in *Almazaida*, it would anſwer his preſent Purpoſe. This he effected by the Aſſiſtance of a Lady who was very intimate with her; who told *Almazaida* all that had paſt in *Abyſſinia* with Regard to *Elphamira*, aggravating the Whole with Circumſtances, which he knew would make *Almazaida* very uneaſy; particularly when ſhe was aſſur'd that *Narzanes* ſtill held a private
Cor-

Correspondence with her. His Design succeeded to his Wishes: For in a short Time this Lady, by her artful Insinuations, prepossess'd the Mind of *Almazaida* with so many extravagant Notions, that she grew unwarrantably jealous of *Narzanes*, even to a Degree of Madness; so that all the Endearments which they mutually enjoy'd in the Beginning of their Marriage were now turn'd into suspicious Reproaches on her Side. So sudden a Change in *Almazaida* gave *Narzanes* a Deal of Uneasiness, who used his utmost Endeavours to clear himself: But whatever he could say or do, 'twas all in vain; the more he labour'd to dissuade her from her Jealousy the more it rag'd, and *Elphamira* was the perpetual Theme of her Discourse.

Thus was *Narzanes* for some Years perplex'd in his Domestic Concerns, without discovering the secret Spring from whence all these Discontents flow'd; whilst on the other Hand, the *King* made it his continual Study how to raise him to greater Honours, which indeed it was scarce possible for him to do: For by this Time he was so highly in the Favour

vour and Efteem of his *Prince*, and his Power fo unlimited, that he govern'd under the *Monarch*, the whole Kingdom without a Competitor. But of what Avail is all the Pomp and Glitter of Fortune to a troubled Breaft! The Love and Jealoufy of his Wife were now become a Torment to him; for tho' her Jealoufy, like a raging Diftemper, was grown to fuch a Head as not to be immediately cur'd, yet it did not leffen her Love, which alfo was of a moft extravagant Caft. So that what with thefe jarring Paffions of *Almazaida*, and the intricate Affairs of State he was then imploy'd in, he had enough to do, to behave towards every one with that Evennefs of Temper, which ufually gave a Grace to his whole Conduct.

He had two Children by *Almazaida*, a Son and a Daughter, of whofe Education fhe took an uncommon Care, in order to recommend herfelf the more to his Affection; and in all Probability, they wou'd have been crown'd with Felicity, had not *Euryphax*, by fo barbarous a Contrivance, fow'd thefe Seeds of Difcord in his Family. However, *Narzanes* being a Man of great Wifdom and
Dif-

Difcretion, he conceal'd *Almazaida's* Weaknefs from the Knowledge of the World; and, as he was naturally complaifant, he bore her various Caprices with all the good Humour imaginable.

About this Time, the Treafurer-General of *Perfia*, Father to *Euryphax*, was feiz'd with an Illnefs, of which he fhortly died; and as this was a Place of great Truft, there were many Competitors for it: But the *Emperor*, who was a judicious *Prince*, would not difpofe of that Employment, till he had firft confider'd who was the fitteft Perfon to fill it. Amongft others, *Euryphax*, who was of a vain and ambitious Character, being of Opinion that the *Emperor* could not refufe him his Father's Employment, without doing him the greateft Injuftice, made a vigorous Application to him for the Grant of it: But fetting afide his Years, which were then under Thirty, he had no Abilities which might intitle him to a Place of this Truft; for which Reafon the *Emperor* gave him a flat Denial. This *Monarch*, who was well fkill'd in the Knowledge of Men, had for fome Days caft his Eyes round the Court, in order to make choice of an able Treafurer;

furer; but could think of no Body fo deferving of it as *Narzanes*, and accordingly he declar'd his Intention to him. This generous *Minifter* being fufficiently fatisfied with the Favours which his *Sovereign* had indulg'd him, and not willing to engrofs all his Bounties to himfelf, he therefore made a proper Apology for his Refufal of the great Honour he intended him; and earneftly defir'd him to confer it on *Euryphax*, who, he faid, had no Preferment, and was then fuing for fome: But the *Emperor* would not be prevail'd on by any Means, fo that *Narzanes* was forc'd, tho' with the utmoft Reluctancy to acquiefce with his Will and Pleafure.

Euryphax, who was of a turbulent and fiery Spirit, feeing all his Expectations thus fruftrated, immediately revolv'd a thoufand vile Projects in his Mind, in Prejudice to *Narzanes*, all which he only waited for an Opportunity of putting in Execution. He now faw his Rival in Poffeffion of the only two Things which could have gratified his Vanity and Ambition, the Lady whom he lov'd with the utmoft Excefs, and his Father's Poft; and notwithftanding the
Pains

Pains this *Minifter* had taken, to make him senfible that he had us'd his utmoft Intereft with his *Sovereign*, in his Behalf; and that he would not have accepted of this laft Employment, had not the *Emperor* laid his abfolute Commands upon him for that Purpofe; yet *Euryhax* was unwilling to believe that he had the leaft Obligation to *Narzanes*; but rather look'd upon him as his moft inveterate Enemy, an Opinion he had no other Grounds for, but his own wicked Imagination. However he had Policy enough to conceal his fecret Diffatisfaction, left the other fhould guard himfelf againft his pernicious Defigns.

Narzanes being now poffefs'd of the two firft Pofts in the Empire for Power and Intereft, had the whole Affairs of the *Perfian* Nation committed to his Management; and indeed it may be faid, that he was as upright in the Adminiftration of the one, as he had been fuccefsful in the other: For he had not been *High-Treafurer* many Months before he increas'd the Revenues confiderably, and highly diftinguifh'd himfelf by the wife Choice he made of his Subalterns. In a Word, no *Minifter* before him had ever made

made so great a Figure in the *Persian* Empire, and his *Master* esteem'd himself happy in such a Subject.

Such was the Posture of Affairs in that Empire, when a neighbouring *Prince*, who was very powerful, declar'd War against the Emperor of *Persia*; and had already march'd his Forces into the *Persian* Dominions, before any considerable Preparations could instantly be made for so sudden an Irruption. However, by the Diligence and Activity of *Narzanes*, a potent and flourishing Army soon enter'd the Field, in order to oppose the Designs of the Enemy. The Beginning of this War prov'd fortunate, and the *Persian* Arms were, for some Years, victorious; till at last, several other Princes having entered into an offensive Alliance, they poured in upon the *Persian* Territories like a Torrent; and had like to have caus'd a general Destruction throughout the whole Kingdom. This unhappy Turn began to create mighty Divisions in *Persia*; and many seditious and disaffected Persons made this a Handle to fly in the Face of the *Ministry*. *Euryphax* had not as yet unmask'd himself, but was plotting under-hand against *Narzanes*;
and

and fancied he had now met with a fair Opportunity of working his Ruin. The two chief *Men* with whom he enter'd into a Cabal were *Alharzaman* who had formerly held a Place under his Father in the Treafury; and *Salem* then Governor of *Sigiftan*, both of the *Perfian* Monarch's Privy Council. Thefe three *Men* could not behold the rifing Greatnefs of *Narzanes* without Hatred and Envy. They were equally proud, hot-Headed and ambitious; and ready for any defperate Attempt, in which they might fecure themfelves, and promote the Downfal of others.

Euryphax now enjoy'd a very plentiful Fortune left him by his Father, which plac'd him above Dependence; but his extravagant Way of living, and the large Sums of Money he employ'd in keeping up the Spirit of a factious *Party*, foon convinc'd him that his Eftate was not fufficient to fupport his Expences; and that nothing lefs than the Adminiftration of the Treafury, could gratify his Ambition, and give Succefs to his Defigns. This was the only Object he aim'd at; and therefore refolv'd by fome Stratagem or other, to bring his vile Project to bear.

His two other *Associates*, who were Men of the same wicked Principles, and had also their own private Views; did not in the least doubt, but he being made *High-Treasurer*, they of Course would be promoted to the Dignity of *Secretaries* of State; and thus they all three, in Concert, conspir'd the Ruin of *Narzanes*; and had, as is the Custom of all such wild *Projectors*, dispos'd before Hand of his several Employments to themselves; as tho' their Design could not possibly meet with Disappointment.

But during this Interval, a remarkable Incident happen'd, which, for some Time put a Stop to the Proceedings of these factious *Men*. As the good or ill Success of Affairs in a Nation, is generally imputed to the Conduct of a *Ministry*; so long as a Government is prosperous and flourishing, the *Minister* who presides, is applauded, and almost worshipp'd; whether the Happiness they enjoy be owing to his Management or not. On the other Side, if Affairs prove unsuccessful, the same *great Man*, who, but a Moment before was the Idol of the People, is now aspers'd, vilified, and condemn'd right or wrong; and not the
least

least Regard had to his past Services. This was almost *Narzanes*'s Case, who upon every little Turn of Fortune was exclaim'd against, and insulted by an ignorant Multitude; whilst his *Sovereign*, who was throughly sensible of the Integrity and Abilities of his *Minister*, never laid any of those Reverses to his Charge; but approv'd all his Measures, which were well concerted, and encourag'd him so far in the Execution of them, as to be answerable himself for the Events.

However, the *Persian* Affairs were now at a very low Ebb, when, in the Beginning of the Year, the confederate *Princes*, with their innumerable Forces, had over-run a considerable Part of the Country; and propos'd, in a Campaign or two, to subdue the whole *Empire*. On the other Hand, *Narzanes*, who was inform'd of their Designs, took Care to re-inforce the *Persian* Army with the choicest Troops of the Nation, which he had called from the remote Provinces, where he apprehended no Danger from any Incursion of the Enemy. Thus prepar'd on both Sides, they enter'd the Field; and the first Battle that was fought, decided the Fate of *Persia*; for after

after a bloody Engagement, which began at Day-Break, and lasted till the setting of the Sun, the *Persian* Army gain'd a complete Victory over the united *Princes*, whose scatter'd Forces were pursu'd with so much Vigor, that they were oblig'd to quit the *Persian* Dominions.

This joyful News being brought by an Express to Court, where they were very dubious of the Event, gave a new Turn to *Naizanes*'s Affairs, as well as to those of the *Emperor*. For the Success of this great Victory was immediately ascrib'd to the wise and prudent Measures of his *Minister*. And those *Persons* who were labouring secretly at his Ruin, were now struck with Confusion to see and hear him universally applauded. Yet the more the World extoll'd his Wisdom and Merit, the sharper Edge it gave their Malice and Hatred; and tho' they did not dare to shoot their Venom at him openly; yet these restless *Conspirators* villainously imploy'd their dark Emissaries to blacken and defame his Character.

NEVER-

NEVERTHELESS, this wife *Statefman* ſtood his Ground with uncommon Reſolution, and purſued all his Meaſures with unparallel'd Courage. He had now acquir'd a large Experience, and was no Stranger to the Intrigues of a Court, tho' he himſelf abhorr'd the Practice of them; and as he was not tainted with any ungenerous Paſſion, he had a Soul above employing baſe Methods to revenge the Injuries of his *Enemies:* Accordingly, he bore their abuſive Reproaches unmoved; and was ſo conſcious of his Integrity, that he would not even ſuffer any one to write in his Defence, or make the leaſt Reply to the numberleſs ſcandalous *Libels* which were daily publiſh'd, from dark Corners, againſt him; but was often heard to ſay, that he look'd with Pity on the wretched *Authors* of them; and only wiſh'd they could employ their Pens more to their Credit; whence we may infer, that a Man whoſe Heart and Hands are pure, is above taking Notice of thoſe foul Inventions that are hatch'd to his Prejudice, and which flow wholly from a Spirit of Rancour.

By this time, the *Perfian* Empire was again reftor'd to its former Tranquility, and every thing at home feem'd to promife a lafting Peace; but the Affairs abroad wore a different Afpect; for the neighbouring *Princes*, who had been defeated the foregoing Year, exafperated at their ill Succefs, and jealous of the *Perfian* Grandeur, were refolv'd to enter into a ftronger Alliance, and call in other *Powers* to their Affiftance. *Narzanes* having receiv'd timely Notice of the great Preparations they were making for a fecond Invafion, took proper Meafures for fecuring the *Empire* from their Attempts: And as he had the Army at his Devotion, and the Treafury at Command, he could eafily bring Matters to bear at home; but the Difficulty was how to caufe fuch Diverfions without Doors, as might check the Defigns of the Enemy.

Here he projected an Expedient within himfelf, which, if fuccefsful, would redound greatly to the Advantage of his *King* and *Country*. As he had carry'd on a Correfpondence for feveral Years with *Elphamira*, meerly out of Gratitude and Friendfhip; and that her Father, who

who had entertain'd him in so courteous and splendid a Manner, during his Residence at the *Abyssinian* Court, was now rais'd to the Dignity of President of the *Emperor*'s Council, an Employment of great Power and Interest: *Narzanes* was of Opinion, that in Case an Alliance could be concluded between the *Emperor* and the *King* his Master, it would be of important Service to the *Persian* Government at this Juncture. And for this Purpose, he immediately dispatch'd a Person in whom he could confide, with proper Instructions to *Elphamira*, who was to communicate them to her Father, and by his Interest endeavour to bring about this grand Alliance.

Elphamira, who was a Lady of a superior Genius, and had a better Notion of political Negotiations than Women generally have; was pleas'd with being entrusted with the Management of an Affair, which might turn to the Advantage of *Narzanes*, for whom she ever entertain'd a sincere Esteem. The Moment she receiv'd his Proposals, she took the Business in Hand; and by her wise and well-concerted Measures, brought over

over her Father entirely to the *Emperor* of *Persia*'s Interest.

BUT a Negotiation of this kind, could not be carry'd on without a considerable Charge to the *Crown*; and as the War had already been vastly expensive, the *Emperor*'s Exchequer was now very much drain'd; which put *Narzanes* to some Difficulty, how to raise the necessary Supplies for the present Exigencies. He was unwilling to lay new Taxes on the People; and yet the Treasury had not sufficient, at this time, to pay the Army at home; and furnish him with such Sums as he was oblig'd to send abroad, for the Support of this weighty Alliance with the *Abyssinian* Monarch, whose Council would not come into the *Emperor* of *Persia*'s Measures without a handsome Consideration; besides the Maintenance of the auxiliary Forces, who were to be paid at the *King's* Expence. However, as *Narzanes* was possest of immense Riches, and preferr'd the Interest of his *Sovereign*, and the Good of his *Country*, to all other Considerations; he resolv'd upon so worthy an Action, as perhaps no *Minister* had ever done before him.

HERE-

HEREUPON, without communicating his Design to any one, he immediately rais'd a large Sum of Money out of his own capital Funds; and having made such Remittances to *Elphamira* as were agreed upon, her Father undertook to manage the Affair with the Members of the *Emperor*'s Council, to whom he made such Presents as he thought proper; by which means this important Alliance was soon completed, to the entire Satisfaction of the *Emperor* of *Persia*, and the whole Nation in general.

THIS Master-stroke of Policy, which had been concerted with all imaginable Secrecy, broke the whole Measures of the confederate *Princes*, whose Forces were already upon their March. For as the Empire of *Abyssinia* border'd almost upon their Dominions; they were apprehensive, that whilst they should be carrying their Arms into *Persia*, the *Abyssinian* Monarch, with a formidable Army, would instantly fall upon their small Kingdoms, and make himself Master of them, before ever they could be able to make Head against him. These Considerations prevail'd with them to lay aside the Execution of their Design; so that

that inſtead of attempting any farther Acts of Hoſtility againſt the *Perſians*, they made the firſt Propoſals towards an Accommodation, which in Time brought about a moſt advantageous Peace to the *Perſian* Emperor.

Narzanes, in the mean time, could not break the ſeditious *Spirit* of his *Enemies* at home. He was perpetually ſerving his *King* and *Country* at the Expence of his own Fortune, and without any View of Reward; whilſt a Set of ſelfiſh and ambitious *Men*, who were prompted by no other Views but thoſe of Self-Intereſt, were contriving his Deſtruction. *Euryphax* was at the Head of this factious *Party*, who were now encreas'd to a great Number; he having drawn into his pernicious Cabal, ſeveral Members of the *King's* Council, with many other diſaffected Perſons who were all as deſperate as himſelf, and equally ready to promote Miſchief. Theſe inſatiable *Creatures* could not be at reſt, unleſs they had the Adminiſtration of Affairs in their own Hands; and were angry to find that *Narzanes* could ſo happily govern the State, and complete all his Schemes without their Aſſiſtance and
Parti-

Participation; and what incens'd them ftill more, was to find that all their Under-hand Oppofitions, and open Provocations, could not once ruffle his fteady Temper.

AFTER what has been obferv'd with regard to the Conduct of *Narzanes*; we may naturally fuppofe that this great *Minifter* had made no Addition to his Fortune; but on the contrary, had very much impair'd it, in the fecret Services of his *Sovereign* and his *Country*, tho' his *Antagonifts* were of a quite different Opinion: For as he was free from all Vanity and Oftentation, he had conceal'd the Merit of his Negotiations from the Knowledge of the Public; and been cautious even of acquainting the *Emperor* his Mafter, that he had purchas'd the *Abyffinian* Alliance with his own Money; left he fhould think it were merely out of Self-Intereft, and with a Defign of obtaining new Favours. This gave a Handle to *Narzanes*'s Enemies to make a ftrict Enquiry into the State of the Treafury, which, for the Reafons above-mentioned, had for fome Time been pretty much drain'd.

'Twould be needlefs to take Notice of all the little, undermining Arts which were now employ'd by thofe defigning *Men*, in order to blacken the Character of the beft of *Minifters*, whofe greateft Pleafure was to do good, even to his moft inverate Enemies; not that he was afraid of them, or propos'd to recommend himfelf to their Favour and Approbation, by fome generous Act; but becaufe it was a fix'd Maxim with him, that he ought to treat Mankind in general with good Nature and Humanity. *Euryphax* himfelf, as alfo *Salem* and *Alharzaman*, his two principal *Affociates*, had experienc'd his Benevolence towards them; he having on feveral Occafions follicited his *Prince* in their Behalf, who had rais'd them to great Preferment at *Narzanes*'s Requeft. But his unparallel'd Goodnefs was intirely thrown away on thefe ungrateful *Difturbers* of the public Peace, who could not bear to fee any one in Power but themfelves.

However *Perfia*, which for feveral Years had labour'd under the Inconveniency of a very expenfive War, was at laft reftor'd to a flourifhing Condition by the

the wife and prudent Adminiſtration of this zealous *Patriot*, who aſpir'd at no higher Glory than that of being ſerviceable to his *Country*, and his *King*. But as he had hitherto employ'd his whole Time to this Purpoſe, and had found no Leiſure Hours to attend his own private Concerns; he began to think that a Receſs from public Buſineſs was the only Step could ſecure him a perfect Tranquility during the Remainder of his Days. He was entirely reconcil'd to *Almazaida*'s Humour, who now had found out her Error, and was reclaim'd from her former Jealouſy; and as ſhe had brought him a Son and a Daughter who were grown up, and adorn'd with all the Virtues which embelliſh human Nature; he propos'd to himſelf a real Satisfaction in a retir'd Life, where he might cultivate their excellent Inclinations, and govern his Family, free from thoſe Dangers and Difficulties which generally attend the Management of *State* Affairs.

In this Diſpoſition of Mind, *Narzanes* took an Opportunity of communicating his Intentions to the *Emperor*; whom he told, with all imaginable Submiſſion, that

that the only Reward he defir'd for his paſt Labours, was to have Leave to reſign all his Employments, and retire into the Country. But the *Perſian* Monarch was too well acquainted with the great Capacity and ſhining Qualities of his *Miniſter*, to comply with his Requeſt; and therefore refus'd abſolutely to indulge it; adding, that he wonder'd how he could propoſe to forſake him, ſince he might be perſuaded there was not another Perſon in the Realm, in whom he could repoſe ſo much Confidence. So gracious a Reply from a *Sovereign* to a Subject would have rais'd the Vanity of any other Man: But *Narzanes*, all whoſe Actions were grounded upon the moſt juſt Principles, receiv'd this handſome Denial with a more than ordinary Concern; and could have wiſh'd he had a leſs Share in his *Prince*'s Favour and Affection. The Integrity of this great *Miniſter* was now ſo well grafted in the Opinion of his *Maſter*, that one would have thought it almoſt impoſſible to be remov'd by any Stratagem that could be invented; but Virtue itſelf, tho' guarded by Power, is never ſecure from the baſe Attempts of Envy and Detraction.

F o r

For now *Narzanes*'s Greatnefs is affaulted on every Side. His vile *Oppofers* are contriving not only to ruin his Reputation, and difpoflefs him of his Employments, but are even plotting againft his Life. *Euryphax* and his Party had brib'd fome of the Subalterns of the Treafury, which was the only Repofitory of all the Royal and National Funds in *Perfia*; by which Means they obtain'd a very imperfect Abftract of the Accounts which had been paft in that Office, from the Beginning of *Narzanes*'s prefiding in it, to that Time; and after having ftrictly enquir'd into the whole Affair, they found a great Deficiency in the Revenues, which they immediately imputed to the Male-Adminiftration of the *Treafurer*; and accordingly thought *that* a good Foundation for an Impeachment, but not of Weight fufficient to compafs their wicked Defign. Therefore, *Euryphax*, who had been very active in difcovering the Correfpondence which was carried on between *Narzanes* and *Elphamira*, having intercepted fome Letters relating to Remittances of Money and political Negotiations, contriv'd to have others forg'd to the fame Purpofe; in which it was intimated that *Narzanes* had

had remitted confiderable Sums into *Abyssinia*, and that he himfelf intended foon to take a Journey thither, in order to diffolve the Alliance which had been made with that *Emperor*; and enter into a Confederacy with other *Princes*, who were now ready to invade the Kingdom of *Perfia*. Thefe Letters, tho' anonymous, were fuppos'd to be written by *Narzanes* and *Elphamira*; and this Scheme was fo artfully manag'd, that *Euryphax* had even impos'd upon moft of his *Party*, fo far as to perfuade them that thefe Letters were genuine; no Body being let into the Secret, but his Bofom Friends *Salem* and *Alharzaman*, who were chiefly concern'd with him in carrying on this black Confpiracy.

ONE Circumftance to be obferv'd here, is, that the *Emperor* of *Perfia*, having repos'd an intire Confidence in his *Minifter*, had therefore never requir'd him to produce the Particulars of fuch Sums as had been expended in carrying on the War, in forming Alliances, and other fecret Services: But relying fo much on his Integrity, was throughly fatisfied with his Conduct in general. And as to *Narzanes*, whofe Actions had already prov'd him

him the greatest *Man* of the Age, both for the Practice of all the Moral Virtues, and his powerful Skill in the Arts of Government; it could never be surmiz'd that he wou'd in any Manner deceive his *Prince*, and employ the public Funds to his own private Use, since he had given so many Proofs to the contrary. But as he was sensible that a *Minister*, in all political Transactions, ought to carry on his Designs with the utmost Secrecy; he so strictly observ'd this Maxim, that he scarce intrusted any Person with his Negotiations; but kept private Journals written with his own Hand, of every Particular that had been transacted during his Administration, which made it almost impossible for any one to dive into the State of Affairs without his Knowledge. And certainly a *Minister* who acts upon these Principles is not to be blam'd; nor is his Candor and Honesty to be disputed, because he is throughly vers'd in *Politicks*; since that Talent discreetly manag'd, is the only Support of a *Government*. But the Conduct of a *Minister*, be his Actions ever so good and glorious, can never please ambitious *Men*; who, to gratify their Passions, are always ready to destroy the best concerted Schemes, and lay them open to the Enemies of their *Country*. For at this very Juncture, whilst *Narzanes* was taking the best Measures possible, to secure an advantageous and lasting Peace to the *Nation*, whose Welfare he had so much at Heart; *Euryphax* and his *Adherents*, were traiterously carrying on a secret Correspondence with foreign *Powers*. They had represented the *National* Affairs to them in a very false Light; and buoy'd them up with the Hopes of an approaching Civil-War in *Persia*, which was the only Thing the confederate *Princes* could wish for, in order to form some new Attempt against the *Empire*. And this horrid Contrivance had like to have obstructed all *Narzanes*'s Measures; as it not only caus'd a general Stagnation in Trade, but also put the *Crown* to very unnecessary Expences, which might otherways have been avoided.

Such was the infectious Spirit that rag'd in *Euryphax* and his *Party*, which by their false *inuendos* and malicious Insinuations, had already tainted a considerable Part of the *Nation*, especially the worthless Part of it; who daily clamour'd mour'd not only againſt the *Miniſter*, but even againſt the *Emperor* himſelf, for no other Reaſon, but becauſe they were not let into the Secrets of his Government; as tho' a *Prince* were not at Liberty to chuſe his own *Miniſters*, unleſs a *Miniſter*, when choſen, were to be accountable for his Actions to the *prying* Multitude; and oblig'd to gratify their impertinent Curioſity, by diſcloſing his *Maſter*'s Secrets, which in the Opinion of every Man of common Senſe muſt abſolutely tend, not only to the immediate Prejudice of a *State*; but at laſt prove its Deſtruction. And if this were the Caſe, what *King* would ever find a *Miniſter* to aſſiſt him in the weighty Cares of *Government*? And what *Miniſter* would ever undertake ſo hazardous a Province, ſince he muſt perpetually be expos'd, either to forfeit his *Prince*'s Favour by diſcloſing his ſecret Negotiations, or incur the People's Hatred for not revealing them? and thus either Way, ſink under a Burthen too heavy for his Shoulders; and right or wrong fall a Sacrifice to the diſſaffected *Party*.

Now after what has been obſerv'd, 'twould not be natural to ſuppoſe, that ſuch

such a *Sett* of Men as compos'd *Euryphax*'s Party, would have the least Regard either to the Wisdom of a *Prince* in his Choice of a faithful and able *Minister*, or to the Integrity and conspicuous Merit of that *Minister*, in whom he thought fit to repose a Confidence: We shall therefore see the Methods which they employ'd to undermine and destroy him.

Euryphax being Master of all the Address and Subtilty, requisite for the *Ring-leader* of a Faction; and having ready Money enough to gratify those whose Assistance he wanted for the carrying on of his destructive Design, began now to take off the Mask, and declare himself *Narzanes*'s Enemy. He had prepar'd Articles of Impeachment against him, all which were grounded upon false Inventions of his own; and these he laid before the *Emperor*'s Council, most of whom were already prejudic'd against this great *Minister*, meerly by *Euryphax*'s Flattery, and artful Insinuations; who had so far impos'd upon their Credulity, as to persuade them that he was guilty of the Crimes he laid to his Charge, and that his Doom was inevitable

table; which, with his specious Promises that they in Conjunction with himself, should govern the *Nation* after *Narzanes*'s Fall, had wrought so strongly upon them, that they blindly acquiesc'd to whatever he propos'd.

THE *Emperor*, who all this Time had not been appriz'd of the vile Designs which were carrying on against his *Minister*, had Occasion to call a Council upon some Affairs of Moment, who met at the Time appointed: But before the *Emperor* could explain his Intentions, they began to exclaim heavily against his *Minister*, who was present, and accus'd him with being a Traitor to his Country, and other high Crimes. *Euryphax*, *Salem*, and *Alharzaman*, had undertaken to open the Charge; and as they were *Men* of a smooth Tongue, they had work'd up their Speeches with so much Art, and in so specious a Manner, that no Body could have suspected them guilty of the least Falshood or Disguise. And indeed the whole Council were almost persuaded that their Accusations were true. The *Emperor* himself was startled at first to hear these *Men* lay open such a Scene of Villainy, attended

tended with so many plausible Circumstances: But being a *Prince* of great Prudence and Moderation, he was resolv'd not to give his Judgment, till he had throughly examin'd the whole Matter.

Narzanes, who had been inform'd of what was hatching against him, and was conscious of his own Innocence heard them with a Calm, which no Danger or Adversity was able to ruffle; and when they had done speaking, he ask'd them if they had any Thing farther to alledge against him; but the Council being silent, he made a handsome Speech in which he laid open their base and unjustifiable Proceedings; but said very little in his own Defence, hinting only, that as the greatest Part of them were concern'd in the Accusation, they were therefore unqualified to be his Judges; and that in his high Station, he was accountable for his Actions to GOD and his *Sovereign* only: Then turning to his *Master*, he told him that he was ready to answer, in private, any Question his *Majesty* would please to ask him. Upon which, there arose great Debates in the Council, who look'd upon *Narzanes*'s

Behaviour

Behaviour as an Act of the higheſt Contempt; and therefore would at that very Inſtant have nominated Judges to try him as a *State* Criminal; but this Motion being over-rul'd by the *Emperor* and ſome of his Councellors; *Euryphax* was very hot upon this Occaſion, and mov'd that *Narzanes* might be immediately confin'd under a ſtrong Guard, leſt he ſhould attempt to make his Eſcape, before they could bring him to Juſtice; which Motion was approv'd by a Majority, and accordingly it was reſolv'd, that his Perſon ſhould be ſecur'd till he might be brought to a Trial.

The *Emperor*, notwithſtanding all his Power and Authority, could not prevent the Execution of this Order; and therefore thought it prudent not to oppoſe the Council, till ſuch time as he could find an Opportunity to allay this raging Storm; but in the mean while he ſent for ſome of his principal Officers, and order'd them to go forthwith to *Narzanes*'s Houſe, and ſet his Royal Signet on all his Books and Papers, which was accordingly done.

This

This wife *Prince*, having taken proper Measures to prevent any Violence from being offer'd to the Person of his *Minister*, to whom he perceiv'd the *Party* bore a most inveterate Malice, summon'd the Council to attend him on a certain Day; when upon mature Deliberation, he order'd *Narzanes*'s Accusers to produce their Articles of Impeachment, which the *Emperor* himself perus'd; and having consider'd the whole, he told them that Justice should be done, and that his *Minister* should take his Trial in a fair and legal Manner, Judges being appointed for that Purpose. But at the same time, he declar'd with a solemn Oath, that in case *Narzanes* should be clear'd of the Crimes they charg'd him with, his *Accusers* should undergo the same Punishment they intended to inflict upon him. The *Party* was highly offended at this severe Declaration: And some of them who were not so hot as the rest, and did not expect any great Advantage from this Combination, began to repent they had ever been concern'd in it: But for *Euryphax* and his chief *Adherents*, as they were desperate *Men* and Slaves to their Ambition, they were
resolv'd

resolv'd to pursue their wicked Design, whatever might befall them.

HENCE we may see the fatal Consequences of a *factious* Spirit, which prompts Men to build their Fortune upon the Ruin of others. When once they involve themselves in cruel and unlawful Practices, and have carried their Malice and Envy to such Lengths as to become odious and contemptible to all Men of Honour, they are deaf to the Voice of Reason, and run all Hazards to succeed in their abominable Attempts, without even so much as providing for their own Safety: A Lesson to all rash and ambitious *Competitors*, if we may give them so soft a Name.

IN the mean time, *Narzanes* bore his Confinement with undaunted Steadiness of Mind: So happy it is for a Man to be conscious to himself, that he has always acted pursuant to the Dictates of Honour and Justice. He was sensible that his Books and private Journals when produc'd, would clear him of all the false Imputations which were laid to his Charge; but then he at the same time knew, that in case his Secret Negotiations

tions should once be expos'd to public View, 'twould prove very detrimental to the Welfare of the *Perfian* Nation, and Prejudice his *Sovereign*'s Interest in *Abyssinia*; where he himself, at this very Juncture, supported the Alliance at his own Expence, by the Pensions he paid annually to several Members of that *Monarch's* Council: a Circumstance he had not communicated to the *Emperor* his Master; who, had he known it, would have set a just Value on this important Service.

Now to shew how artful a turbulent and factious *Person* may be in the Contrivance of a wicked *Stratagem* when subservient to his Purposes; *Euryphax* had hit upon one of the most hellish Inventions that could have been imagin'd; an Invention which had like to have compleated *Narzanes's* Ruin. As he was well inform'd of the secret Correspondence he carried on with the *Abyssinian* Court, he did not doubt but there were several authentick *Writings* and *Memorials* among his Papers, which might justify him upon his Trial: But as the *Imperial* Seal had been put upon them, and consequently they were not to be view'd, view'd, he thought that in cafe he could find out Means to burn his Houfe down, they would be confum'd in the Flames; and hereby put it out of his Power to clear himfelf. To this End, he brib'd fome of his Creatures, whom he order'd to go by Night in Difguife, and fet fire to the feveral Entrances of *Narzanes*'s Houfe, to prevent the People from getting in to give Affiftance, which horrid Project was executed with the utmoft Difpatch and Secrecy: But Providence was fo favourable to *Narzanes*, that timely Notice having been brought to the *Emperor*, he fent a Party of his Guards to the Houfe, with Orders to fave the moft valuable Part of the Furniture; and particularly the Books and Papers that were mark'd with his Seal, and bring them immediately to the Palace, which was accordingly perform'd.

By this time, a multitude of People, notwithftanding the Oppofition of the Guards, were enter'd the Houfe in order to plunder it; and fome of them having laid hold of whatever came firft in their Way, were going off with their Booty; when among others, a Man richly laden was feiz'd, and upon ftrict Examination

mination, finding him to be one of the Incendiaries, he was fecur'd and put in Irons. *Euryphax* had his Emiffaries all this while, who from time to time gave him an Account how things paſt on this Occafion; and hearing that one of the Incendiaries was taken, it ſtruck him at firſt; but his Uneaſineſs was ſoon over, when he reflected, that he had made, as he imagin'd, a Party ſtrong enough in the Council to complete his execrable Deſign.

THE Day appointed for *Narzanes*'s Trial being now at Hand, great Preparations were making for it. The *Emperor* had order'd a confiderable Body of Men to be drawn up within the Courts of his Palace, to prevent any popular Commotions; and having ſummon'd the Judges and Council, he repair'd thither as uſual, that the feveral Formalities of Juſtice might be obſerv'd on this Occaſion. *Euryphax* on his Side, had muſter'd up a Crowd of *Miſcreants* and falſe Witneſſes, who, he flatter'd himſelf, were ready to ſwear and ſet their Hands to all the Depoſitions that would be made againſt *Narzanes*, and thus the Trial began: But the *Emperor* would not ſuffer the

the Seals to be taken from the Papers, till he had heard what his *Accusers* had to say. *Euryphax* open'd the Charge, and was seconded by *Salem* and *Albarzaman*; after which several other Persons were examin'd, when Matters seem'd to go so very hard against *Narzanes*, that the *Emperor* himself scarce knew what to think; nevertheless, when he consider'd the Calm and Serenity he discover'd in his Behaviour, at a time when his Life was in Danger. he could not be persuaded that he was guilty. The Council indeed, being misled by false Informations, and prejudic'd against this great *Man*, were of a different Opinion, and had already pronounc'd that his Crime deserv'd Death.

But as *Traitors* seldom prove true to their *Fellow-Conspirators*, it happen'd that those *Men* being call'd in, who were to prove *Narzanes* and *Elphamira*'s Hand-writing to the Letters and Papers which *Euryphax* had produc'd; they would not answer to their Examination, till they were assur'd in the *Emperor*'s Name, that provided they would declare the Truth of what they knew, with Regard to those Writings, in case they

they had been guilty of any *Male* Practices, they fhould obtain a free Pardon. Upon which, as they were afham'd of the abominable Act wherein they had been already concern'd, and their Confcience flying in their Faces, they could no longer refolve to be the Inftruments of fhedding innocent Blood; but readily confefs'd that all thofe Letters were forg'd, and that they themfelves had drawn them up by the Inftigation of *Euryphax*. At the fame time, one of the Incendiaries who had made his Efcape after having fet fire to *Narzanes*'s Houfe, came voluntarily and depos'd before the *Emperor* and Council, that three other Men in Conjunction with himfelf, had receiv'd a certain Sum of Money from *Euryphax*, upon Condition that they fhould put this deteftable Villainy in Execution.

These unexpected Depofitions gave a new Turn to the whole Affair; upon which the *Emperor* immediately order'd that the feveral Books and Writings belonging to *Narzanes* fhould be produc'd; when the Seals being taken off, they were laid open to the Perufal of the Council, who afterwards comparing fome of of *Narzanes* and *Elphamira*'s Letters, with thofe which *Euryphax* had fram'd for his Accufation, the Forgery was manifeft; and upon Examination of one of the Books it plainly appear'd, that this injur'd *Minifter*, fo far from having embezel'd the public Funds, had, on the contrary, expended very large Sums of his own Money for the Service of the *Crown*, which was then confiderably indebted to him. So many undeniable Proofs were more than fufficient to convince all Men of *Narzanes*'s Integrity, and root out every Sufpicion. But let us fee in what Manner his *Accufers*, who were now fill'd with Defpair and Confufion, will extricate themfelves. The *Emperor* infifted that all thofe who had employ'd fo many villainous Engines to ruin his *Minifter*, fhould be brought to condign Punifhment; and having declar'd his Royal Intentions to the Judges and Council; 'twas determin'd, that as the Evidence was ftrong enough againft them for their Conviction, they fhould all be condemn'd to die without any farther Trial, and their Eftates confifcated to the Ufe of *Narzanes*.

Here this great *Minister* might have triumph'd completely over his *Enemies*, and have fully reveng'd himself of all their Malice and Treachery: But so far from taking any Advantage of the Power and Authority to which he was now restor'd, he employ'd it in their Favour; and us'd his utmost Interest with his *Sovereign*, in order to obtain their Pardon: However, as such notorious Crimes, when committed with Impunity, often prove as dangerous to a *State* in general, as to a *Minister* in particular; the *Emperor* judg'd that it was consistent both with Prudence and Justice to make a public Example of them, and accordingly a Day was appointed for their Execution.

In the mean Time we shall see another Instance of *Narzanes*'s generous Disposition in the Person of his inveterate *Enemy*. He could not think with Unconcern of *Euryphax*'s being put to Death, tho' he had been the Author of all these Evils; and therefore resolv'd if possible to save his Life. With this Design he waited on the *Emperor*, to whom he said that all the Honours he had conferr'd on him were merely of his bestowing;

ing; that his *Majesty* was sensible he had never sued for any single Employment, or ask'd any Favour for himself; but that now he had a Request to make him, which, if granted, would lay him under greater Obligations to his *Majesty*, than all the Instances he had before receiv'd of his Goodness: This *Prince*, not knowing what his *Minister* had to propose, told him, that in Return for the considerable Services he had done the *Crown* and *Nation*, he could not well deny him any Thing; upon which *Narzanes* addrest him in Behalf of *Euryphax*, and us'd the strongest Arguments imaginable to extenuate his Crime, which he imputed wholly to the many Disappointments he had met with; and withal represented earnestly to his *Sovereign* that 'twas much more glorious to give, than to take away Life; and concluded with assuring him, that this was the last Favour he would ask of his *Majesty*, either for himself or any other Person.

THE *Emperor* was astonish'd at the generous Conduct of his *Minister*, towards an *Enemy* who had us'd him so barbarously; and would have offer'd some substantial Reasons for not complying

ing with his Request: But *Narzanes* pleaded for *Euryphax* in such persuasive Terms that he at last obtain'd Mercy. This incomparable Man endeavour'd also to procure a Pardon for *Salem* and *Albarzaman*; but here the *Emperor* was deaf to all his Intreaties; so that in a few Days after, they were both executed according to their Sentence, together with some other Criminals who had been concern'd in this abominable Plot.

AFTER the good Nature and Generosity which *Narzanes* had extended to *Euryphax*, and the many Steps he had taken to save his Life, and restore him to his Fortune; it were but reasonable to suppose, that Gratitude alone would have made some Impression on his stubborn Spirit, and have reclaim'd him from those vicious Inclinations, which had so long led him to the Practice of all that was base and wicked. But when we consider how seldom the violent Impulses of Envy and Ambition are suppress, when indulg'd by *Men* who have no Regard either to Virtue or Honour; we shall not at all wonder at the Manner in which the ungenerous *Euryphax* acknowledg'd so great an Obligation.

ON

ON the very Day that *Narzanes* had obtain'd his Pardon, he himself went to the Place where he was confin'd, and told him that he was very sorry any Thing had happen'd that could give him the least uneasiness; and that as he was willing to forget whatever was past in Relation to himself, he hop'd to find him in the same Frame of Mind: That he was now come to acquaint him, that upon his Intercession, the *Emperor* had granted him his Life; and that the only Thing he desir'd in Return was his Friendship. *Euryphax*, Thunder-struck at the Sight of *Narzanes*, was for some Time speechless: But recovering from his Surprize, he fix'd his Eyes on him, and with a furious Countenance told him, that he could not bear his Presence without Horror; that of all the Misfortunes which ever had befallen him, none could be so afflicting as the being indebted to him for his Life; that his Soul was stung with the bitterest Remorse, and that he preferr'd Death to the greatest Honours the *Emperor* could bestow on him. Saying these Words, he drew out a Dagger, which he had conceal'd under his Robe, and plung'd it in his own Bosom in the Presence of *Narzanes*. Thus fell that perfidious
Man,

Man who, for so many Years had been labouring at the Destruction of this excellent *Minister*; and at last receiv'd from his own Hand the Punishment due to his complicated Guilt.

By this time the *Persians* were become formidable to their Enemies abroad, and enjoy'd a happy Peace at home; being now deliver'd from a vile Sett of *Men*, who had they succeeded in their wicked Attempts, would not only have depriv'd their *Sovereign* of one of the best of *Ministers*; but also have undermin'd the whole *Constitution*. Such are usually the dire Effects of *Ambition*, which, when not check'd in time, commonly prove destructive to a *Nation*. And as it is the Duty of a *Sovereign* to reward the good Services of his *Subjects*; so on the other side, 'twill be thought just and prudent in him to punish those *restless* Spirits, who by their Evil Practices are perpetually endeavouring to blacken his *Ministry*, and disturb the *publick* Tranquility: For altho' Clemency in a *Prince*, adds the greatest Lustre to his Diadem; yet when his *Ministers*, who act immediately by his Authority, are unjustly struck at; and the Safety of a *Nation* endanger'd by the pernicious Arts of infatiably-*ambitious* Men, who prefer their private Advantage to the Welfare of a *Government*; then I prefume, a *Sovereign*, who is to be confider'd as the Father of his *People*, muft be under a Neceffity of having Recourfe to fuch Methods, as will moft effectually tend to the Prefervation of both.

We fhall here leave *Narzanes* exalted to the higheft Grandeur, and conclude with a Word or two on the diftinguifh'd Character of this *Great* Man, tho', after what has been faid, it feems needlefs to expatiate upon it: Yet as his wonderful Conduct in all Affairs, has plainly prov'd that he was not cloath'd in borrow'd Ornaments; but poffeft within himfelf fuch confpicuous Virtues, as made him a moft accomplifh'd *Statefman*: We may juftly affert without Flattery, that when a *Monarch* is affifted in his *Government*, by fo able and upright a *Minifter*; it muft be equally glorious to the *Crown*, and advantageous to the *Subject*, who always feels the happy Influence of his *Adminiftration*. And as no *Man* was ever better qualify'd for fo high a *Station*, or could difcharge the Duties of it

with

with greater Honour and Integrity; we may with Juſtice conclude, that no *Miniſter* ever had a better Title to the Favour and Eſteem of his *Sovereign*, or more truly deſerv'd the Love and univerſal Applauſe of his *Country*.

FINIS

The Unparallel'd Impostor

Anonymous

Bibliographical Note:

This facsimile has been made from a copy in the Beinecke Library of Yale University (British Tracts 1731 M78)

THE
Unparallel'd Impostor:
Or, The whole
LIFE,
ARTIFICES *and* FORGERIES
OF
JAPHET CROOK,
ALIAS
Sir PETER STRANGER, *Bart.*
With all the Proceedings againſt Him.

CONTAINING,

I. An Account of the ſeveral Employments he followed in *Hertfordſhire* (under the Profeſſion of a *Quaker*) as Brewer, Malſter, Grazier, Chapman, Merchant, &c. Of his Marriagees, Amours, Breaking, and Running away.

II. Of his Rambles to *Ireland*, *Scotland*, and the *North* of *England*, the various Pranks he played in all theſe Places, and of his being taken up during the *Preſton Rebellion*, and defrauding the *King's Meſſenger* of a conſiderable Sum of Money, and afterwards cheating his *Widow.*

III. Of his twice becoming a Bankrupt. His Artifices, to impoſe on Mr. *Hawkins.* Copies of his *Wife's* Laſt Will and Teſtament to *Him*; and his own *Will* to Mr. *Hawkins*; in order (as he did) to draw in that Gentleman to leave him his Eſtate. Alſo Mr. *Hawkins's* Will.

IV. A Collection of his Original Letters, ſetting forth his Negotiations with the Dutcheſs of *Kendal*, Duke of *Somerſet*, Lord *Carliſle*, Lord *Bleſſington*, Sir *Robert Walpole*, Lord *Townſhend*, General *Pepper*, Colonel *Kempſton*, Sir *John Eyles*, and many others.

Peter, *throughout his Life, has been a Ranger;*
And, *to no Fraud whatever, is a* Stranger.

LONDON:
Printed in the Year M.DCC.XXXI. [Price 1 s.]

PREFACE.

THE *Publick will soon perceive, that what is here laid before them, is neither Romance nor Forgery; but inconteſtable Matters of Fact, ſupported by authentick and legal Vouchers,* viz. Crook's Indictment *for* forging Deeds *of Mr.* Garbutt's *Eſtate;* the Brief *of the* King's *Counſel;* the Libel *exhibited againſt him in* Doctor's-Commons; *and his own* Original Letters; *wherein he tells us, that his Father was a* Buccanier *in the Service of his King. This is indeed, I confeſs, a Poſt of Honour I never heard of, tho' our Hero has often boaſted, that he followed his Father's Example.*

I have now in my Poſſeſſion, a large Collection of Sir Peter Stranger's *Letters, recounting many Paſſages of his private Life, Amours, and very odd Adventures*. *Together with several Schemes he laid in* Ireland, Scotland *and* Cumberland, *concerning the Duke of* Somerset's *Mines*, &c. *relating to the Iron Works at* Whitehaven. *Also a regular Correspondence which he held for above four Years with Mr.* Hawkins. *These I intend shall soon follow this* Narrative, *according to the Notice given at the End of it.*

But, before I take my Leave, I cannot but observe the Goodness of our Legislature, *with relation to this most notorious Crime of* Forgery; *who from the flagrant and* unparallel'd *Practices of this* Impostor, *have now made it* Felony; *for by an Act of Parliament since his Conviction, one* Cooper, *a Victualler, at* Stepney, *for forging a Bond of* 25 l. *in the Name of* Holme, *a Grocer, near* Hanover-Square, *has been tried, convicted, and executed for the same, on* Wednesday *the* 16th *Instant; so that the Hopes I have expressed, in the Close of my* Introduction *to this Narrative, are by this just Law now fully accomplished.*

And now, I am the Reader's Humble Servant,

Hampstead,
June 21. 1731.

JAMES MOORE.

A Full and Authentick

NARRATIVE

OF THE

Artifices and Forgeries

OF

JAPHET CROOK, &c.

INTRODUCTION.

WHEN Mankind become Popular, either through the Motives to good or bad Actions, the Enquiry of the Publick after them proceeds from one and the same Cause; and the Thirst of Curiosity is raging upon them till they are let into the Original and Course of Life of the Saint or the Sinner:

A plenteous Crop of *each* our Annals boast,
But here the *former* in the *latter*'s loft.

The *Knight*, of his own making, now before us; may for his Tranfactions, be faid to have outdone the Age he lived in, and feems by Nature made to bear the Weight of thofe enormous Endowments for which he has been fo remarkable, and for which he is here handed down to Pofterity as a Villain of the firft Rank. And I cannot but in this Place thoroughly lament the Deficiency of our *Laws*; when I reflect upon the *Mildnefs* of a Punifhment for the *Blackeft* of Crimes, which I look upon *Perjury* and *Forgery* to be ; nay, Crimes of a deeper Dye, than even *Murder* it felf. It is the *facred Law*, that *he who* fheddeth *Man's Blood, by Man fhall his Blood be fhed.* What *Punifhment* then does that Wretch deferve, who through *Perjury* and *Forgery* attempts to deprive whole Families, and all that fpring from them, of their Subftance, and obliging them to pine away their Lives in Want and Mifery ? A poor Fellow is fure to be hanged by *one* Act of Parliament, who picks a Pocket but of a Twelve-Penny Handkerchief; when by *another*, the *Forger* of Deeds (the only Method by which every Man's Property can be fecured to him) is *only* to *lofe his Ears*, and
ftill

still *enjoy his Thousands.* This partial Distribution of Justice might well make the Poet cry out,

—— *Little Villains* must *submit* to *Fate*,
That *great Ones* may *enjoy* the World in *State*.

But as the Administration of Justice is duly dispensed in our Courts of Judicature, especially in the Example now before us, and the Complaint here made, being not against the *Dispensers* but the *Makers* of our *Laws*; it is to be hoped, that this trifling *Ear-Statute* will be repealed, and that Mr. *Ketch*'s Anodine *Necklace* will hereafter *cut off all false Swearers* and *Forgers* from the *Land of the Living*.

CHAP. I.

Of the Birth, Family, Education, and Marriage of Japhet Crook, alias *Sir* Peter Stranger.

I Am credibly informed that this most notorious Forger was born in *Hertfordshire* about the Year 1662 (some say at a Place called St. *Margaret*'s; *) was educated in the precise Persuasion of *Quakerism*, and when

* There is no Place of that Denomination in *Hertfordshire*, but there is St. *Margaret's-Roding* in the County of *Essex*; tho' I believe neither County will wrangle for the Honour of his Birth.

at Years of Manhood, became Servant, *alias* a Drayman, to Mr. *Ralph Hawkins*, an eminent *Brewer* at *Walthamstow* in *Essex*.

In a short time he turned *Malt*-Jobber, and very dexterously in that way practised his *Frauds*, in *selling* by Samples of *one* sort, and *delivering* another, (*i. e.* damaged Goods) to his Customers.

He had the Luck, much too good for him, to become the Son-in-Law of a very honest Man; by marrying *Mary*, the Daughter of Mr. *Joseph Benning* of the County of *Hertford*, with whom he had a tolerable Portion.

By his base Practises his Character became soon established, but being then, as he still is, void of all Remorse, or Shame; he acquired the Ability to purchase something of an Estate at St. *Margaret*'s, as before-mentioned, for the Life of himself, his Wife, and his Brother. This Estate he mortgaged for the Sum of Six Hundred Pounds to one Mr. *Robert Cooke*, being the full Worth of it, and before he had repaid Mr. *Cooke* any part of his Debt, he mortgaged the same Estate a *second* time to *John Hawkins* Esq; of *Walthamstow* in the County of *Essex* (Son of the before-named *Ralph Hawkins*) for the Sum of Sixteen Hundred Pounds. Of this *John Hawkins*, we shall have Occasion to say much more in the Course of our Narration.

CHAP.

CHAP. II.

Of Japhet Crook*'s coming to* London, *&c.*

AFTER fraudelently acquiring an Estate, and getting Two Thousand, Two Hundred Pounds into his Clutches by twice mortgaging the same, our *Forger* makes the Grand Tour of *London.* From *double* Mortgages he now proceeds to *double* Marriages; and wedded another *Mary*, Sister of Captain *Nash* of *Tooley-Street* (*alias* St. *Olave's*) in *Southwark*, with whom he had a considerable Fortune. By his first Wife he had *one* Son, and by this *second, one* Daughter.

By the Artifices and Pranks he played in Town, after his second Marriage, upon the unfortunate Death of Sir *John Freind* (who suffered on the Account of the Assassination-Plot against King *William*) he became Master of that Gentleman's Brew-House near *Tower-Hill.* But, as *ill got Goods seldom thrive*, tho' he has been a fatal Exception to this well meant old *England* Proverb; yet, he felt one Instance of its Veracity, and commenced Bankrupt, tho' he had not the Honesty to surrender himself to his Creditors, but run away to *Ireland.*

CHAP.

CHAP. III.

Of his Pranks in IRELAND, *&c.*

CORK, in that Kingdom, he made the Place of his Residence, where he had the Modesty to Honour himself with a sham Title, though he had the Assurance to give out, that Queen *ANNE*, on account of some signal Secret Services which he had performed, conferred on him the Honour of Knighthood, under the Denomination of,

Sir PETER STRANGER.

Here he dropt his Scripture Name *Japhet* [*], and we do not find that he ever, here, acknowledged his two elder Brethren *Shem* and *Ham*, or any of old *Noah*'s Progeny. The faithful Inhabitants of *Cork*, were not wanting in paying their Respects to our *strange* Knight, but honoured him with a Stone Doublet, sending him to Jail for some Impostures committed there; from whence to obtain his Liberty, he procured one *Hooker*, in order

---

[*] *Shem, Ham,* and *Japhet,* the three Sons of *Noah.* See the Bible.

order to be his Bail, to swear himself worth Five hundred Pounds, which he accordingly did; and his honest Agent being proved perjured, lost *one* Ear in the Pillory (which, had *Japhet* had but the least Spark of *Grace*, or *inward Light*, would have been a shrewd Prognostick to him to have taken more Care of his own *two*.) After giving *Hooker*, his Bail, this Specimen of his Friendship, Sir *Peter* made off privately for *Dublin*, and there pretended he had such great Interest at the Court of *Great Britain*, that he could procure them her Majesty's Patent *for digging their own* Coals, *and for the opening other* Mines *in that Kingdom*.

Here it was, that he likewise drew in that honourable Gentleman Colonel *Kempson* to be Security for him, on some pecuniary Account, and for which the Colonel, to the great Detriment of his Family (having a Wife and six Children) suffered an Imprisonment of several Years, for what our impudent Knight was pleased only to call, *a Milk Score*.

At *Dublin*, Sir *Peter* married a *third* Wife, one *Mary Savage*. His second Wife *Mary Nash*, hearing of this, went with her Daughter over to him. From *Dublin*, by some Means which we cannot assign, he trapanned both her and the Child to *America*. The Mother died of Grief at *New-England*. She had, during her vile Husband's Excursion to *Ireland*,

Ireland, fubfifted her felf and her Daughter, on part of a Legacy of Thirty Pounds a Year, left her by her Brother, Captain *Nafh,* the greateft Share of which Legacy, Sir *Peter,* by his Artifices, applied to his own Ufe, neither regarding Wife or Child.

Being obliged to leave *Dublin,* our Knight left his *third* Wife with Child behind him, and went to *Scotland;* in which Kingdom he played the fame Game, and continued fhuffling the fame Cards on all Accounts. Firft, he married here a *fourth* Wife, alfo named *Mary,* and the *Scots* Laffes being generally plentiful Breeders, by her he had feveral Children; and after a Ramble of twenty Years returned again to *England,* leaving likewife his *Scots* Family behind him.

CHAP. IV.

Of his Behaviour after his return into ENGLAND.

UPON his Arrival in *London,* finding, after a very ftrict Enquiry, that moft of his Creditors were dead; he prevailed with a
Widow

Widow Gentlewoman, one Mrs. *Davis*, to whom he owed a confiderable Sum, to take out a *fecond* Statute of Bankrupt againft him, by which he was cleared of his Debts, yet had not either the Honefty or Humanity to pay her. But fome Folks were up with him, and for his ufual Rogueries got him confined in the *Gate-Houfe* at *Weftminfter, viz.* for fraudulently obtaining and detaining *Deeds of Eftates and other Writings thereunto belonging.* Under this Confinement he was reduced to a very miferable Condition. But, by his Contrivances, he once more got loofe, flunk down into *Hertfordfhire,* put on a mock Repentance, and ingratiated himfelf fo far as to live again with his firft Wife. Her Father being dead, and having devifed an Eftate at *Barkhamftead* to her, of which *Japhet* found her poffeffed, was the Motive of his pretended Contrition for his paft Offences. But upon Enquiry finding that this Eftate was only fettled by Mr. *Benning* upon his Daughter for Life, and after her Deceafe was to devolve to his Nephews and Nieces. Our honeft *Japhet* foon got himfelf poffeffed of the *Deeds and Inftruments,* and immediately mortgaged this Eftate likewife to *John Hawkins,* Efq; of *Walthamftow,* for Five hundred Pounds, and to get the farther into his good Graces (Mr. *Hawkins* being almoft fuperanuated and very rich) *Japhet* pretended to recover

recover the Eſtate at St. *Margaret's*, which he firſt mortgaged to Mr. *Cooke* (as before-mentioned) by filing a Bill in Chancery againſt one Mrs. *Owen*, a Widow, to whom, at his Death, Mr. *Cooke* had bequeathed it. Our Impoſtor *Japhet* and his Nephew, by ſome Stratagem, got into Poſſeſſion of the ſaid Eſtate, and totally defrauded the Widow *Owen* and her Children of the ſame. *Thirdly*, He mortgaged to Mr. *John Hawkins* aforeſaid another Eſtate at *Endfield* for two hundred Pounds, which alſo belonged to another poor Widow, and was all ſhe had to live on.

He likewiſe found means to mortgage ſome *Waſte Lands* in the County of *Northumberland*, for two thouſand Pounds, which was held by a Grant from King *Charles* II. and not of any intrinſick Worth, *Japhet* having purchaſed the ſaid *Waſte Lands* for a hundred Pounds. And in order the better to impoſe on Mr. *John Hawkins*, *Japhet Crook* becoming acquainted with Mr. *Joſeph Garbutt* and *Elizabeth* his Wife, now living in *Tothill-Fields* in *Weſtminſter* (and who were entitled to an Eſtate called *Jawick-Park*, in the County of *Eſſex*) by his frequenting Prayers at the *Abbey*, and his ſeeming religious Deportment; and did in the Year 1727, apply to Mr. *Garbutt* and his Wife, either to purchaſe or take a Leaſe of the ſame; which they refuſing, he procured ſham Deeds to be drawn and engroſſed,

groſſed, cauſing the Names and Seals of Mr. *Garbutt* and his Wife to be ſet thereunto, and mortgaged the ſaid *Garbutt's* Eſtate to *Hawkins* for Four thouſand five hundred Pounds, in three Days after he had finiſhed the clandeſtine Writings. The ſaid 4500 *l.* with many other conſiderable Sums of Money he actually received of Mr. *John Hawkins,* pretending all he did was to ſerve him; and, to give his Villainies a better Gloſs, and induce Mr. *Hawkins,* who was worth above Threeſcore thouſand Pounds, to make him the Heir of his Eſtate; *Japhet Crook* made his Will, leaving Mr. *Hawkins* ſole Executor of all his Effects. This Stratagem obtained the End propoſed by *Crook,* and wrought ſo far upon the poor old Gentleman Mr. *Hawkins,* who thinking *Crook's* Intention to be ſincere, and that he meant no other than a mutual Exchange of Friendſhip, by making the Survivor the Inheritor of each other's Fortune, Mr. *Hawkins* accordingly made his Will, and left *Crook* his ſole Executor; as will be found in the Cloſe of this Narrative.

CHAP.

CHAP. V.

Of the Death of Mr. Hawkins, *&c.*

THIS laſt Scene of *Japhet Crook*'s Roguery, for which the *Devil* reſolved honeſtly to pay him the Shame he owed him, was effected in little more than a twelve Month. *Crook* became acquainted with Mr. *Garbutt* and his Wife, but in the Year 1727, of whom when he found he could neither Purchaſe their Eſtate, nor take a Leaſe of it, he was reſolved to take it from them as above-mentioned. Mr. *Hawkins* died in the Year 1728, this Forgery of *Crook*'s was detected by Mr. *Garbutt* about the Month of *September*, and the worſhipful Sir *Peter Stranger* was convicted of it, in the Court of *King*'s-*Bench*, in *February* 1728-29.

The following Letter is a full Confirmation of the Contents of our Narration; and which we received from a Gentleman who has inſpected all the Proceedings, *viz.*

To

To JAMES MOOR, Esq;

SIR,

Whatever uncertain Accounts you may have of *Japhet Crook* I know not, but what I here send you may depend on for strict Truth.

He is near seventy Years of Age, and was born at *Hunsdon* in *Hertfordshire*, of honest Parentage, of the People called *Quakers*. He himself was brought up a *Quaker*, and appeared as one, for many Years, whilst he traded as a Malster in *Stansted-Saint-Margaret's*, and at *Ware*, and *Hertford*, and the neighbouring Towns, till the Year 1702.

During the time of his living in *Stansted*, he got acquainted with many Brewers in *London*; and particularly with Mr. *John Hawkins*, then, and for many Years afterwards, a considerable Brewer at *Norton-Falgate*, without *Bishopsgate*.

He has since assumed the Character of a Merchant, in order to give the better Credit to his Forgeries; as by the following Extracts, from the *Brief* of his Majesty's *Counsel*, will appear.

The *Indictment* for *our Lord the King*, againft this *Impoftor*, fets forth, that,

Jofeph Garbutt, Gent. in Right of his Wife *Elizabeth*, on the 21ft of *Sept. Ann.* 1. Geo. II. were feized in Fee of certain Meffuages, Lands and Tenements, called *Jawick cum ptiu*, in the Parifh of *Clackton*, in *Com. Effex.*

That *Japhet Crook*, of the Parifh of St. *Dunftan*, in *Com. Middfx.* did forge a falfe Writing fealed, purporting to be fealed and delivered by Mr. *Garbutt* and his *Wife*, as an Indenture of Bargain and Sale for one Year, bearing Date as above-mentioned, fuppofed to be made between *Jofeph Garbutt* of the City of *Gloucefter*, Gent. and *Elizabeth* his Wife, of the one Part, and *Japhet Crook*, of *London*, Merchant, of the other Part, That in Confideration of 5 *s.* in hand paid to Mr. *Garbutt* and his *Wife*, they did agree to fell to *Japhet Crook*, and give him Poffeffion of *Jawick-Park*, in the Parifh of *Clackton*, in the County of *Effex*, being about eight Miles in Circumference, and containing by Eftimation 4000 Acres, with all Rights, Privileges and Royalties thereunto belonging; to have and to hold the fame for one Year, paying a Pepper-Corn the laft Day of the Term, with Intention that by Virtue thereof, he might be in Poffeffion, and be enabled to take a Grant of the Reverfion, to him and his Heirs, to

the

the Damage of Mr. *Garbutt* and his *Wife*, againſt the *Statute*, and againſt the *Peace* of our Soveraign Lord the King.

To this Indictment, *Crook* pleaded *Not Guilty*, and *Iſſue was thereon joined.*

He was, as your Narrative ſets forth, Servant to Mr. *Ralph Hawkins*, a Brewer; and did afterwards ſet up to be a *Malſter*, a *Brewer*, a *Grazier*, a *Timber-Merchant*, and ſeveral other Trades at one and the ſame time, in which his chief Practiſe was to outwit and deceive thoſe he dealt with, and he took a certain Pleaſure in ſo doing, and would frequently boaſt of his Exploits that way.

He borrowed of Mr. *John Hawkins* 1650 *l.* upon the Eſtate you mention at St. *Margaret's*, which *Crook* had twice mortgaged before for more than the Value, ſo that Mr. *Hawkins* never had any Benefit of his Mortgage.

A Statute of Bankrupcy was taken out againſt *Crook*, 1706, and he thereupon abſconded, and from that time to 1725, wandered about in *Ireland*, *Scotland*, and the *North* of *England*, having no viſible way of living but that of Tricking under various Shapes, Titles and Denominations; ſometimes pretending to be a Baronet, a Merchant, and whatever elſe might promote his Deſigns.

By this means unwary People were drawn in and tricked out of their Money.

During thefe Tranfactions, his common Appellations were *Peter Stranger*, and Sir *Peter Stranger*. And by the Name of *Peter Stranger* he lay in *Cork* Jail, and *Dublin* Jail, in *Ireland*, and was for a confiderable time in Cuftody as a Perfon concerned in the *Prefton* Rebellion. He at that time pretended to be a Man of Eftate and Fortune, and to have Intereft among Perfons of Quality, and told the King's Meffenger who took him up, that if he would lend him fome Money, he would as foon as he obtained his Liberty pay him again, and it fhould be greatly to his Advantage. He prevailed upon the Meffenger to lend him Money, who dying foon after, *Crook* farther prevails on the Meffenger's Widow, to take out a Commiffion of Bankrupcy againft him as the only Means of getting her Money, which in 1725 fhe did, but never got a Farthing; however, it ferved *Crook*'s ends, for he had thereupon his Certificate and Difcharge.

This was no fooner done, but being in a very neceffitous Condition, he caft his Eye on Mr. *Hawkins*, whom he knew was rich and very covetous, as a proper Perfon to work his Defigns on, and begins by a Letter dated *Anno* 1725, wherein he acquaints Mr. *Hawkins*. " That he had got his Difcharge, but
" that

" that he thought himſelf not diſcharged
" from the Obligations he was under to him;
" and he had a way not only to procure
" him the whole 1650 *l.* and Intereſt, but a
" Surplus of 2000 *l.*" Mr. *Hawkins* pleaſed
with the Thoughts of receiving ſo much Money, of which he never expected one Farthing, liſtened very earneſtly to *Crook*, who
had an extraordinary Talent at Deceiving,
and making the moſt improbable things paſs
for Truth. Now *Crook's* Project was (and it
took Effect) as follows, *viz.*

" *Crook* perſuades Mr. *Hawkins*, that the
" Eſtate he had mortgaged to him for 1650 *l.*
" was worth 400 *l.* or 500 *l. per Ann.* and that
" the former Mortgagees, who had been in Poſ-
" ſeſſion above twenty Years, were over-paid
" 2000 *l.* and he intended Mr. *Hawkins* ſhould
" have the ſaid 2000 *l.* beſides the 1650 *l.*
" due to him, and ſhould alſo have the E-
" ſtate itſelf when recovered, intending no-
" thing for himſelf, it being ſufficient for
" him to ſerve his Friend."

Mr. *Hawkins*, who was very eager after
Wealth, was hugely pleaſed with *Crook's*
generous Propoſal, Money being the ſole Delight of his Heart. *Japhet*, however, intimated to him, that there was an abſolute
Neceſſity of advancing ſome Money to enable him to procure theſe Advantages. Mr.
Hawkins inſtantly lays down 200 *l.* for that

Purpose; and *Crook* the readier to induce him to trust him, pretended to have lately bought a Copyhold Estate at *Endfield*, and would mortgage that to secure this 200 *l.* last advanced, and *Crook* produces a Surrender to himself, from one *Chapman*; but this was all Fraud, *Crook* having no Right or Title to any such Estate.

Mr. *Hawkins* being wholly blinded with the Expectation of getting so much Money, never so much as made the least Enquiry concerning the Title, but was fully contented with the Surrender which *Crook* made of it to him.

Crook pretends, with this 200 *l.* to proceed against the Prior-Mortgagees, and from time to time amused Mr. *Hawkins* with the mighty Services he was doing, and the great Advantages which would soon arise from the Estate of St. *Margaret*'s, provided he would advance some more Money, and so prevails with Mr. *Hawkins* to lay down 300 *l.* more. But to please, and keep Mr. *Hawkins* from Suspicion, *Crook* makes him another Mortgage for this 300 *l.* of an Estate he pretended was come to him from his Wife's Father, when in reality he had no such Estate. This, however, was not so much as looked into by Mr. *Hawkins*, and *Crook* still continues his Amusements of the mighty Services he was doing for Mr. *Hawkins*, and that he was on the

Point

Point of getting Possession of St. *Margaret's*; and for enlarging the Advantages which might thereby be made, *Crook* proposes to have a Store of *Sheep*, ready to put on the Lands, magnifying the Profits which were to be made by their Grazing; and so gets Mr. *Hawkins*'s Consent to buy seven hundred Sheep, which *Crook* told him cost 700 *l*. which Sum Mr. *Hawkins* paid for them. Soon after *Crook* buys eight hundred Sheep more, and likewise received of Mr. *Hawkins* 800 *l*. for them, on no other Security than his own Note, and a Bill of Sale of the Sheep.

In a little time afterwards, *Crook*, by some means or other, got Possession of an old Grant from the Crown of fifteen thousand Acres of Waste Land in *Holy-Island* in the County of *Northumberland*, of no Value whatsoever. With this Royal Grant *Crook* goes to Mr. *Hawkins*, and assures him, that with laying out 3000 *l*. it would bring in a vast Estate. For, says *Crook*, in a Letter to Mr. *Hawkins*, " The Land is proper for sowing of *Rape*, " and a thousand Acres so sown, will, " if but half an usual Crop rise, bring in " 10,000 *l*." And *Crook* proposed to make over this *Grant* as a Security for all the Money he had had. This was another Bait which readily took with Mr. *Hawkins*, and *Crook* procures by it no less than the advance of a farther additional Sum of 2500 *l.* And now Mr. *Hawkins* thinking himfelf fufficiently fecured by a Mortgage of this *Holy-Ifland*, and always retaining an extraordinary good Opinion of *Crook*, and all his Tranfactions, infomuch that he entirely credited whatever he propofed. And the more to oblige *Hawkins* (as you have hinted, Sir,) *Crook* made his Will in Form, and devifed to Mr. *Hawkins* the entire *Fee* of his great Eftate, and all other the Eftates (of our wealthy Sir *Peter Stranger*) and leaves it in the Hands of Mr. *Hawkins.*

This was highly agreeable to Mr. *Hawkins*, who, in Gratitude to fo good a Friend and Benefactor, made his Will, and gave *Crook* all his Eftate. But *Japhet* not willing to wait the Uncertainty of his Death, determined to have a good Share of the Eftate in Mr. *Hawkins*'s Life-time; and in order thereto, in fome fhort time afterwards, *Crook* applied to Mr. *Hawkins*, and pretended he had met with an extraordinary Bargain of an Eftate, eight Miles in Circumference, and in *Effex* the very Country where Mr. *Hawkins* lived, and he was to pay only 4500 *l.* That he was to have a Conveyance, and be put into Poffeffion on Payment of 1500 Guineas, and that there was room to get a great deal of Money by the Bargain, and affured Mr. *Hawkins*, that, if he would advance the Money,

Money, he would bring the Purchase-Deeds and make over the Estate to him by way of Mortgage: Likewise he would take care that Mr. *Coningsby*, his Counsel, should examine the Title, and the Deeds should be duly executed.

Mr. *Hawkins*, still giving Credit to his good Friend *Crook*, advances the 1500 Guineas. Some few Days afterwards, *Crook*, by Letter, sent word that he had got Possession, paid the 1500 Guineas, and given his Note for the Remainder of the Purchase-Money. Soon after *Crook* brought Mr. *Hawkins* two Deeds of Conveyance by way of Lease and Releafe, from *Joseph Garbutt* and *Elizabeth* his Wife, to himself; and also a Mortgage of the same from him to Mr. *Hawkins*, with a Receipt on the Back thereof, for the 4500 *l.* so draws from Mr. *Hawkins* the whole 4500 *l.* which, with other Sums he had before fraudulently obtained of him, amounts to the Sum of 13,000 *l.*

In a little time after this, Mr. *Hawkins* died, and his next Relations taking Possession of his Effects, finds the Deeds (of Mr. *Garbutt's* Estate) among the Deceased's Writings, and making Enquiry among other Matters, into this Security, they discovered that these Deeds of Conveyance were forged, and the whole a Fraud and Imposition on the deceased Gentleman: And for forging these
Deeds

Deeds of Lease and Release, and publishing the same to defraud Mr. *Hawkins*, the Indictment against *Crook* was brought, and of which he has been found guilty, and justly by our Legislature punished, tho' not in a manner (as you well observe in your *Introduction*) adequate to the Heinousness of his Offence.

Inner-Temple,
June 15, 1731.

I am, Sir, Yours,

J. W.

C H A P. VI.

The Proceedings against Crook, *in the* Ecclesiastical Court, *and his Pretences to Interest with Persons of* Distinction.

IN the *Libel* exhibited against our *Impostor*, and now depending in the Ecclesiastical Court, it is attested, that *Japhet Crook* being several times told, particularly in the Month of *August* 1728, *His Forgeries would bring him to the* Pillory. He answered boldly, and with an uncommon Assurance, *He did not value that, so he got Mr.* Hawkins's *Estate.* And he has frequently made his Boasts in the Years 1725, 1726, 1727, and 1728, of the great personal Interest he had

had with several Persons of Quality, and of the first Distinction, particularly in the Dutchess of *Kendall.* In a Letter to Mr. *Hawkins,* bearing Date the 24th of *May,* 1725, he thus expresses himself, in his own Orthography,———*I have such Runing and Atendeing of this Greate Duches of* Kendall *and this Generall* Peper *that I am allmost weried out of my Life.*———(And in the same Letter, mentioning his *Endfield* Estate, he thus delivers himself, viz.)———*I have got the Surrenders of the estate att enfild Chase but the Generall hath Demolished my Pocket and put me In sum Debt.*———(Then solliciting Mr. *Hawkins* for more Money, to induce him thereto, he says, in the same Letter,)———*I will If Posibell put her Graces of the Afare of the Holy Island til that she Returns back from Hanover* *——— This Letter he signs P. S. (for *Peter Stranger*) and under it writes at large *Japhet Crook,* adding this remarkable Postscript, viz.

I was advised by My Counsell to take the estate at enfeild In the name of Peter Stranger and they Assured Me it was as well as Japhet Crook for I being the same Person and haveing Passed this 20 *years by that Name and Aquired it with out any fraud It was all one.*

We

---

* He means thus, that, he intended *to put her Grace in mind of the Affair of* Holy Island: *But that it could not be accomplished till her Return from* Hanover.

We next come to the Right Honourable Sir *Robert Walpole*, the Lord *Townſhend*, and the Lord High Chancellor of *Great Britain* (the Earl of *Macclesfield.)* All of whom he gave out, *had ſo great a Regard for his great Skill, Knowledge, Integrity and Judgment, that they conſulted him on all Occaſions. And, that he was ſoon to be made a Lord or Peer of this Realm, and have a conſiderable Title and Eſtate beſtowed upon him, and that he ſhould be then able to do great Things for the Family of the* Hawkins *.

Theſe Aſſertions the late Mr. *John Hawkins* believed as true; but he, poor Gentleman, was at that time deprived of his Underſtanding, and thereby not capable of judging properly of ſuch ridiculous Stories and Inventions; contrived on purpoſe by *Crook* to impoſe upon and gain Credit with Mr. *Hawkins.* Adding to all the reſt, as an *Inſtance* of the *good Opinion* the *Right Honourable* the Lord Chancellor had of him; That he did, in the Preſence and Hearing of *John James* and others, tell Mr. *Hawkins,* that Mr. *Vaughan* came into Court, and ſwore before the Lord Chancellor, that, " The ſaid *John Hawkins*, Eſq;
" was dead. And that he the ſaid *Japhet*
" *Crook* happening to hear the ſame, immediately came into Court, and then told the
" Lord Chancellor, that what Mr. *Vaughan*
" had

---

* *Extract*, from the *Libel* in the *Commons*, Artic. 58.

"had sworn was a Lye, or False; for that
"the said *John Hawkins* was alive. And
"that thereupon the Lord Chancellor gave
"Credit to the *Word* of him the said *Japhet
"Crook*, before the Oath of the said Mr. *V*⸺
"affirming, that this Instance *was* and *is*
"true *, *viz.* that *Crook* so gave out; but is
"*false* in *Fact*."

At length *Crook* triumphs in his Estate-Royal of *Holy-Island*, and on the 13th of *February* 1726-7, sends Mr. *Hawkins* the following elegant Letter; *viz.*

Worthy Sir
"Inclosed in the Bage is the *Grant* from
"the Crown with the other Writeinges be
"pleased to Take them home with you and
"at your owen Laziour Peruse them and If
"it May be your Pleasuer to be Consernd
"or to serve Me int I shall make the Tittell
"as good and ferm as any on earth and all
"that I have Afirmed of it is truth."

Your Most obledged obeidant Humbell Servant
Till he's I: *Crook* &c

By this *Northumberland-Grant*; forging the Deeds of Mr. *Garbutt*'s Estate; and his Management of making *Wills*; he drew in Mr. *Hawkins* to make him his Heir.

* See the *Libel*, ut supra, *Artic.* 59.

CHAP. VII.

Containing Mary Crook*'s* WILL *to her Husband.* Japhet Crook*'s* WILL *to Mr.* Hawkins, *and Mr.* Hawkins*'s* WILL *to him.*

IN *the Name of God, Amen.* I *Mary Crook* of *Barkhamsted,* St. *Peter*'s, in the County of *Hertford,* Wife of *Japhet Crook,* late of *London,* Chapman, being sick and weak in Body, but of sound, perfect, and disposing Mind and Memory, Thanks be therefore given to Almighty God for the same; and calling to Mind the Uncertainty of this present mortal Life, do make and ordain this my last *Will and Testament* in Manner and Form following, (that is to say) First and principally, I do commend my Soul into the Hands of Almighty God that gave it, hoping assuredly through the only Merits of Jesus Christ my Saviour and Redeemer, to be made Partaker of everlasting Life: For my Body, I do commit the same to the Earth, in decent manner to be buried, at the Discretion of my Executor herein after-named: And as touching such worldly Goods and Estate as it hath pleased Almighty God of his Goodness to bless me with, I do hereby give, will and be-

bequeath the same as followeth. *Imprimis,* All my real and personal Estate whatsoever I shall die possessed of, as Heir at Law to *Joseph Benning* of *Barkhamsted,* St. *Peter*'s, aforesaid, deceased, my late Father, I do hereby give, will and bequeath unto the abovesaid *Japhet Crook,* my Husband, and to his Heirs and Assigns for ever. And I do hereby constitute, ordain and appoint him the said *Japhet Crook* sole Executor of this my *Last Will and Testament,* utterly making void all former and other *Wills* by me made; and I do hereby pronounce and declare this, and no other, to be my said *Last Will and Testament.* In *Witness* whereof, I have hereunto set my Hand and Seal, this three and twentieth Day of *October,* in the twelfth Year of the Reign of our Soveraign Lord *George,* by the Grace of God, of *Great Britain, France* and *Ireland,* King, Defender of the Faith, *&c. Annoq; Dom.* 1725.

Mary Crook ⊕

Signed, sealed, published, pronounced, and declared by the above-named *Mary Crook* the Testatrix, as her *Last Will and Testament,* in the Presence of us,

John Howard,
Frances Hawes,
Mary Martin.

Item, My Will and Mind further is, that an handſome Grave-Stone be ſet or laid over the Graves of my Father and Mother.

Teſt.

John Howard,   *Mary Crook.*
Frances Hawes,
Mary Martin.

IN *the Name of God, Amen.* I *Japhet Crook,* alias *Stranger,* of the Pariſh of St. *Margaret,* in the County of *Hertford,* Gentleman, being of ſound, perfect and diſpoſing Mind and Memory, Thanks be therefore given to Almighty God for the ſame; and calling to Mind the Uncertainty of this preſent mortal Life, do make and ordain this my *Laſt Will and Teſtament* in Manner and Form following, (that is to ſay) Firſt and principally, I commend my Soul into the Hands of Almighty God that gave it, hoping aſſuredly, through the only Merits of Jeſus Chriſt my Saviour and Redeemer, to be made Partaker of everlaſting Life: For my Body, I do commit the ſame to the Earth, in decent manner to be buried, at the Diſcretion of my Executor hereafter named. And as touching ſuch worldly Goods and Eſtate as it hath pleaſed Almighty God of his Goodneſs to bleſs me with, I do hereby give, will and bequeath the ſame as followeth. *Imprimis,* All my real and perſonal Eſtate

Eſtate whatſoever, and whereſoever I ſhall die poſſeſſed of, I do hereby give, will and bequeath unto *John Hawkins* of *Walthamſtow*, in the County of *Eſſex*, Eſquire, and to his Heirs and Aſſigns for ever: And I do hereby conſtitute, ordain and appoint him the ſaid *John Hawkins*, ſole Executor of this my *Laſt Will and Teſtament*, utterly making void all former and other Wills by me made. And I do hereby pronounce and declare this and no other to be my ſaid *Laſt Will and Teſtament*. In *Witneſs* whereof, I have hereunto ſet my Hand and Seal, this one and twentieth Day of *Auguſt*, in the firſt Year of the Reign of our Soveraign Lord *George* the Second, by the Grace of God, of *Great Britain*, *France*, and *Ireland*, King, Defender of the Faith, &c. *Annoq; Domini* 1727.

Japhet: Crookee ⊕

Signed, ſealed, publiſhed, pronounced and declared by the above-named *Japhet Crook*, alias *Stranger* the Teſtator, as his *Laſt-Will and Teſtament*, in the Preſence of us,

John Hinton, of *White's-Alley*, near *Chancery-Lane*.
Samuel Bedford, of *Pope's-Head-Court*, near *Chancery-Lane*.
Cath. Wibert, Spinſter, in *Chancery-Lane*, near the *Crown* and *Rolls* Tavern, who ingroſſed the above Will.

In about three Months after *Japhet Crook* had executed his Will to Mr *Hawkins*, he obtained his End; and Mr. *Hawkins* made his own Will, which bears Date *December* 1ft, 1727, confifting of but of three *Items*, viz. *Firft*, He gives to his Brother *Thomas Hawkins*, one Annuity of Five hundred Pounds *per Annum* for Life. *Secondly*, He gives a Charity of One thoufand Pounds to *Chrift*'s Hofpital. *Thirdly*, He gives the Reft and Refidue of his real and perfonal Eftate to his Friend *Japhet Crook*, his Heirs, Executors, Adminiftrators and Affigns. And makes the faid *Japhet Crook* fole Executor.

From thefe Artifices of *Crook*, together with his *many deceitful Suggeftions, Mifreprefentations, and Infinuations in his Difcourfe* with, *and by his Letters wrote* to Mr. *Hawkins*; *and reprefenting his* Relations, *as vile, wicked and extravagant Perfons, and that they wanted his Death in order to divide and fpend his Subftance* *. By thefe falfe, bafe, and notorious Contrivances, he impofed upon and drew in Mr. *Hawkins* to make the Will abovementioned, to the great Prejudice of his Brother and other Relations.

And it is farther manifeft, " That for fe- " veral Months preceding the time of Mr. " *Haw-*

* See the *Libel*, ut fupra, *Artic.* 60.

" *Hawkins*'s making his *Will*, to the time of
" his Death; *Crook* invented and publickly
" told many falſe, groundleſs, and malici-
" ous Stories of Mr. *Hawkins*'s Relations, to
" exaſperate him, and alienate his Affections
" from them, in order to get his Eſtate; and
" which indeed were ſo apparently falſe,
" groſs and groundleſs, and altogether ſo
" inconſiſtent and untrue in the relating, that
" they could not have been received, or any
" Credit given to them by Mr. *Hawkins*, if he
" had been in his *right Senſes*; but on the
" contrary, he muſt have ſhewn the utmoſt
" Reſentment to the Inventor of ſuch Ca-
" lumny *. Moreover, *Japhet Crook*, to in-
" duce Mr. *Hawkins* to make his Will in fa-
" vour of *Him*; did, in the Preſence and
" Hearing of *Robert Floyer*, *Richard Lucas*,
" and others, moſt falſely averr, that he,
" *Crook*, had made great Improvements of
" his Money, and gained a vaſt Eſtate, to
" the amount of Ten thouſand Pounds *per
" Ann.* and upwards, and that his perſonal
" Eſtate was worth Eight thouſand Pounds
" *per Ann.* and upwards, and that he would
" give it all to Mr. *Hawkins* †."

This was the pretended Purport of *Crook*'s Will above-recited. ‖ " And the more ef-
" fectually to work on the weak and decayed
"   Under-

---

* See the *Libel*, ut ſupra, *Art.* 66. † Ibid. *Art.* 67.
‖ Ibid. *Artic.* 71, 72.

" Underſtanding of Mr. *Hawkins*, and cheat
" him of his whole Eſtate, and to cover and
" carry on his fraudulent Deſigns, did from
" the time of obtaining Mr. *Hawkins's* Will,
" to the time of his Death, continually ſend
" as Preſents to him, Wines, and other ſtrong
" Liquors of an intoxicating Nature, pri-
" vately made up and mixed for this Pur-
" poſe by *Crook*, who recommended them as
" the moſt excellent in their Kind, and good
" for his Health; aſſuring Mr. *Hawkins* in his
" *Letters*, that theſe *Wines* came out of the
" King's Cellar, and were ſuch as King
" GEORGE himſelf uſually drank, and that
" *one ſort of them*, which he called *Aſhcolon* *
" Wine, had very extraordinary Virtues.
" *I Kno* (ſays he) *the Jewes are the Cuninges*
" *Pepell in the world and they call it* Long
" Life *and whatever is ſold in England is*
" *ſold to help poor Wines* †. By this Artifice,
" *Crook* ſo far prevailed on Mr. *Hawkins*
" (who received the ſaid Preſents as particu-
" lar Marks of *Crook's* Affection for him) that
" he did every Day drink great Quantities
" of the ſaid Liquors, and thereby became
" intoxicate and ſtupified, ſo as not to be
" able to remember what he did, or to diſtin-
" guiſh *Fraud* from *Friendſhip*, or diſcern the
" moſt open and bare-faced Impoſitions put
"   " upon

* *Aſcalon*, he meant.   † See his *Letter* to Mr. *Haw-*
kins, March 26, 1726.

"upon him. And the said Liquors were
"so far from being good for the Health of
"Mr. *Hawkins*, that in the Opinion of Mr.
"*Thomas Simpson*, and others, who attended
"him during the last twelve Months of
"his Life, and who saw what Effect the
"said Liquors had on him, that they did
"*impair his Health and shorten his Days*. And
"it is not doubted but that *Japhet Crook*
"did mix, prepare, and send these Liquors
"on purpose to impair the Health and
"shorten the Days of Mr. *Hawkins*, that
"he might the sooner accomplish his wick-
"ed Purposes, and possess his Estate. And
"*Crook* hath confessed the same in the Pre-
"sence of *Zachary Cole, Deborah Newton*,
"and others. And Mr. *Hawkins* became
"so stupified by these Liquors, that from
"the time of making his *Will*, to the time
"of his Death, he did not *remember*, or
"*take Notice* to any Person whatsoever, that
"he had *made any such Will*, but the same
"lay about his House in a *neglected Manner*.
"And no doubt, had Mr. *Hawkins* not
"been thus stupified, *he would not have done*
"*any such Act.**

* See the L1BEL, *ut sup*. ARTIC. 75.

F   CHAP.

CHAP. VIII.

The Proceedings in Chancery relating to Mr. Hawkins's WILL.

SINCE the Deceafe of Mr. *Hawkins*, in *Michaelmas* Term 1728, his *Relations*, together with his *Brother*, brought a Suit and exhibited their Bill in the High-Court of *Chancery* againſt *Crook*, in order to have this pretended Will ſet aſide, for the fraudulent Practices made uſe of by the ſaid *Crook* in obtaining it. And upon hearing the ſaid Cauſe, on the 21ſt Day of *July* 1729, the Court *Decreed, Firſt*, " That the ſaid pre-
" tended Will of *John Hawkins* Eſq; made
" in favour of *Japhet Crook*, as to the *real*
" *Eſtate*, ſhould be ſet aſide. *Secondly*, That
" the ſaid *Crook* ſhould bring before a Ma-
" ſter of that Court upon Oath, all Deeds
" and Writings in his Cuſtody, or Power,
" relating to the *real Eſtate* of the ſaid *John*
" *Hawkins*. *Thirdly*, That the ſaid *Crook*
" ſhould bring the Sum of *thirteen Thouſand*
" *Pounds*, received by him, into the *Bank*
" of *England* to be placed to the Accompt
" of the Accomptant-General of that Court.
" *Fourthly*, That the ſaid *Crook* ſhould ac-
" compt for ſuch other Sums of Money
" as he had received of the Eſtate of the
" ſaid *John Hawkins* ſince his Death, and
" pro-

"produce upon Oath all Books of Ac-
"compts and Papers in his Custody, or
"Power relating thereto, and be examined
"upon *Interrogatories*, as the Master should
"direct, and bring what appeared to be
"due into the Bank to be placed to the
"Accompt of the Accomptant - General.
"*Fifthly*, That the said *Crook* should pay
"the Costs of the Suit, and after the De-
"termination of the Matter in the *Eccle-
"siastical Court*, the Plaintiffs in this Suit
"were to apply to the said Court of *Chan-
"cery* for farther Directions."

And it is not to be doubted, but that the *Ecclesiastical Court* will confirm this just *Decree* of the High-Court of Chancery.

Mr. *John Hawkins* died a Batchelor, without Father or Mother; and left behind him at his Death, *Thomas Hawkins*, *John Nutt*, and *Dorothy Blount*, and *Catherine Woolball*, his Nephew and Neices, Joint-Plaintiffs against *Crook* in the *Ecclesiastical Court*.

CHAP.

CHAP. VIII.

The Clauses out of the Statute at large, Ann. 5. Eliz. *on which* Crook *was Indicted and Convicted. And of Executing the Sentence on him.*

Be it therefore Enacted by the Queen's most Excellent Majesty, with the Assent of the Lords Spiritual and Temporal, and the Commons in this present Parliament assembled, and by the Authority of the same, That if any Person or Persons whatsoever, after the first Day of *June* now next coming, upon his or their own Head or Imagination, or else by false Conspiracy and Fraud with others, shall wittingly, subtilly and falsely forge or make, or subtilly Cause, or wittingly Assent to be forged or made, any false Deed, Charter or Writing sealed, Court-Roll, or the Will of any Person or Persons in Writing, to the Intent that the Estate of Freehold or Inheritance of any Person or Persons, of, in, or to any Lands, Tenements, or Hereditaments, Freehold or Copyhold, or the Right, Title, or Interest of any Person or Persons, of, in, or to the same, or any of them, shall or may be molested, troubled, defeated, recovered or charged; or after the said first Day of *June,* shall pronounce, publish, or shew forth in Evidence any such false and forged Deeds, Charter, Writing, Court-Roll, or Will, as true, knowing the same to be false and forged, as is aforesaid, to the Intent above-remembred, and shall be thereof convicted, either upon *Action* or *Actions* of forging of false Deeds, to be founded upon this *Statute,* at the Suit of the

Party

Party grieved, or otherwise according to the Order and due Course of the Laws of this Realm, or upon *Bill or Information* to be exhibited into the Court of the Star-Chamber, according to the Order and Use of that Court, shall pay unto the Party grieved his double Costs and Damages, to be found or assessed in that Court where such Conviction shall be; and also shall be set upon the Pillory in some open Market Town, or other open Place, and there to have both his Ears cut off, and also his Nostrils to be slit and cut, and seared with a hot Iron, so as they may remain for a perpetual Note or Mark of his Falshood, and shall forfeit to the Queen our Soveraign Lady, Her Heirs and Successors, the whole Issue and Profits of his Lands and Tenements during his Life; and also shall suffer and have perpetual Imprisonment during his Life; the said Damages and Costs to be recovered at the Suit of the Party grieved, as is aforesaid, to be first paid and levied of the Goods and Chattels of the Offender, and of the Issues and Profits of the said Lands, Tenements and Hereditaments, of such Party convicted, or of one or both of them; the said Title of our said Soveraign Lady the Queen, Her Heirs and Successors to the same notwithstanding, &c.

After Mr. *Hawkins*'s WILL was set aside, by a Decree in the High-Court of *Chancery*, and the farther Proceedings relating thereunto referred to the *Ecclesiastical Court*. *Japhet Crook* was indicted upon the Statute above-recited. And being convicted thereof, *Ann.* 1729, had a Respite of above two Years

Years to prepare what he had to offer in Arrest of Judgment. But having recourse only to farther Frauds, and seducing a Gentlewoman of a good Family, to use means to spirit away one of the chief Evidences against him; this Point could not be gained, and he was therefore called up, together with the Lady *Lawley*, to have Sentence passed upon them, which was accordingly done in *Hilary* Term 1731.

I. The Lady *Lawley* was fined 300 Marks (*i. e.* 200 *l.*) and to suffer one Month's Imprisonment.

II. *Japhet Crook*, alias Sir *Peter Stranger*, had the Sentence of the Statute pronounced upon him; and it was put in Execution accordingly. The common Hangman cut off his Ears, slit up his Nostrils, and seared them on the *Pillory* at *Charing-Cross*, June 10. 1731. From whence he was carried back to his Jail, (the well-known *Golden-Lion* Spunging-House kept by the Widow *Pearson*) near the King's-Bench-Prison, *Southwark*, with whom, as we are assured, he has *run on Tick* ever since his Confinement, not only for his own Subsistence, but that of his amiable Handmaid, *Mary Madelin*, impiously called by *Crook*, *Mary Magdalen*; and to keep his Landlady in Humour, it is said, that *Japhet* is treating with her about becoming his *fifth* Wife, and likewise for making a *double* Match between

Master *Pearson* and Miss *Madelin*, whom *Crook* calls his Ward, and promises her Mr. *Hawkins*'s Estate. Flushed with this good Fortune, the Widow *Pearson* has sent down her Son to *Walthamstow*, in order to survey the same.

As a Confirmation of the Facts, related in this Narrative, we shall close it with a Collection of *Japhet Crook*'s Original Letters, that both the present Age and Posterity may have a genuine Account of his Honesty, signed by his own Hand.

Litera scripta manet.

We shall first produce his Letters sent to *Ireland*, to Colonel *Kempston*, &c. the Gentleman mentioned in *pag.* 7. of our Narrative, and thus directed.

For Cornnall *John Kempston*, &c.

London y 29th of *June* 1725

Dear Comrade,

SIR the True Reason of my Writing now is that I cant send Mr. *Harison* of * this Day as I Did expect and that you might be Ready to Assist him as soon as he Landes and that you Might Make your self fuly master of Where they May By † the Salmon fish Cheapest

I

---

* off, *it should be.* † Buy, *he means.*

I Do think that at *Limberick* muſt be the Places they muſt ſalt at and may Buy there fiſh ſum there and from all the Rivers In the county of *Kery* they may Bring there Salmon on horſes Backes from the County of *Kery* to *Limberick* and there ſalt them and Pack them into terſes which muſt be gott at *Dublin* and ſo cary the Tearſe by Land to *Limberek* or where they can by the Terſes Cheapeſt I Bought them at four ſhilings ſix pences *per* Terſe in *Cork* Sir I Beg you may Lett Mr. *Hary Kempſton* Know I have Wrot him by Mr. *Hariſon* to ſerve me in this Afare the Gentillman that Advances this money is as wee call him on *London* Echange A Dubell Plum Man Alias 200000 pounds and if this ſucceedes I will ſoone Draw enough to *pay of your Milk Scores* In *Irland* (be pleaſed to Turne) I Beg you Would ſend for Mr. *Mathu Quin* and Diſcourſe him ſuly In this Afare I Beleve he may be as Proper A Perſon to Aſſiſt and help forward this Afare as any Perſon Indeed you Muſt Doe it with as Littell Charge as may bee for the Perſon is a very ſtrict man and will narrowly ſcrutyny into Mr. *Hariſon*'s Acounts and the Salmon fiſh are to be Imported into *England* as food not as A Perticalar Rarity for Gentillmen and Woomen they will bring over Salt to Cure them With as alſo full Inſtructions I Beg you Will make it your Study to git

your

your self (fuly) Master Against Mr. *Harison* comes over I hope on *Tusday* he shall set out here at fartheft he Bringes over in silver hilted Swordes Buckells and Butons and Eie Water and sum Water with a Cleanseing Pouder for teeth to About 70 pounds and the Rest in Gold Indeed I cant see how this Can faile he paying hand Mony the Prise at *Limbreck* and the Rivers in *Kery* was four pences *per* Salmon and 2 *d. per* peale but all this Depends on the fish taken and the Buyers Demands yours Intierly Till hes *Peter Stranger.*

Deare Comrade

May Heavens be unJust to mee if I forgitt my Promisses to you send Word by the first Post how much mony will Cleare you and likewise If the 70 poundes Judgment is to bee Bought In and how much will Doe it of my Lord *Blesintowns* this doe the first Post as to the 350 ginas there is five hundred Pounds Borrowed on my Bond and Lord *Blesintowns* Judgment this day Sir *John Illes* * Promised me (hes now our Lord Mayor) Love to all frindes as Esq; *Eckells* and Esq; *o haro* I have bin worse Plaged to come at my owen and this day have Bin before A Master in Chansery of an Acount of 6600 *l.* and have Another to Come on of up-

* *i. e.* Sir *John Eyles.*

wardes

wardes of 32000 *l.* that It makes mee wely mad If you write Directe to Sir *Peter Stranger* as ufual and it will come to his hand thats youers

In All fencerity Till hes

the 22d of *no.* 1726
Lo'e to Honeft *Pi ill*
Mull Patruk

Peter Stranger

London the 22d of *Aguft* Thurfday

Dear

COmrade I wrote you on *Saterday* the 17th on the Back of Mr. *Savage* To me from *Egermount* ad finds my fears are Com truths for Mr. *Hen. Kempftons* walking of and not Clearing the Cuntry Mr. *Slackes* Runing in Debt and he and his Sons Runing away leaveing all the Debts he contracted unpaid hath Gave the Cuntry with the Dukes Commifhoners fuch an Ill opinion of the whole that I find that Letter to be what I took it to be at firft Reading A modeft Deniall that they will have no more to do with us thus ftands our Credite at *Egermount.*

As to Mr. *Hen. Kempftons* Refleckting on what I wrote for if they had followed my Directions In bying the Woodes of and if they were fold but for twenty ginas and If Honeft *Phill. Mulpatrick* had not have
made

made eighty Pounds of the Barke let me note him be Credited for nothing After and If there had not bin feaven hundred Pounds made of the Iron neat Profite after all Charges Deducted let me meet with no Credite on any thing I fay or here After fpeak on this head or any thing elfe I mention indeed as to what Capt *Slack* or his Son *Will.* faid I fhall not mention nor will I beleve Capt *Slacke* after what he offered to me for there was never A Defign for to Build A fortune from Mr. *John Kempftons* mony or Could I ever Prevaile on them To ftay and not go over as they did but over they would Run indeed I well kno that it was the opinion that I was under fuch A Defparate Confinement that who ever Bailed me was undun and that fham letter that was wrott to the old Lady *Kempfton* was all vilanie but I muft end this with A ftory of my fathers when Liveing that when he com home from the *Weft-Indies* he brought home his effects in thre fhipes when they came in to the Chanell they Run the fhip on a Rocke the Capt blamed the Livetenant he blamed the mate In fhort every man Blamed each other the fhip ftuck faft every man for faveing of his Life and fleeing out of the fhip my father walkeing not with out great Confern hereing they Blameing each other heres an old skillfull faying that If all the failes was ftrained and backed and when the Tide made If the wind fhould fpring A Loffe (I kno not If I fpeak the Proper Language) the helmalee) it was poffible the fhip might be faved my father Being an old Buckanere for his Prince (then King of *England*) Dru his fword took the whole Command of the fhip on him all imedately obeyed his Command well knoing two thirds of the Carco was his the minfter Did his Duty all ask the Blefeing of (God) Immedately After took the skillfull failers Directions brought the fhip of and came fafe into harbour (the Morall is with us) Mr. *H. Kempfton* blames *Stranger* and he the whole Conduct here is 100 ginas of Mr. *John Kempftons* mony fpent Mr. *Franfes Savage* Reqireing moor (the reft of the Partners flead whats now to be Dun all I can fay (the Account I will not medell with) I am Indebted to Mr. *H, Kempfton* one Gina to Mr. *Franfes* fixteen fhillings and A noat of two ginas on Mr. *Dods* Papers A Horfe I have which will Return In as good order as receved what I want is an order from Mr. *H. Kempfton* to pay it to Mr. *Savage* with Mr. *H. Kempftons* orders to Mr. *Franfes Savage* (who * * * him felf all matters) this is what is expected from him thats your Free Comrade

Peter Stranger.

Dear

Dear

COmrade Sir you cant thinke I take Pleaſwer In Rideing of 800 miles a wild gooſe Chaſe as I Did into the *Hylands* of *Scotland* and to Do it in 18 Dayes to try my ſtrenth that hath bin fully tryed before now wittnes the holes in my Caue Skin (Angry I am but what will that Prevaile me) I Kno I am farr enough of and I am Afraide my Comrade yet hath ſo good opinion of his owen four Quarters that he will be ſtill telling of his mighty Deeds of Chevalrey and Charity as giveing Poor Mrs. *Savage* A ſix pences or two and weekely her and her Children two Loafes of Bread *per* weeke for twelef months Indeed you was not bound to Do it or had Mr. *Savage* (had that Regard to his family he might have prevented) by ſaveing ſum Pences out of his owen on this ſide the water I Kno one word I ſaid was made ten yet (I cant ſay my Comrade can Gaul me moor then hereing him Praiſe him (ſelf) which is good *Iriſh*) but not my Coarſe Hedg Hog Dialogue for I had Rather have a frind Rebuck na A broken head or ſhin (then any of that Curſed oyle of flatery gave me when I Kno the harts full of Poyſon and be told I am a Prety Gentillman when I Kno the Revers) as to any money that you have gave me or Dun to or for my Dear *Maſon* depend ont its bread ſtrewed on the water that ſhall be gratefuly Repayd and altho I cant ſay ſhe is mine I can ſay I am fathfuly and ſincerely

hers

hers and I am fure I am young enough for her and I cant beleve but Kno fhe is all Above twenty old enough for me however I have nothing to fay of her or will I beleve any thing Lefs but that fhe is fhamelefly belyed by any that faith any thing Ill as to her Virtue I Kno this Is truth and hopes fhe will Prevent any gaine fayes by her Prudent Conduct for the futor as to Mr. *Danill Sharp* I am fum Pences out for him and Beleves It might be worth your while to git his noat for what your Pleafed to fay he oweth you as to Mr. *John Gilbreath* I muft pay feaventeen fhilings fix pences for the Charge you put me to on his Acount as to his Afare there If his Part of the thoufand Pounds is good to him If he out Lives his mother but If he Dies before its noon of his indeed he may fell it you and fo After to ninteen moor and the Laft and firft the fame Titell for as he can be poffefed of nothing till his mother is Dead he can only fell nothing (nor If you have any moor Nothings to fend over to your Comrade that he muft pay mony out of his fmall moite for) I Doo advife you to fend them over here to me for my part being in *England* this five yeares you may beleve I muft want Buffines as to Mr. *Noguere* and *Dilkes* there can be no mony made of (at Prefent and *July* will be the fooneft any money will be had) however I will be anferable that you fhall have no

Flemifh

Flemish Acount from me nor Mrs. *Dod* If I could have onces Acount of Mrs. *Dods* Receveing them Papers sent (you should have such Acount of the Rest) but Assure your self they will not stand A court of Record therefore I will make sum end as soon as I can with them here so much in Anger (Turn over)

Dear Comrade you have Read mine on that Part I have sent you to give Mr. *H: Kempston* and now what my father Did I am Resolved on for I am not for Runing or Rideing any moor Idell wild Goose Chases but now will look out therefore as soon as This comes to hand I desire you may be pleased to Command *Phil: Mulpatrick* to obey the under writen for I have sum thing yet in view that will make you and my family hapy and let me fight as much as I will by the help of (God) I will bring you from that Confinement but Remember (Gods) time is the best and must and will be obeyed and I shall allways agree with his holy will be Dun and not mine here hath bin a Reverd Divine a Cannon of St. *Pauls Ludgate* and he would Gladly Imbrafe the Revrd Doctor *Finlases* Liveing Pray let me have your Positive Answer to it by *Philip Mulpatrick* as also my Answer to all mine to you by him and If you can depend that Cornal *Jones* may be Relyed on to Do any thing for you as to Mr. *Savage* Pray Do you and Mr. *H:Kempston* write Planely ly too for hes to Rely on what you two write to him and as 1 told you I ſhall not medell betwixt you and your family as to your owen Perſon I take to be my Family and ſo will Do for it and as to the reſt any frindly Servis Depend I ſhall be Ready to Do that in me lieth my Harty love to Kind frind and I have her Ring on my finger (my Deare Liefs on my hart) and is

Your True Comrade whileſt

Peter Stranger

Phill: Mulpatrick as ſoon as this Comes to your hand If wind and wether offers you are to take ſhiping for *Whitehaven* and as ſoon as you Land you are to Come to the Black Cock at *Egermount* you are to Doe as *Joſeph* ſaid to his brethren (not to Regard any thing they had in *Canan*) for the Good of the fate Land of *England* is before you therfore Look you make no ſtay but Come Imediately Away and you ſhall be there Attended by him thats yet your

Friend *Peter Stranger*,

Dr.

Dr. *Mason* the other Day as I was at Diner after I had satisfied my *Hyland* stomake with sum good Plates of A sarline of *English* Beef I was surprised with a fitt of Laughter the Gentillmen was as much surprised for I cant say I have Dun the licke the Lady seeing noon woud ask commaned to Know the cause (Lady must be obeyed) the Rome was full of sconses and as every one eaten I having Dun see all the Rest bussey on there Danties of the second coarse had time to look on the company and seeing the Ladys Gentillman standing at my Back with a Lase neckles and Lase Ruffels and A long bow wigg and I In my habit I had in *Ireland* at a noblemans table It did not surprise me how ever it went of with A faint sight when I thought of my Dere Life *Phill* : *Mullpatick* will bring your Commands to him that is Ready and willing to Obey them thats yours Interely whilest hes

Peter Stranger.

Dublin 1o.ʳ y.ᵉ 3d 1722

To Mr Kempſton *to be left with Mr* William Savage *att the Cuſtome houſe* Whitehaven

Gentillmen,

BY ſum thing I hard this Day I find Capt *Slack* Is for going to *Branton* and hath ordered his Letter for him at Mr *Lamberts* at *Branton* I Kno not how farr he may go farward In that Afare by him ſelf or how his Corroſponds here may Incorage him I am Credibely Informed he hath 1000 pounds In Gold and Good Bills with him and what ſums he hath To follow or what Dependances he may have on any under hand Contract made before he went of

You have mine before now and I am yet of the ſame mind you ſhould Perſue what I there wrot In makeing A bargainne for the oar by a Leaſe and to Agree for the furnes and ſuch Woods as are in the Compas of Mr *Williamſon* Sir *William Penintons* excepted all wich may be Dun with the ſume of five hundred pounds wich ſume may be Commaned with eaſe and only waite on and watch *Slack* for I muſt Tell you Gentillmen its eaſeyr to make Contracts (then to find mony and Punctaly Perform them) and this you may Aſſure your ſelves that

as

as you have Gentillmen and Noblemen of the firſt Rank to Deale with (your Buſſineſs is to Keep them your frinds) to make no Contracts with them nor there Agents (but ſuch as you can Perform) and by Doing of which you would do well to have allways the mony Lying by you to Perform ſuch Contracts (as ſoon as made) or to make none

I fear a founder muſt be had out of this Kingdom and as Great as your Capt may Apere there his Carrector Is as mene and Bad here Amongeſt all ſorts of workemen That have had any Dealeing with him ſo that Mr *Hary* muſt be here in *Febarary* and A founder muſt be hyred from hences and Carred ouer for as to Capt *Slack* I Take him to be A Rent Charg on the Partners for If he Cant Go on In his under hand Defineing way he will Deſtroy the worke and the Partners

To Prevent which you are to follow this Schem wich I wrote you word In my Laſt but the Truth will allways Bere twiſe Telling and is as followeth

Aſſone as this Comes To your hands you are to make A firm Bargaine for the *Oar* (that is by Takin A Leaſe from his Graces the Duke of *Sumerſead* her Graces being newly Dead as our Coroſponds write from *London*) which I hope may not hinder or
Delay

Delay the Comiſhonor from giting your Leaſe.

You are to Take the furnes as well and as Cheap as you can at A yearly Rent or otherways but ſecure it You are to ſecure all the woods with In the Compas of *Joſeph Williamſon* and to care In your Artickelling that you leave no Loſe end for Rangling but have Rome enough for Diging and Cuting of couering of Coale Pitts and ſeting and Burning Coale with all uſall convencys for the working and cuting of the woods and to Take time In making of your Payments for the woods not to ſone and Qick upon the Partners for mony that muſt be Laid out will Run A way faſt enough before any will Com in

As to your going upon any ſerching for Coale I fere you will only ſpend mony and git in none which will be wrong

The thoughts of the *Hyland* woods I think nothing of for as to *Galbraiths* Credit In *Scotland* I beleve my own as Good and as to the *Scottiſh Hylandmen* I Ken them well and I can By woods there nere the ſea and That any Priſe I ſhall ſay (and the Payments when and at what Time I Pleaſe) but Gentillmen you have only ſeen the Earle of *Carliſle* woods I will give you my word you have not ſeen A 5th Part of the woods that I will cary you to In *Cumberland Northumberland* and *Weſtmerland* and if
you

you will give me Leave to tell you that if by your owen Mifmanedgment thofe noblemen fhall court you and the Partners to by and Deale for all there woods and Lands &c (and not you them) and you fhall find I will make my words Good, for I Kno the Perfons that can and will do it:

But the only thing I want is to fee the furnes makein fow Iron and the forge hammers Drawing out Iron for I Love to fe mony coming In at fmale expences

Gentillmen when you have fecured all as I have wrote To you which I hope you will have Dun by *Chriftmas* I beleve it to be for the Advantage of the Partners that you write to *David Littell* and let him be Doun with at *Egermount* and let him waite on Capt *Slack* in your Abfences and give him his full Inftructions for I Kno he will Do all things that you order and he Doth not Love Capt *Slack* nor can Capt *Slack* make A motion In your Abfences but he will Kno it and give A True Account of it to the Partners and fince the Partners pays him his wagges he will be fure to obeie your Commands but you muft order him fume mony To *London* to Bere his Charge Down to you and git him Down to *Egermount* before you Leave the Cuntry and give him his Charge and then all things will be fafe with the Partners and Capt *Slack*

Direct

Direct yours for *David Littell* to the Care of Mrs. *Sarah Davis* at the *Tennis* Court Coffee house in *White Hall* and put Your Letter under Couer

And Direct it To Mr *Joseph Richardson* at the Right Honourable the Lord Viscount *Townhsend* offices In the Cock Pitt *White hall*

Gentill: I am your

Most Humble Servant

The 4th Desemb 1722   Peter Stranger.

To the Same

the 14th *Jany* 1722 *Dublin*

Mr *Kempston* Mr *Savage* and Capt *Slack*

GEntillmen In my Last I have wrot fuly what Remaines is this to lett you Know what is in Closed in this of Mr *Slack* wich Pray Communicate to him and If you Comply with it well If not I desier you may be pleased to Return my letter of Atorny by the first post as to matters here they Cant be worse (but when they will mend I Kno not)

Mr

Mr *Savage* you have my Artickells which I beg you may Keep Its not in my power to ferve Mr *Savage* with mony tho hope it will as fone as I Receve an Anfer to this (and you and fhe may expect it fhall be Complyed with to both your Contents)

Gentillmen I am your

Moft Humble Servant

Peter Stranger.

To Mr Francis Savage *at* Tenis Coffee houfe *charing* Crofs London

Gentillmen

MR *Butterfeild* Receved A Letter this Poft from Capt *Slack* which fays that you are to have your full inftruction from his Graces the Duke of *Sumerfead* in order for the Leafe of the mine and that as foon as that is Dun he would with you Go down and Repare the furnes and fet it at worke and that he expected Mr *Butterfeild* would order his Quota of mony According to his Artickells this Is the fub-
ftances

stances of his Letters by the 9th of *Marſh* from *London*

I wrot you fully In my Laſt from us Mr *Kempſton* and I was Reſolved to go on our owen Bottom that wee had made A bargaine behind you and that wee ſhould have 4000 barrells of Barke this ſeaſon and that wee ſhould have Acation for 200 pounds which Mr *Kempſton* hath wrote for wich I hope you will Remit the firſt poſt ouer here that nothing may be wanting on your parts

Mr *Kitellwells* Letter from me I Recomend you too and take Care of *Kittellwells* And *Slacks* being too Great and that they act nothing to our prediieces in the maine between themſelves for *Kittwell* is A man of mony and Capt *Slackes* Honeſty mixed may be of Ill ſervis If not well obſerved and notiſed by you

I am with Due Reſpectes

Yours whilſt

Peter Stranger

The 19*th of* Marſh 1722-3

For Mr Franſes Savage *at* Egermount *To the Care of Mr* William Savage *at the Couſtom Houſe in* Whitehaven *Theſe*

Dublin the 11th of *Aprill* 1723

Mr Hen Kempſton *and Mr* Savage

GEntillmen what now offers *is* that as ſoon As this Comes to your handes that If there be no bargaine of wood that you Can by with In the Reach of *Jos Williamſon* In or nere *Egermount* for what we had to Rely of I cant find the reaſon which wee Relyed on hath Dun what wee Promiſed to our Likeing ſuch woods I would have you Contract for and ſecure and take ſuch time for payments as you Can git ſo that wee may not be made uneaſey to gitt mony and Contract for the furnes at *Egermount* and have not to Doe with any Perſon but Agree for them only by your own Perſon for Mr *Slack* Juner Is all wrong as I wrote In my laſt and Mr *Buterfeild* Is good for nothing and as to Capt *Slack* with you I beleve as bad ſo that I Look on the Partnerſhipp ſigned here of no uſe but finally Broke and Dun with I kno there are woods there that may be bought that the Barke will pay the Purchaſe If carefuly Manedged In bargaineing for at or nere *Egermount*

By

By the firſt Poſt that you can write you are to give Acount of as Above and try how farr any ſuch bargaine be made as alſo to let A True obſervation be had In the Laſt to you to that of workemen for had I bin ſo that I could have bin ouer ſea this great bargaine had not ben thus farr back as now it is and the ſeaſon ſo nere as too Run the haſard to Loſſe it this yeare yet I am In good hopes wee may ſave it for If wee are at worke by the 15th of *May* the ſeaſon may be ſaved therefore mind what I now write and what I have wrot In my Laſt to you to *Whitehaven* The 6th Inſtant About workemen As to your Leaſes I allways told you nothing cold be Dun but at the Land ſetting at the Audite and you Dont ſay what time In *May* the Audite will be pray let us Kno as alſo A letter from you If any thing can be and write by way of *London* as Alſo by the ſhiping from *Whitehaven* to *London* you give ſuch Lame Acounts and ſo Imperfecte that they are very unſatesfactory for how you have ſecured the Reſt of *Nogers* mony you ſay by noat If Its only his owen its very Mean ſecuryty If its A bill Draw on any good Perſon and excepted by that Perſon the bill being Indorſed is Good and you might have had the mony before you Left *London* on A ſmale Diſcount It ſeems here to Look very Indifrantly but I hope you have been wiſer then it Aperes I

ſhall

(59)

shall ad no moor but hopes to have Acount by first Return that can be to Gentillmen

Your most humble Servant

Peter : Stranger.

Mr *Savage* as to Mrs *Savage* you may beleve me she and both her Barnes are in very sober Condition and all the mony comes out of Mr *Kempstons* pocket you would Do well to Consider how that Mr *Buterfeild* hath not paid his Bill Due to Mr *Kempston* or one farthen to Mrs *Savage* and I dont see Mrs *Savage* can Come of to Whitehaʋ̀ to you till wee Kno where to pich our Tents whether where this Contract is made since you went of or at *Egermount* Indeed If it was in my power as much as in my will my littell wooman and two Barnes should not Complain If its the Leafe Dont forgit her and indeed you are better there then here depend ont From him that Is

Sir your True Frind

Peter : Stranger

F I N I S.

Crooke died at his Spunging House 1734.

London : Printed for J. WILFORD, at the *Three Flower-de-Luces*, behind the *Chapter-House*, in St. *Paul's* Church-Yard.

In the Press, and will speedily be published,

ORiginal *Letters,* From JAPHET CROOK, *alias* Sir PETER STRANGER, Bart. To *Colonel* Kempston *and his Three Sons, Mr.* Francis Savage, &c. *relating to the said Sir* PETER STRANGER*'s Negotiations in* Ireland, Scotland, Cumberland, *and the* Mines *and* Iron-Works *at* Whitehaven.

Also, I. JAPHET CROOK's *Account of an Estate of* 2000 l. per Ann. *left him at* Antegoa, *and of his being advised to solicit for the Government of that Island.*

II. *His taking up* 10000 l. *in* Staffordshire, *upon the said* Antegoa *Estate.*

III. *How he was sent by a Gentleman to undertake the* Restoring *of a Lady's* lost Virginity.

IV. *A remarkable Letter of* CROOK*'s to my Lord* Altham.

V. CROOK *gives an Account of the Presentation of two Livings in his Gift, worth* 500 l. per Ann. (viz. Ashley *and* Bridgenorth *in* Shropshire) *which he offers to Colonel* Kempston*'s Son.*

VI. *A Collection of* CROOK*'s Letters to* John Hawkins, *Esq; for near four Years, from* 1724 *to* 1729, *shewing all the Artifices by which he imposed on that Gentleman, and decoyed him out of his Estate.*

The whole being a Series of such surprizing Transactions, as almost seem incredible. Price 1 s.

Foundations of the Novel

compiled and edited by
Michael F. Shugrue
Secretary for English for the M.L.A.

with New Introductions for each volume by

Michael Shugrue, *City College of C.U.N.Y.*
Malcolm J. Bosse, *City College of C.U.N.Y.*
William Graves, *N.Y. Institute of Technology*
Josephine Grieder, *Rutgers University, Newark*

A Garland Series
Foundations of the Novel

Representative Early

Eighteenth-Century Fiction

A collection of 100 rare titles
reprinted in photo-facsimile in 71 volumes

131063